"Putting aside my rodeo days was hard at first," Ty admitted, "but being here on the ranch? It's vastly fulfilling."

He hadn't expected to love this place, didn't want to, but all the same, it was part of him now.

"Then what's wrong?" Juliette asked.

"My dad is always on me about my old reputation." He chuckled. "He wasn't happy when you and I got into trouble with the police chief."

"I have to admit, that day was unexpected."

"But fun?"

She went serious as she met his gaze. "More fun than I've had in a long time."

There was a truth to her words he related to. But as much as he wanted what was happening between them to grow, he had to put his duty to his family first.

"We do tend to bring out that side of each other," he said instead of revealing his true feelings, like how she'd become as vital to him as breathing.

Dear Reader,

Welcome back to Golden. It's autumn in the mountains, my favorite time of year in my favorite place on earth. I love the leaves in their full glory of reds, yellows, oranges and browns. There's a chill in the air that means it's time for sweaters and boots. When you step outside, woodsmoke scents the air. Can you tell I really love this season?

In this book, you'll get a glimpse of Golden at its fall best. Horseback riding in the woods with the fall foliage all around. Standing on the edge of a fast-moving creek to view a cascading waterfall on the opposite side. Festivals and a very special farmers market. Apple cider and pumpkin spice coffee.

For the Golden Matchmakers Club, this is a great time to pair their next couple. Neither Ty nor Juliette is looking for love, but sometimes it sneaks up and surprises you. In life, the road to happily-ever-after is not always straight or easy. But the thing about matchmakers? They see the possibilities and go for it, sure in their hearts that the couple will feel the same.

I hope you enjoy Ty and Juliette's story. The matchmakers are going to take a step back, but you never know where they might pop up in the future.

Tara

Heartwarming

Her Surprise Hometown Match

—

Tara Randel

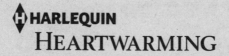

HARLEQUIN
HEARTWARMING

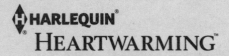

HARLEQUIN®
HEARTWARMING™

ISBN-13: 978-1-335-58487-8

Her Surprise Hometown Match

Copyright © 2023 by Tara Spicer

All rights reserved. No part of this book may be used or reproduced in any manner whatsoever without written permission except in the case of brief quotations embodied in critical articles and reviews.

This is a work of fiction. Names, characters, places and incidents are either the product of the author's imagination or are used fictitiously. Any resemblance to actual persons, living or dead, businesses, companies, events or locales is entirely coincidental.

For questions and comments about the quality of this book, please contact us at CustomerService@Harlequin.com.

Harlequin Enterprises ULC
22 Adelaide St. West, 41st Floor
Toronto, Ontario M5H 4E3, Canada
www.Harlequin.com

Printed in U.S.A.

Recycling programs
for this product may
not exist in your area.

Tara Randel is an award-winning, *USA TODAY* bestselling author. Family values, a bit of mystery and, of course, love and romance are her favorite themes because she believes love is the greatest gift of all. Tara lives on the west coast of Florida, where gorgeous sunsets and beautiful weather inspire the creation of heartwarming stories. This is her tenth book for Harlequin Heartwarming. Visit Tara at tararandel.com. Like her on Facebook at Tara Randel Books.

Books by Tara Randel

Harlequin Heartwarming

The Golden Matchmakers Club

Stealing Her Best Friend's Heart
Her Christmastime Family
His Small Town Dream

Meet Me at the Altar

Always the One
Trusting Her Heart
His Honor, Her Family
The Lawman's Secret Vow

Visit the Author Profile page
at Harlequin.com for more titles.

To all our wonderful Harlequin Heartwarming
readers who look forward to pumpkin spice
season every year!

PROLOGUE

"C'MON, IVY, we're going to be late."

Juliette Bishop glanced over her shoulder at her little sister, lagging behind as usual. Staring at that dog, most likely. The day had started out rough when Ivy wouldn't listen to Juliette's suggestion that she dress warmly to venture to Gold Dust Park. Just another ordeal when it came to caring for her sister. Not that Juliette minded, she understood why both of her parents worked hard. But some days, Juliette wanted to be a normal fifteen-year-old and hang out with her friends, tossing responsibility to the wayside for a few hours. Then she'd glimpse Ivy's adorable face and feel guilty.

Today was no exception. They'd come to the park for the Veterans Day parade and to listen to Mayor Danielson's speech. At least that's what Juliette told her mom. Really, she was to meet up with a boy from math class. She'd been excited, dressing up in her favorite outfit and making sure her makeup was perfect. Only, once they arrived, Brian Barnes never showed. She'd been disappointed and a little humiliated. But she'd stayed so Ivy could take her time on the play set, perched on the outside swing on the right side of the playground. Always the same seat. Juliette had become accustomed to her sister's methodical choices. Having been diagnosed with Asperger's syndrome, Ivy tended to be pretty regimented in her ways.

But the parade of veterans who lived in Golden had ended, the mayor had spoken, and Juliette wanted to go home and hide in her bedroom. Under the covers, preferably. Ivy, it seemed, had other plans.

Juliette stopped and turned to discover her sister standing in the same spot she'd left her. With a huff, she stomped over to take Ivy's hand. The crowd had thinned, but the mayor and his wife were still greeting the townsfolk, the stroller with their toddler daughter inside just a few feet away. The toddler tried to get her parents' attention, but they were too busy schmoozing to notice. As Juliette passed, the mayor waved. She distractedly waved back, more intent on finding out what had caught her sister's attention.

"Ivy, what's going on?"

Ivy pointed across the open space. "There's the dog. I've seen him here three times now."

Juliette squinted her eyes. Sure enough, a scraggly looking mutt, probably a stray, sat at the rim of the park, staring back at them.

"Don't worry, I'm sure there's someone to take care of him."

"Three times," ten-year-old Ivy repeated. "He needs us."

"We need to get home," Juliette reminded her.

"It'll just take a minute."

Now that Ivy's attention was on the dog, nothing else would sway her sister otherwise. Sure enough, Ivy ran in the direction of the mutt. He barked and suddenly made a dash for the park exit.

"Wait," Ivy called, taking up the chase.

"Great," Juliette muttered, following closely.

The dog zipped out of the park onto the crowded sidewalk along Main and crossed to the other side of the street. Juliette nearly crashed into her sister when they lost track of the animal.

"Where did it go?" Ivy asked, becoming agitated.

"Maybe he went home too?"

"But why? I saw him three times."

"Maybe all these people spooked him. If we start walking, we may find him."

This seemed to satisfy Ivy, so Juliette walked in the direction of their house. They weaved through folks making their way to their cars or stopping to browse in shop windows after the festivities. If Juliette could just keep her sister's attention from the dog, they might get home without any other detours.

As Ivy dragged her feet, Juliette took her sister's hand, hoping to steer her through the groups of people still chatting about the day's celebration. The sidewalk in this area of town had a slight downward slope, tricky to navigate if you were in a hurry. Mayor Danielson and his family had joined the crowd, holding court as he and his wife discussed a town issue, the stroller left unattended again. As people passed by, they bumped the stroller and it moved farther from the parents.

Ivy caught sight of the toddler and started in that direction, but at the same time, the dog appeared across the street.

"Look," her sister said, releasing Juliette's grasp, stepping to the curb as if to run across the traffic.

"Ivy!" Juliette grabbed her sister's arm before she ran into the road.

"Three times," Ivy repeated. "He needs us."

With a sigh, she debated what to do. When her sister's face flushed, Juliette sensed an outburst coming and said with a soothing tone, "He'll be fine."

Ivy's face grew redder. "He won't."

"What do you want me to do? We can't cross the busy street."

"Please?"

The cajoling tone from Ivy always did Juliette in.

From his post across the street, the dog watched, giving Ivy more reason to go after it. She made a motion to dart out again. Juliette was faster, reaching the curb to stop her. Ivy tugged to get away and Juliette lost her balance, staggering into the street. At the same time, the stroller rolled in their direction, jumping off the curb and smashing into Juliette. She reached out to stop the stroller's movement—afraid it would run over her toe or bang into her shin—coming eye to eye with the panicked toddler.

As all of this was happening, a cry sounded from the crowd. People started pointing and suddenly the mayor was in the street, waving his arms in a panic to halt traffic. Once the cars screeched to a halt, he grabbed the stroller handle, and Juliette, to drag them back to the safety of the sidewalk.

Juliette, afraid of losing sight of her sister in the throng, pulled away to reach Ivy's side. Now Ivy watched her with wide eyes.

"I'm sorry."

"It's okay. Let's just go home."

"But you saved the little girl."

Actually, she hadn't. They'd just crossed paths at the same time.

They took two steps to continue the trek when the mayor stopped them. "You aren't going anywhere."

Oh, no. Does he think I pushed the stroller into traffic?

Waiting to be disciplined, Juliette watched color make its way into the mayor's ashen face while her stomach plummeted.

"I didn't—"

"Juliette, you went after her."

She blinked. Was he talking about the dog?

"You saved her."

Confused, she glanced at her sister, who nodded her head.

"If it hadn't been for you, the stroller would have rolled farther into the street. Who knows if the traffic would have stopped in time. We could have lost our daughter."

"But I lost balance and—"

"You saved Ellie."

In his relief, the mayor didn't hear the start

of her explanation. He unstrapped his daughter from the stroller and pulled her into his arms.

By then the mayor's frantic wife had joined them. "What happened?"

"Juliette saved Ellie."

"No, I was—"

"Oh, Juliette, how can we ever thank you?" Mrs. Danielson hugged her, enveloping Juliette in her heavy perfume. Juliette wrinkled her nose and tried to explain again, but the woman wouldn't let go.

By this time others had gathered around them, murmurs advancing through the crowd. Juliette had saved the mayor's daughter. How noble of her. She should receive a prize.

Juliette blinked. Why wasn't anyone listening to her? She'd been after the dog, not stopping the stroller.

Mr. Danielson handed a whimpering Ellie to his wife and took Juliette by the shoulders, bending at the waist to meet her gaze head-on. "You're a hero."

"No, I was only—"

"Doing your civic duty."

Ivy came up beside her, slipping her trembling hand into Juliette's, refusing to make eye contact. Juliette needed to get her sister out of the crowd. Too much social interaction with this many people would overstimulate her.

"I need to get Ivy home."

The mayor noticed Ivy and nodded. "Of course. We'll talk later."

Juliette tugged her sister down the sidewalk, away from the people who had eyes on her. Later, she'd tell the mayor it was a fluke. That she fell into the street the same time as the stroller. No heroics, only timing. Once she explained, it would get straightened out.

Ivy pulled to a stop and stared across Main Street. Juliette followed her gaze.

The dog, still seated in the same spot, cocked his head and met Juliette's eyes, then trotted away.

CHAPTER ONE

Fifteen years later

"C'MON, C'MON, C'MON," Juliette muttered under her breath as she circled the courthouse parking lot for the third time.

This morning, of all days, she hadn't been able to find her keys. After searching for ten minutes, she'd realized they'd probably been moved when her sister visited the cottage yesterday afternoon. Once a week, Ivy arrived after work to have dinner with Juliette and then "tidy up." It had started as a way to introduce Ivy to healthier foods. Her sister was a very picky eater and hated to have her diet changed. For some reason, she'd only eat food suggested by Juliette. So she'd made a deal with her parents to entertain Ivy, to get her to try at least one new item, and then let her clean up, a routine that brought Ivy pleasure.

It also meant that Ivy put things in places that made sense to her, but not Juliette.

"I am so going to be late."

Trying not to let mounting frustration overwhelm her, she called her sister, popping a minty antacid while she listened to Ivy recite the entire list of things she'd put away, repeating each location before announcing where the keys were. Last, of course. Juliette rushed to the apple bowl on the kitchen counter and sure enough, the bright green four-leaf clover key ring that Ivy had made for her was inside. So far this morning, luck had not been on her side.

"And before you go, Mom said we could get a dog. I want a puppy who snuggles with me. Will you help me pick him out?"

Every few years, Ivy went on a puppy kick. They would go look, but Ivy couldn't make up her mind and then overwhelmed and frustrated, they'd leave empty-handed. "Sure, we can look at the rescue shelter website so you can scroll through pictures and we'll read the backstories."

"Thanks. I picked out a name. Bruno. What do you think?"

"It's very nice. Honey, I need to run but we'll talk later."

"Bye."

Juliette finally ended the call and rushed out to her silver sedan, only to get stuck behind a school bus stopping to pick up students the entire way to her destination.

Cloud cover obscured the Friday morning sunlight. Chilly October weather had arrived. To ward off the nip in the air, she'd thrown a multicolored, crocheted sweater over her conservative green dress, paired with tan booties, just before leaving her cottage. She generally enjoyed this time of year, with the leaves changing color and the crisp temperatures that made hiking in the forest a delight. Usually she took time to appreciate the natural panorama of this Georgia mountain community, but this morning her mind was focused elsewhere.

Juliette was going to be late and Judge Murphy was not going to be happy. The stern woman was already miffed at Juliette for showing up in her courtroom for the second time in six months.

To say she had a reputation in Golden was an understatement. It wasn't Juliette's fault, really. If the town council hadn't proposed a cut in funding for the city's special needs program, she wouldn't have had to block the meeting room door in town hall. Yes, attaching a rope through the handles and wrapping the remainder around her waist to prevent the council from entering made a statement, informing each and every member just what was at stake. But her actions also ticked people off. Although Police Chief Davis agreed with her and hadn't liked the cut to funds, he had a job to do: remove her. Using hedge clippers to cut the thick rope, the chief then slapped on cuffs when she resisted arrest. In the end, she stood by her decision. The cause was too important, too near and dear to her heart, to not make waves.

So maybe she'd crossed a line. Maybe she shouldn't have used those exact measures to get her point across. Drastic measures had been needed and once again she was in the spotlight.

If she didn't speak out for those who had no voice or weren't listened to, who would?

That was the problem with living in Golden. People knew her. Or at least they thought they did. She strived to live up to their expectations but would never attain that goal.

"Are they having a sale on building permits toady?" she wondered out loud. Why had everyone picked today to go to the courthouse?

The Federal style, redbrick courthouse, was built in 1840 after the population of Golden had grown significantly. It featured white doors and trim around the windows, black shutters, and a portico over the main entrance. Located two blocks east off Main Street, it served a dual purpose. Courtrooms and judge's chambers were located on the first floor, the town business offices on the second.

As she moved slowly through the parking lot, Judge Harrison waved. She tried not to cringe. The retired judge had always been a champion in her corner, which was sweet, but unnecessary. She could take care of herself.

And you're doing a bang-up job.

Hush, she censored herself.

Except for the years she went away to college and then grad school, Juliette had spent her entire life in Golden. Why, when she had the chance to escape completely she hadn't done so, still amazed her. But as it had always been, she'd missed Ivy and her parents and couldn't imagine living elsewhere.

So she bit the bullet, so to speak, and settled down in Golden. Bought a cute little cottage downtown. Worked as an occupational therapist at a rehabilitation facility serving the community. If it hadn't been for the past and the title she didn't deserve, she'd love it here.

The mountains and scenic overlooks were

beautiful during any season, boasting water-falls, hiking trails and Golden Lake, a huge tourist draw. The town itself was quaint and welcoming.

Downtown consisted of six blocks of tree-lined sidewalks built on an increasing incline. Gift shops, restaurants, lodging and profes-sional offices were painted in vivid colors to draw a visitor's eye. Old-fashioned, ornate cast-iron lampposts lined the main street, supporting large planters overflowing with seasonal flowers, right now featuring sunny yellow chrysanthemums. Halloween deco-rations could be spotted in the windows and doors.

The people were generous, lovable and, un-fortunately for her, possessed long memories. The day she'd "saved" Mayor Danielson's daughter—she let out a nervous laugh—had sealed her fate. She'd tried to explain it was a fluke, that while she'd been trying to calm her sister and keep her safe, she'd stumbled into the street in the process. The mayor refused to listen. Told her he admired her modesty. And before she knew it, the story had taken on a life of its own and she'd become a town hero. Even her parents were impressed by her selfless act. It had all piled up and since no one listened, she'd stopped trying to explain.

Once the hubbub had died down, Juliette moved past the events of that day, just like everyone else. At least that's what she'd told herself. When Mayor Danielson's term was over, the family moved to Atlanta for his new high-profile job, taking the pressure with them. So much time had gone by, why was it still a big deal?

Because you're a fraud.

It was over and she should let it go. Almost did, until the family moved back to Golden two years ago. Mr. Danielson ran for mayor again and won. Old regrets took up residence in the forefront of her mind and she was afraid they'd never go away.

Today would be much of the same. The judge had probably decided her sentence.

She was just about to circle around to another row when she noticed an empty space near the front steps of the building. Finally, something going her way.

"Thank goodness."

Stepping on the gas, she flipped on her blinker. A battered, black truck approached from the opposite direction. She turned the steering wheel to angle into the open spot at the same time as the truck, which didn't stop. She slammed on her brakes, hoping not to collide with the vehicle. What was the driver thinking?

A horn blared at her. She squinted her eyes to stare at the other driver. Hadn't he seen her blinker indicating she was moving into the spot?

They sat there in a standoff, the man's hands draped over the wheel, neither one willing to back up to let the other in. Juliette could hear the clock ticking in her head and nearly broke out in a sweat. The judge would have it out for her for sure when she finally rushed into the courtroom.

Just when she hoped the man behind the wheel would give up and back away, he opened the door, hopped out of the cab and strode her way. He was dressed in a flannel shirt, jeans and boots, and a black Stetson obscured his face. Were they going to clash over the space? Taking her eyes off him for a moment, she put the car in Park and rummaged in her purse for the can of pepper spray she carried with her. When a sharp rap sounded on her window, she jumped.

He rolled his hand, motioning for her to lower her window.

"No," she said loud enough to be heard through the glass.

"Lady, I need this spot. I'm late."

"So am I."

"Then it looks like we have a problem."

"I was clearly here first. You'll have to wait until another spot clears out."

"I've circled the lot four times."

She felt his pain but wasn't backing down. Lowering the window an inch, she pleaded with him. "Can't you just be a nice guy and give me the space?"

He tipped back his hat and Juliette was greeted by eyes the color of aged whiskey. Her breath lodged in her throat and she made a funny squeaking sound. His eyes narrowed. Swallowing hard, she noticed the man's overlong sable-colored hair, deciding it suited him. She couldn't tear her gaze from him, despite the irritation clearly lined on his tanned face.

He opened his mouth when a horn blared. Another car had pulled up behind the truck.

"Now I'm not going anywhere for sure," he muttered, but refused to move.

Indignation welled up in her. This guy trying to take *her* space was the last straw on a day that had gone from bad to worse. Juliette opened her car door, making the man jump back to avoid getting hit, channeled her inner fierce, and took a determined step to face the man. He crossed his arms over his broad chest, spread his stance and scowled at her.

Okay, clearly not going anywhere. What could she do to make him change his mind?

"One of us has to move or we'll be stuck here," she reasoned.

"I should have parked on the street." He removed his hat and ran a hand through his wavy hair. The motion made the shirt sleeves pull tight against his muscles.

She watched the movement, then shook herself. No time for admiring his good looks when they had a situation on their hands.

"Instead of creating a scene, why don't you let me move into the space and then you can go out to the street."

He stared at her for a moment, his eyes heated, but she couldn't decipher his expression.

She continued after his nonresponse. "At this point we're both going to be late. Let's not make matters worse."

"Why can't *you* back out and let *me* in?" His scratchy voice sent a shiver over her skin. She swallowed, then pulled herself together.

"Because I had my blinker on."

A wrinkle marred his forehead. "Yeah, my turn signal is broken."

"Your lack of maintenance isn't my problem."

"Your lack of timing isn't mine."

They glared at each other until the car behind the truck backed away.

"You can leave now," Juliette pointed out.

"And give up?"

A slow, unexpected grin spread over his face, changing him from merely handsome to plain out gorgeous. Juliette lost her train of thought for a second, until another car horn shook her back to reality.

"You must be new in Golden," she said, hoping to successfully cover her reaction to the stranger. "You can't charm me to get your way."

His smile ramped up a notch. "You think I'm charming?"

"That's not the point." She crossed her arms over her chest and tapped a foot. "I'm not moving."

He slapped his hat back on his head. "Then it looks like we're at an impasse."

She pressed her lips together, her eyes moving to the empty spot and the sign at the curb. Reserved for the Golden Police Chief.

Disappointed and relieved at the same time, she said, "Seems neither of us can park here."

"Why not?"

She pointed to the sign. "It's reserved for the police chief."

Some of the man's ire slipped away.

They both approached the sign, standing so close that Juliette could feel his body heat. She was enveloped by his cologne. The scent reminded her of pine trees and a touch of citrus. She hadn't noticed this many details about a man in forever.

She cleared her throat. "Stalemate?"

He shook his head and stepped directly to the sign. What was he up to?

"You don't believe me?"

"It's not that I don't believe you," he answered as he circled the metal post, reaching out to touch something on the back side. With a chuckle, he turned on his boot heel and strode to the truck. In the bed, he swung open the top of an oblong metal chest, then rummaged around. He finally pulled out a tool, grinning as he made his way back to the obstacle in their way. He began using the wrench, his arm moving in time as he worked.

"What are you doing?"

"Solving our problem."

"Why do I think you shouldn't be doing what you're doing?"

"Because you're probably right."

He finally stuffed the wrench in his back pocket and shook the plaque completely off the post. With shock, and a little bit of awe, Juliette watched him hold up the sign in victory.

"Looks like we don't need to worry about that any longer."

Her mouth fell open before Juliette marched over. "You can't remove that sign."

"I just did."

"Well, put it back."

He grinned at her.

Did he just dare her to make him put it back? Not one to surrender a cause, she reached out and yanked the sign from his hands. "I'll return it."

"You don't have any tools."

She narrowed her eyes at him. He made a good point, but she wasn't giving in either.

He threw up his hands in defeat. "Be my guest."

"I need your wrench."

He moved a hand behind him and his gaze shifted to something over her shoulder.

Clearly her stellar reasoning skills had malfunctioned today, which was confirmed when a voice behind her said, "Care to explain, Juliette?"

She closed her eyes and silently grimaced, then turned to face the Golden police chief, the sign still in her hands.

SHE WAS GOING to rat him out. It was written all over her lovely face.

Furious green eyes flashed at him. "It's his fault," she accused.

"Me?" he asked in all innocence, keeping his hands behind his back.

"Who is your partner in crime?" the chief asked the woman.

"I…ah…don't know."

"Ty Pendergrass," he said, politely reaching out to shake her hand before realizing he still held the wrench. The one he'd have given her if the law hadn't shown up. He'd been curious to see if she knew how to screw in the bolts he'd removed.

The chief zeroed in on the tool. Busted.

Ty felt a little guilty at the scene before

him. *Little*, being the operative word. Juliette, as he now knew her, had decided to buck him on the day he was running on fumes and a short temper.

He'd been waiting for over a week on a building permit and had finally gotten the call this morning to come get it. He'd lit out of the farm as fast as his old pickup would take him, not expecting to confront a beautiful woman who stood in the way of him completing his mission. If it wasn't for the fact that she'd stood up to him, he'd almost be sorry they got caught.

"Ty." The chief nodded at him then the woman. "Juliette."

She closed her eyes for a moment.

"Someone needs to explain here."

A crowd was starting the form, the first inkling that Ty's recklessness was going to bite him. Again. Before he could say a word, Juliette beat him to it.

"Brady, we were vying for a parking space. I had no idea he was going to act like a delinquent."

"Hey!"

She shot him a glare. "When we both tried to pull into the space, it turned into this whole competition before we realized it was your reserved spot."

Brady? She was on a first-name basis with the police chief? *Does it matter?* They were both in trouble here. Caught red-handed.

The chief, who looked to be in his midthirties, around the same age as Ty, sent him an impressive frown.

"She's right. We were trying to decide who would park in this space and things got out of hand."

The chief reached out for the wrench. "Is this the tool you used to remove the sign from the post?"

"Guilty."

Ty handed it over. The chief weighed it in his hand—or was he weighing the situation?—before giving it back. "You're going to fix this," the chief told Ty. Then turned to Juliette. "And you're going to help him."

"But…"

Not wanting to be in more hot water, Ty said, "Sure thing."

Ty returned to the post, Juliette in his wake, a hint of peppermint in the air. From her? She held up the sign and he screwed the nuts and bolts back on.

Once the job was finished, Juliette moved

away as quickly as possible, taking her scent with her. Shame. He liked mint.

He watched her from the corner of his eye. Her name fit. Juliette. He imagined her in stories of old, with her green eyes flashing, her curly auburn hair a cloud around her pretty face, resting on her shoulders. Her skin, creamy with a touch of crimson high in her cheeks, made him want to know more. But the way she held herself, arms crossed in a defensive motion, gave him pause. He was pretty good at reading people and he was convinced there was a whole lot going on under the surface. She seemed to have her guard up, as if prepared for battle.

Yeah, the woman intrigued him. Too bad they had to meet this way.

"I'll find another space," Juliette was saying to the chief. "If I make Judge Murphy wait, she'll be furious."

"That's not your only problem. You and your buddy need to answer for this mischief."

Panic replaced the fury in her eyes. "Are you going to charge us?"

"That depends."

She shot a glance at Ty. He saw her throat move as she swallowed.

"You'll both agree to clean up Main Street

or I'll charge you with tampering with city property."

"Done," Juliette said. So quickly, Ty did a double take.

She sent him an imploring glance and darn if a protective streak rose up in him. He decided not to buck the system, since he wasn't doing that any longer. They were in trouble and she seemed pretty wigged out at the thought of having to face a judge. Which had him wondering what she'd done to summon her before a judge in the first place. Captivated by her, he wanted to ask, but she was beginning to look a little green.

If he thought about it for too long, he might feel the same way. This was not quite the auspicious introduction to the fine folks of Golden he was hoping for.

Moving to this small town was supposed to curb his freewheeling lifestyle. At least that was the plan and he was one hundred percent on board. His family needed him to make good decisions, which he'd been proud to say had been working. Until Miss Juliette brought out the rebellious side he thought he'd tamed.

Or not.

He glanced at Juliette, then said, "Yes, sir, we'll clean up."

"Tomorrow morning. I want to see you out here bright and early with a broom, trash bag and window cleaner. Got it?"

Window cleaner? Had the chief walked down Main Street lately? The shop owners took meticulous care of their shops. Windows shone, doorways were swept and all around the town was tidy. Was he goofing them?

"Yes," Juliette answered for both of them.

Huh. Turned out she was an annoying Goody Two-shoes.

"I'll be keeping an eye on both of you," the chief said. "Especially you, Juliette. You don't need another mark against you. I don't want to come across a stunt like this again."

What did the chief mean by a mark against her? Her trip to see the judge? He glanced over to see Juliette's face color.

The chief turned to leave, but stopped and swung back. "And please remove your vehicles. I need to park."

Ty could have sworn he heard the chief chuckle as he strode away.

"Now look what you've done," Juliette hissed at him.

"Sounds like it's not your first rodeo."

She waved her hand. "Doesn't matter. I don't need trouble."

A desire sparked in him to mess up Juliette's squeaky-clean opinion of herself. Even though he'd come to Golden to fix his own act, he couldn't resist her allure.

"Says the troublemaker."

Her brow furrowed. "Let's just show up in the morning, get the cleaning done and then we never have to see each other again."

"In this small town? Hardly. And it sounds like you're notorious. How are we going to avoid each other?"

"I didn't know you before today, so we've managed not to cross each other's path."

"Ouch."

"Sorry, I just meant—"

"I know what you meant."

A horn blared from somewhere in the lot.

"We should get moving," she said, starting toward her sedan.

"Good idea. I don't want the chief coming back."

"So tomorrow?" she said. "How does ten sound?"

"That works."

"I'll see you then."

Juliette picked up her pace and when she reached the car door, Ty called out, "Good luck in court."

She stumbled, but climbed into the driver's seat without a word. Before long she'd backed up and moved on to find a different parking spot. Hopefully one she didn't have to wrangle for.

Ty returned to the truck, whistling as he went. Sure, having the chief discover them in the act of vandalism—well, him at least—wasn't great, but it definitely could have been worse. Tossing the wrench in the chest, he secured the lid before sliding in behind the wheel of his pickup to vacate the parking lot. He found an open space on the side street, parallel parked and climbed the steps to the courthouse, hoping to avoid any more skirmishes.

CHAPTER TWO

"WE'RE NOT OFF to a great start."

Gayle Ann Masterson watched Brando Pendergrass move the spoon around at his place setting. The Golden Matchmakers Club had convened a meeting this Saturday morning at Laurel's Corner Cafe to discuss future plans for Brando's son Ty and the woman they hoped to match him with, Juliette Bishop.

"It can't be that bad," Alveda Richards, co-founder of the club, said from her place beside the man. She tucked a strand of gray hair into her tight bun and straightened the sweater over thin shoulders.

"Juliette can be a bit skittish," Wanda Sue Harper informed the man who was new to town.

"And besides," Judge Harry Carmichael added, "we've only just begun."

"You got any sway over the police chief?" Brando asked.

All eyes moved from one to another.

"Come again?" Gayle Ann asked.

Brando let out a long sigh. "There was an incident in town. Ty and Juliette were involved in a tussle over a parking space at the courthouse and things got out of control. The two have to meet this morning to clean up Golden."

Bunny Wright, an additional member, glanced at Gayle Ann. "Did we put that in motion? Because I don't remember agreeing to anything about breaking the law."

"Of course I don't condone breaking the law," Gayle Ann said, her gaze meeting those of the retired judge.

"It couldn't have been too serious if Chief Davis only gave them community service," he said.

Brando sighed. "Still, I'd hoped Ty had gotten over his wild days."

"Wild in what way?" Alveda asked.

"From an early age it was clear that Ty was a natural on horseback. I encouraged the talent and when he got old enough to join the rodeo with me, it kinda went to his head. He was always taking chances, but once he got in the limelight, he was hooked."

"How did your family end up in the rodeo?" Bunny asked.

"I started the family tradition." He rolled one shoulder and grimaced. "Was a bull rider until I had so many aches and pains, I had to give it up. Liz became a competitive barrel racer and Ty took to trick riding. Once we formed our own show, the kids were a hit. My oldest, Scott, ran the show until the multiples sclerosis became too much for him to manage. He's at an assisted living facility and as soon as it can be arranged, he'll move here."

Alveda reached out and squeezed his arm. "Brando, we're so sorry to hear that."

The big man swallowed. "Tore me up on the day he couldn't live with us any longer."

The group went silent. They'd all had some type of tragedy in their lives, one way or another. Who didn't, Gayle Ann thought.

This was why the club was important. Assisting young ones to find their match was a calling Gayle Ann took seriously. There was no better antidote to life's ups and downs than love.

Sitting tall, she patted the pearl necklace she'd added to her ensemble before leaving the house this morning. With a chill in the air, she'd worn one of her power suits in pale blue, with slacks instead of a skirt. She'd visited the salon yesterday, her white hair in its usual style, her tone modulated to one in control. This group looked to her for leadership and she would never let them down.

Brando cleared his throat. "Anyway, we had to downsize and Ty's been pretty even-keeled since. I even think he likes it here. But after the latest episode…"

"This is a hurdle we can work with," Gayle Ann said, opting for positivity.

When she'd come up with the idea to start the club, Gayle Ann had been concerned that her youngest grandson would never find happiness. He'd let work rule every waking hour and she wasn't having that. She'd enlisted Alveda and before long, they matched him to a lovely young lady. Since then, they'd added Wanda Sue's daughter, matching her to a town police officer and Bunny's nephew, who fell for an ambitious gal who worked for the Golden Chamber of Commerce.

Harry had joined the group from the onset. Little had Gayle Ann known that his ulterior motive was to court her. She'd been surprised, and flattered, especially since she had no clue this was his plan from the beginning. They were dating now, which sounded so odd to Gayle Ann at their age, but he was convinced they belonged together. Their family and friends heartily agreed.

She met his dark gaze and couldn't believe her luck. The silver-haired fox was all hers.

"You sure this'll work?" Brando asked.

He'd approached the group at the end of the summer to ask for their help matching Ty and so far he wasn't convinced his son would find the right woman to settle down with.

"You can't rush into this," Alveda informed him. "But the fact that they have to work together gives us a starting point. Brady got the ball rolling without us."

"I don't know," Brando hedged. "When we moved here, I was excited to become part of the community. Golden is a great place to start our business, but I don't want Ty to become famous in a bad way."

"The club is all in, ready to match the stubborn young people of Golden with their true loves," Gayle Ann assured him. "We agree that Golden is attracting more businesses. Part of the reason we wanted to get these young couples together is so they'd stay here and continue the town legacy. The plotting and maneuvering doesn't come without its challenges, but so far we've accomplished our goals, so don't give up before we get started."

"Are we sure Juliette is the right choice?" Wanda Sue asked. "I've noticed her acting up around this time of year."

Brando frowned. "What goes on this time of year?"

"Juliette is the town darling" Gayle Ann explained. "Fifteen years ago she saved the mayor's daughter when her stroller rolled into Main Street. Despite the traffic, Juliette rushed into the street and stopped the stroller before it was hit by a car. It was such a selfless act and to this day, everyone in town calls her a hero."

Alveda's forehead wrinkled. "But you're right, Wanda Sue. In the past few years, she has gotten mighty reckless."

Wanda Sue nodded. "That stunt with the town council got her in hot water with the judge for sure."

Brando's eyes went wide in his weathered face. "I don't want my son hooked up with a woman who goes before a judge. I want the exact opposite."

Gayle Ann reached over to cover his work-roughened hand with hers. "Juliette is a good person. I think she and your son could be the answer to both of them settling down. Looking for a steady life instead of drawing attention."

"I don't know..."

"Brando," the judge said. "Gayle Ann has an uncanny knack for picking people who might not look like they belong together on the surface, but once they go deeper, they form meaningful relationships. I've seen it with my own eyes and all I can ask is that you trust her." He waved his hand to encompass the group. "Us."

Brando ran a hand over his shaved head. "This is more than I bargained for, but I sure haven't come up with any better ideas."

"So we can proceed?" Gayle Ann asked.

Brando stared out the window, watching the passersby strolling up and down Main Street. Tourist numbers were up due to the change of the season.

The cool fall weather, along with the seasonal changes, created a natural masterpiece for tourists to enjoy. The local B and B and the Mountain Spa Center were booked solid, as well as Gold Cabins located out by the lake. Hikers were enjoying a jaunt through the forest to find hidden waterfalls or experience the occasional deer sighting. Shops were busy. Before they knew it, the holidays would be upon them, but for now, Gayle Ann would keep the group focused on what was important. Matching Ty and Juliette.

Brando returned his attention to the group. "I'm with you. Just promise me my boy won't get hurt."

"Has true love ever taken an easy path?" Gayle Ann sent him a soft smile. "I can't guarantee what will happen, but know that each one of us is only after the best interests of your son."

"We want all our young'uns to be happy," Alveda said. "Every person, no matter the age, deserves that."

"And everyone needs a little push in the right direction." The judge's silver moustache quivered when he smiled. "After thinking about Juliette's legal issues, I have an idea or two that might keep those two in each other's company."

Impressed, Gayle Ann said, "Harry, do tell."

He tapped a finger to his temple. "Needs a little more time to formulate, but I believe I'm on the right track. I'll call Judge Murphy as well and keep her in the loop."

Gayle Ann beamed. "I, for one, look forward to hearing your plan."

Bunny rolled her eyes. "Could you two get any more sappy?"

"Stop." Wanda Sue fussed at her friend. "I think they're cute."

Pure pleasure crossed Harry's face.

Brando straightened his shoulders. "Okay,

then, I'm counting on you all to work your magic."

Gayle Ann grinned. "Oh, we intend to."

JULIETTE GRABBED A clean towel from her bag sitting on the floor beside the elliptical machine, wiped her face, then pulled out her earbuds. The workout had been necessary this morning. She'd tossed and turned all last night, whiskey brown eyes and a charming smile filling her dreams. She'd risen before dawn and as soon as the doors to the exercise club at the fashionable Mountain Spa Center opened, she was the first inside.

This early, there were a few regulars getting their workout completed before a busy day, along with guests of the spa taking advantage of the state-of-the-art facility. The wide, open space, with floor-to-ceiling windows along one wall to offer a view of nature, was lined with treadmills and elliptical machines. Juliette loved watching the morning light filter through the tree branches to land on the manicured lawn as she pushed herself, working up a sweat. There were weight machines and an area for free weights available, which Juliette used when she was especially stressed. She eyed them now.

"Feel better?" her good friend, Addie Lane, the spa manager, asked with a knowing smile.

She was around Juliette's height, but while Juliette was slim, Addie had more of a gymnast's build. Gifted with girl-next-door looks featuring blond hair, blue eyes and a sunny smile. Juliette had once dyed her auburn hair the same shade as her friend's and disaster ensued. At the time, she'd been thinking she wanted to be someone else. Not a great move and it never reached its intended purpose. She was still the same person.

"For the moment," Juliette said as she paused the music app on her phone. "Unfortunately, I can't stay on the machine all day."

"As much as I love seeing you here, you're right. You have a life to live."

"Can't I call out today?"

"Doesn't work that way."

Didn't Juliette know it.

"So," Addie said, leaning against the nearby machine. "What's got you rearing to go this morning?"

Running the towel along her neck, Juliette draped it over her shoulder and took a long swig from her water bottle.

"Wow. Whatever is going on must be complicated. You're procrastinating."

Juliette swallowed. "Not really."

Addie rolled her eyes. "Oh, yeah? I think whatever it is, it's big."

This was the problem with having a good friend who could read you. You didn't get away with obfuscation.

"Can't I get through a workout without twenty questions?"

"I only asked two, so I'm just getting started."

A young woman jumped on a machine next to her. Juliette moved out of the way.

"Fine. If you must know," Juliette reported, "yesterday went from bad to worse."

"The court date?"

"I was late." She held up a hand to halt Addie's questions. "I'll explain, but first, the hearing."

"Bad?"

"Could have been worse."

Addie knew bad. Her husband had been killed in the line of duty, working a burglary case for the Atlanta PD. She and her young son, Jacob, had moved back to Golden to be with family. In the grand scheme of things, Juliette's penalty was minor.

"Judge Murphy told me she isn't happy with my behavior, like that's a surprise."

"You have been a little…much."

"Much? Is that a nice way of saying I'm out of control?"

Addie shrugged.

"I'll take that as a yes. Anyway, since blocking the doors was my first real offense—if you don't count the traffic jam I caused when my rally to shed light on early Alzheimer's treatment spread from the park to Main Street—she gave me community service."

"Thankfully it wasn't worse."

Juliette nodded. "I'm hoping I can somehow tie the hours in with my pet project, but I don't know where I'll serve."

"Still haven't gotten any of the local stables willing to cosponsor your program?"

"Not yet."

The Mountain Rehabilitation Center, where she worked, was located between Golden and Clarkston. It offered programs for patients with work injuries who needed rehab or pain management, along with a pediatric and geriatric department. She mainly enjoyed working with autistic children, since she had experience. She was always looking for interactive ways to include play, along with learning and socializing.

"Most folks either don't have horses with temperaments that would work with the program or they're giving lessons or whatever and are too busy. I need a firm commitment that once I start, it'll be for the long haul."

"Your boss still putting on the brakes?"

"Yes. Even though I'm certified, Dr. Johnson wants me to focus on the rehab center, but I really think reaching out to kids is important."

"Don't give up, Juls. It'll happen."

When Juliette had started riding in her teens, she'd discovered a freedom that came from being on horseback, exploring the beautiful mountain trails. Taking a slow and steady route, her cares would melt away as she and the horse enjoyed the quiet of the forest.

Before she'd convinced Ivy to take lessons, there'd been a long time when her little sister wouldn't get near a horse. The big animals scared her. But Juliette was convinced that once Ivy gave it a try, she'd be hooked. Over time, Juliette went slowly, introducing Ivy to the animals, making her feel secure and finally getting her sister to mount a horse. Ivy's eyes had been wide with fear, but as Juliette took the lead and walked the horse around the paddock, Ivy had smiled. Thrilled by her sister's reaction, it had cemented Juliette's idea to implement the therapy program.

But soon after, the farm owners she'd worked

with sold the property for a tidy profit to a developer who bought with the intention of building a resort. Juliette lost the one place willing to support her dream.

She shook off the depressing reality and focused on the conversation.

"Still, I was hoping to keep low this fall."

"But?"

"There was an incident."

Addie grinned. "Of course there was."

"An unintended incident."

"Okay, those are rare."

Good thing she loved Addie or her witty observations might hurt.

"I was late for the hearing and the parking lot at the courthouse was full. A space opened up and a truck tried to beat me in, but we both stopped before we collided. We argued over who was there first—" she pointed to herself "—me. And the next thing I knew, he was unscrewing the sign claiming the space was reserved for the police chief."

Addie snorted out a laugh. "He didn't."

"Oh, he did. I was shocked. I grabbed it from him to insist we put it back just in time for Brady to catch us."

Eyes wide, Addie said, "You have got to be kidding."

"Trust me, I couldn't make this up if I tried."

She still couldn't figure out how Ty had pulled her into his scheme so easily.

"Hmm." Addie's lips curved up at the corners. "So who is your partner in crime?"

Juliette didn't like the sound of that. Or what Addie was insinuating. "He's not my partner. There is no partner."

"He sounds like a partner."

Juliette drew in a breath and held it for a ten count. Jumped when a heavy weight clanged on a machine. Maybe if the spa were a little more crowded, Addie could focus on her guests and not Juliette.

Her friend's gaze never wavered.

"His name is Ty Pendergrass."

Addie's eyebrows shot up. "The rodeo guy whose family bought the old Perkins farm?"

"I guess."

"I watched him perform in the Eureka Games this summer." Her expression was one of awe. "The guy can seriously ride a horse."

Now, that piqued Juliette's interest. Another lover of horses? "Sorry I missed it."

"That's right, you were out of town for that event." Addie wiggled her eyebrows. "If I remember correctly, he was cute."

Ty's amazing eyes, the shade of aged, warmed whiskey, flashed before her. How his smile transformed his face from interesting to handsome. How he was a charmer, no doubt, which brought her to her latest predicament.

"I don't want cute. I want responsible."

Her friend's pert nose wrinkled. "Like Bentley Abbott? He was responsible and you were bored to death."

"That's not true."

Addie sent her a disapproving frown.

"Okay, a little true."

"He wanted to move here from Atlanta and you talked him out of it."

Because Juliette didn't date guys from Golden. They knew her history, well, the part the mayor had told, so she didn't risk it in fear that the truth would come out and she'd be revealed as a fraud and then dumped.

Ever since the mayor moved back, the stress and tension that came with her secret had magnified. She kept waiting for someone to figure out the truth and then she'd be sunk.

Addie continued talking as if Juliette hadn't just taken a detour down memory lane, which made things worse because Juliette had never confided to her closest friend what really transpired that day.

"You two dated on and off for a year and when he moved to California for a new job, you didn't even shed a tear."

She hadn't. Did that make her cold? Unfeeling? These days, she didn't know anymore.

"You have to give someone a chance."

If Addie was fishing, Juliette wasn't taking the bait. Yes, there was no denying that Ty was handsome in a bad boy kind of way. Even though his hair was a tad overlong, and with the battered Stetson angled on his head just right, charm oozed from him in waves. Not that she was paying attention.

Really? Then why does his face appear every time you close your eyes?

Amusement creased the corners of Addie's eyes. "Sounds like you've met your match."

"I hardly think so," Juliette scoffed. "He's clearly a troublemaker."

"Pot calling the kettle."

"I want change. To better our town and the people who live here. He just wanted to get into the courthouse."

Addie grinned but she clearly didn't buy her story.

"So what did the chief do?"

Juliette sighed. "Made us put the sign back up and told us he wouldn't press charges if we showed up this morning to clean Main Street."

Addie looked confused. "Our Main Street? In Golden?"

"That's the one."

"Wait, clean up what?"

Juliette shrugged. "I don't know. Litter?"

Addie's eyes sparkled with humor. "Have you ever seen litter lying around in Golden?"

"No." Now that Juliette thought about it, she realized her friend was right. "I suppose we could clean windows."

"The already shiny store windows?"

The merchants in Golden were nothing if not neat and orderly around their storefronts.

"I'm sure we'll find something to do. The point is, I have to meet him at ten."

Addie glanced up at the clock on the wall. "Looks like you have plenty of time to get a shower and meet your par—"

Juliette sent her a ferocious glare.

"—fellow rule breaker."

Apparently there was no changing her friend's opinion. Or the fact that she was soon to meet up with the handsome stranger.

"He's not that and I can get in thirty more minutes on the treadmill."

"Pushing yourself won't change anything, Juls," Addie said in a soft tone.

No, but if she could keep her mind off what today would bring, the better.

Addie got a light in her eyes. One that Juliette recognized and knew didn't bode well.

"You know," Addie said in a nonchalant tone. "Maybe this guy could be boyfriend material."

That was Addie, always the optimistic one.

"I highly doubt it. He was more concerned about his trip to the courthouse than being gentlemanly."

"Fair, but you can't deny he got your attention."

There was something about Ty that struck a chord deep inside, a feeling Juliette had never experienced with a man before. Mostly because she never let herself become so engaged, but Ty had managed to light a fading ember inside her.

"I don't want to discuss this."

A sly grin curved Addie's lips. "Which means you're attracted."

"How on earth does not wanting to talk about him jump straight to attraction?"

"I can see it in your eyes. You're hooked, my friend."

Juliette looked away. "That's ridiculous."

"Really? How long has it been since we've had a conversation about you and a guy?"

Haltingly meeting her friend's gaze, she said, "How should I know? I don't keep track of these things."

Addie placed her hands on her hips. "I do. It's been over a year. You've gotten so wrapped up with work that you forgot to have a personal life."

Right, because if she focused on her life, she'd have to come to terms with the fact that she was a coward and a fraud. No, thank you.

"I could say the same about you."

Addie's face went blank, and Juliette could have kicked herself.

"Sorry, that was incredibly insensitive."

"No, you aren't wrong. I guess I've been hiding behind Jacob and the job. It hurts less that way."

Juliette reached out to clasp her friend's hand. "It's been five years. It wouldn't hurt for you to have a life either."

With a shake of her head, Addie's voice was wry when she said, "What a duo we are."

Juliette laughed. "At least we have each other."

"True, but I'd give up any extra time with you to see you happy with a significant other."

"Ditto."

Juliette's heart cracked over her friend's sad expression. Before she could say anything else, an employee beckoned Addie to the front desk.

"Gotta run. Call me after you leave your partner. I want details, girl. Details."

"There is no partner."

"Keep telling yourself that," Addie called

over her shoulder as she sauntered away, the words hovering in the air.

Juliette picked up her bag and headed to the treadmill. As she placed the earbuds back in place and cranked up the '80s dance music that made her keep a swift and steady pace, Ty's smirk appeared in her mind. He was the exact opposite of the type of man she needed. Steady, grounded and compassionate were her romantic goals. So what was it about this totally contrary guy that had grabbed her attention? And how was she going to work with a man who pushed her buttons?

Addie was sure to get details. Juliette just wasn't sure if they'd be the good kind.

CHAPTER THREE

ARMED WITH A thermos of freshly brewed coffee, Ty jumped on a four-wheeler and headed from the farmhouse to the barn as the sun lifted over the mountaintops. This was his favorite time of day. The quiet soothed his busy mind so he could concentrate on the task at hand, the barn that had put him at town hall yesterday.

He chuckled, thinking about his nemesis with curly auburn hair and green eyes. Man, she'd really wanted that parking space. He'd gotten a charge out of her indignation and the way her cheeks flushed at her show of temper. Nothing like that had affected him for a long time. And despite the fact that they'd gotten in trouble, he was looking forward to seeing her again in just a few hours.

He'd been able to get the permit even though he had to park a block away from the town office. Now they could start the project. One less chore on the vast list of repairs needed around

Crestview Farm, as the family had renamed it. Just when they thought they had tackled one issue, another popped up, like the sketchy well pump that supplied water to the stable and barn. And that was before they talked about building a house for his sister, Liz, and her son, Colton, on the far side of the property.

When they'd purchased the farm from Mr. and Mrs. Perkins and moved here four months ago, they'd known it was run-down, but it was in their price range. Ty and some local friends had emptied out the barn at the end of the summer only to discover much of the wood had rotted and needed to be replaced. Under further inspection, they saw that the wall studs were also affected, so it was not only a matter of replacing the outer boards but shoring up the entire structure. The new, responsible Ty took money from the contingency fund and, not taking a chance to do the work without a permit, had applied.

Winter would be here in a few months and he wanted this job finished by then. First thing this morning he was tearing off the damaged boards so he could get a better idea of what it would entail to get the barn back in shape. Once safe and secure, the barn was integral to their plans to open the farm to the public.

They wanted to sell goods at some point and this structure would be a great showroom.

Around eight, his nephew strolled into the barn, dressed in jeans, a flannel shirt and boots, a near replica of Ty. With shaggy, dark brown hair, tall and lanky at fifteen, Colton was already Ty's height. A mostly black Australian shepherd named Shep, with white and brown coloring, followed on his heels.

"You're up early," Ty commented as he yanked down a board with gloved hands.

"I heard you and Grandad talking about how this was going to be a big job. I couldn't sleep, so I thought I'd come out here and help you."

That's what happened when three adults and a teenager were living under one roof. It had its challenges, but Ty had promised his father to put in the work to make the farm a success and he was determined to keep his word. For too many years Ty had shirked his duty, but now he was all in.

The farmhouse was the first real home the Pendergrasses had lived in since Ty's mom passed. The interior was dated, but they could take their time deciding what needed to be upgraded down the road.

"Well, Grandad is no spring chicken, so I appreciate the gesture."

Colt stared at Ty like he'd just spoken a foreign language. Which, given his young age, probably was.

Ty removed his denim jacket and rolled his sleeves up. "Grab a pair of gloves and you can help me tear out the boards."

"On it."

Before long, most of the damaged wood created a pile in the grass and they were able to get a good picture of the rebuild ahead.

"I was right when I thought the studs would need to be replaced." He pointed to the affected areas. "We'll order new lumber so we don't have problems down the road."

"I didn't think we'd have to do so much work once we moved here," Colt commented.

"We knew the previous owners and they warned us up front. They were an elderly couple and the place had gotten away from them. But they gave us a price we could afford for all the plans we have. Good thing none of us is afraid of a little hard work."

"Looks like more than a little."

"You get my point."

Colt clearly didn't, but Ty refrained from explaining their decisions. It was bad enough that the kid's dad had taken off when he was a toddler, leaving Liz to figure out next steps.

The family had pulled together in tough times. The farm was the hope for their future.

"Do you think the idea of an interactive farm will draw tourists?" Colt asked.

"In time. Your mom already started offering horseback riding lessons, which was our first step. You've been tending to the goats we used in the show, but once we get some more livestock, we can start to monetize this farm." He swept the back of his glove over his overheated forehead. "I started research on beekeeping. I'd like to sell honey at some point and then branch out to other products like candles and soap."

"Think we can pull it off?"

"I do. It's going to take some time to get established, but tourists love it here in the mountains. We can do well. Maybe grow some produce and add a farmer's market too."

They stepped outside the barn for a break. Ty yanked off his dusty gloves and finished off what was left of the coffee. Colt downed a water bottle. The temperature had risen along with the sun, promising a temperate day. Perfect weather to keep busy, either here on the farm or downtown with the woman who brought out his wilder side. In all his life, he'd never defaced a sign just because a woman got under his skin. Guess there was a first time for everything.

"Do you miss riding?" Colt asked out of the blue.

Loaded question.

Ty had loved the rodeo circuit. The freedom of being on the road. He'd had a knack for riding even as a young kid, and since his dad had already made a name in the rodeo circles, it didn't take long for the crowds to be thrilled by the exploits of another Pendergrass. In his early twenties, when he joined the circuit full-time, Ty had enjoyed his daring act. Loved the celebrity that came from being a top billed trick rider. When Ty was featured, the show sold out. He'd never deny it went to his head, but it had a cost.

He met his nephew's gaze. "Every day."

When his brother was first diagnosed with MS, Ty left the rodeo circuit to join the family show. In the early stages, Scott had been able to manage the disease, so after a short period when it looked like things were under control, Ty took off for the limelight again, which ticked off his dad.

It's time to quit sowing your wild oats.

But Ty hadn't listened. Then Liz called, begging him to come home. He did, reining in the carefree attitude to help pay medical bills and assist his widowed father to make ends meet. Unbeknownst to Ty, the Wild West Rodeo Show was falling into deeper debt because they needed money to keep his brother in an assisted living facility.

"So why give it up?" Colt asked.

"Family."

Colt nodded. "At least you rode this past summer during the Eureka Games."

Ty smiled. The thrill of performing always simmered just below the surface. "I enjoyed showing off my skill before the crowd. It was fun to team up with a bunch of my old partners at Golden's summer blowout."

"You used to do stunts with those guys on the road?"

"I did."

The Wright brothers, Adam and Colin, along with Jamey Johnson, the owner of Smitty's Pub, a local hangout, had joined the traveling show for a few summers during high school. When Ty and his dad were looking for a place to plant roots, they decided on Golden because of the good friends they'd made, as well as access to this farm.

"I wish I could ride like you," Colt said, his tone wistful.

Ty clapped him on the shoulder. "It's in your blood. Between me doing tricks and your mom having been a champion barrel racer, you should be a natural on a horse."

"I like to ride, but when I try to do some of your tricks, I chicken out."

"Time, buddy. It doesn't happen overnight."

"I guess. But now that we're here, I have chores and school. It cuts down on my riding time."

Ty understood. Being responsible had been far from his mind when he was competing. At the time, he couldn't imagine anything worse than living a conventional lifestyle. Until his father confessed that he'd run the finances of the family traveling show into the ground. A myriad of emotions had swallowed him. Why hadn't his father said anything sooner? Because of the chasm between them? As a result, he and his father's relationship had become even more strained, but they forced those feelings aside for the sake of the family.

They were fortunate to sell off most of the livestock and remaining equipment in order to purchase the farm and start an entirely new family business, but the tension between he and his dad had never completely gone away.

Taking a more perceptive look at his nephew,

Ty said, "You look like you've got something else on your mind."

Colt ran the toe of his scuffed boot in the dirt. "I don't want to bother Mom about it."

Colt wasn't missing much, his father had been a disappointment, but he had Ty, Scott and Brando as positive male influences in his life.

"What's up?"

"This is my first year at one school since we stopped traveling."

"Right. Junior year. Are you settling in?"

"I guess." Colt's shoulders inched up to his ears in a shrug. "Still getting razzed all the time since I'm the new kid, but I met some guys I think I can be friends with."

They moved back indoors. Dust and specs of hay hung in the beam of sunlight shining through the open slats.

"Are you going to try out for sports?"

"I've been thinking about it. Right now, I just want to fit in."

Ty grabbed a board and pulled. "And how is that going?"

"Okay. I like my classes and the teachers are okay."

Ty sensed there was more. "So, any other friends besides those guys you mentioned?"

"There's this girl, Kelsey, in my chemistry class who's real cute. We talk between classes and she asked me to be her lab partner."

"Go, Colton."

The teen shrugged as if this was no big deal, but his neck flushed.

"You're light-years ahead of me than when I was in school."

"I doubt that."

Ty chuckled.

Colt surprised Ty by saying, "You've always been successful with the ladies."

Ty nearly choked. "Where did you hear that?"

"Mom. She was talking to one of her new friends."

Jeez. He wanted to leave his reputation behind, not have his family cementing it in stone.

"Don't believe all the hype," Ty assured his nephew.

Point in case—Juliette.

He'd been drawn to her immediately and had to wonder why. Okay, he'd bungled things for sure by taking down the sign, but had a chance to make a better impression later this morning. He was determined to pour on the charm, to win Juliette over. It had always worked for him before, why not in Golden?

"Do you have any advice?"

Did he? No matter what Ty told Colt, the teen would have to test those waters on his own, just like every young boy who had a crush and no clue what to do with it.

"Be nice and respectful. Listen to her. Just be yourself, Colton."

"Sure that'll work?" he asked with misery in his tone.

"She's already talking to you, right?"

"The homecoming dance is soon. I was thinking about asking her to go with me." He rolled his eyes. "The dance my mom agreed to chaperone."

Ty chuckled. "I know it's not ideal, but it's a way for your mom to meet other parents. Make friends."

"I guess."

Ty slapped him on the back. "Just ask Kelsey to go. She obviously sees something special in you, so you have that going for you."

Colt's face lit up. "Yeah, you're right."

A goofy grin crossed Colton's lips and Ty decided his job here was done.

"That it?"

"Hmm...."

"There's more?"

"Not about school." While he hedged, Ty waited. "About Mom."

Concern washed over him. "Is something wrong?"

"No. I just… Sometimes she seems lonely. I've got school and I'm making friends but she's sort of…stuck."

"That's why being a chaperone is one step toward solving that problem."

After Liz had decided to file for divorce and raise Colton alone, she'd poured her life into her son. But he was growing up. That had to put Liz at sixes and sevens.

"Don't worry, Colt. She'll figure it out."

"Can I do anything?"

"The fact that you're concerned about her is enough. But she's an adult and can figure this out on her own. She'd hate you worrying about her."

"Is that the Pendergrass pride Grandad is always warning about?"

"One and the same."

"He makes it sound bad."

"It can be. But honestly, I don't think you have much of our stubbornness. You'll be fine."

A long pause halted the conversation.

"And Uncle Scott?"

"You let us figure out how to get him home." Colton nodded.

"Besides, you have a certain young lady to think about."

The tips of Colton's ears turned red.

"Why don't we call it a day. I have an appointment so I need to hit the shower."

"Thanks, Uncle Ty."

"You bet."

"Shep and I are going to check on the goats."

Colton had taken a few steps when Ty called out, "By the way, I fixed the latch on the pen. Shouldn't have any more escapees."

Colton waved in response. As he and his companion took off, Ty headed back to the farmhouse, excitement building in his gut. Like Colt figuring out his attraction to a schoolmate, Ty was looking forward to seeing a particular redhead again. Not that he needed a distraction, he had plenty keeping him on the go. The barn. Getting the business up and running.

When they'd started this new life, he'd made a promise to his dad. Stay focused. Bring Scott closer to the family. Make ends meet. He didn't need trouble, or the woman who came with it.

On the heels of that last thought, he couldn't

contain a grin. After meeting Juliette, staying out of trouble had lost its appeal.

Yeah, no pressure.

He tried to fight off the impending gravity of proving himself, but it didn't work. Instead, he pictured his new friend's pretty face.

Ty and Juliette might not have met on favorable terms, and he had no business being attracted to her, because it could go nowhere, but she'd made moving to Golden a lot more interesting.

JULIETTE, MANNED WITH a broom and a bucket filled with cleaning supplies, rubber gloves and paper towels, watched as Ty headed her way. His long stride ate up the sidewalk, his boots clomping on the concrete sidewalk. Today he was minus his Stetson, but dressed in worn jeans and a long-sleeved T-shirt. She looked much the same, except for sneakers instead of boots, and a baseball cap protecting her sensitive skin from the sun.

Her stomach did a funny dip when he stopped in front of her. Brushing off the sensation, she said, "The sooner we get started, the sooner we can go our separate ways."

"Sounds like someone got up on the wrong side of the bed this morning."

"It's Saturday. I have things to do."

Which was partially true. She did want to clean her cottage. Really clean, not Ivy's version of moving things around. Plus, she had some new resource material to read, so yeah, she was busy.

He rubbed his hands together. "Okay, I'm ready to work, and by 'work,' I mean I'm going to stand here and watch you use all those supplies."

Her mouth fell open. "They're for both of us."

"I knew you had a type A personality," he said with a smirk.

"How could you possibly come to that conclusion?"

"Because you had your blinker on when you tried to steal my parking space."

She held back a flip remark. From the moment Ty had walked her way, he'd sent her blood boiling and she didn't like it.

"One," she said as reasonably as possible. "I was there first. And two, it's a good thing I brought supplies or we'd have to make a run to the store."

The traffic on Main Street was heavy this Saturday morning, folks out enjoying the autumn weather and doing some early holiday shopping. A car honked. Juliette glanced over to see Addie driving by, a huge smile on her face. In the passenger seat, her son, Jacob, waved so hard he looked like he might hurt himself.

Despite guessing correctly what was going on in her friend's head, she returned the wave.

Ty's voice held humor when he said, "Are you going to be waving at people all day?"

"Are you going to be critical all day?"

They stared at each other.

Finally, she broke the trance. "Look, this is ridiculous. Why don't we start over." She held out her hand. "Hi, I'm Juliette Bishop, your cleanup partner today."

Did she just call him partner? Ugh. Addie was in her head.

Ty waited a beat before taking her hand in his. As calloused fingers grazed her skin, a shimmer ran up her arm. Unwelcome, but exciting all the same.

"Ty Pendergrass. Pleased to meet you."

Juliette quickly slipped her hand from his. "Now that we've been properly introduced, where do you want to begin?"

He shrugged. "Beats me. You've got the lowdown on this town."

She went still. "Why would you say that?"

"I asked around and learned you were born and raised in Golden."

"I was."

"I've only been here four months, so I don't have a clue."

Right. That made sense. It wasn't like he was trying to uncover her deep dark secrets.

Then, when remembering Addie's suggestion that Juliette was acting a little bit more tense than usual, she froze. Wait, was she giving off a deep-dark-secret vibe? She sent him a sideways glance, relieved when he seemed more focused on the area around them than her.

They stood midway on Main, decked out in Halloween finery, leaving them to head in either direction. "Let's go south a few blocks. We can make our way back this way and then cross Main at the top of the hill."

To her surprise, he reached down to pick up the bucket. He must have noticed the surprise on her face.

"Believe it or not, I have some manners."

"I didn't…" She pressed her lips together. "Thank you."

Before long they were outside of the T-shirt Depot. Folks went in and out, so Juliette handed the broom to Ty and donned the gloves in order to spray and wipe the window.

"I don't mean to speak ill of the chief, but what was he thinking ordering us to clean up?" Ty rested a hand atop the broomstick. "There's not a lick of litter out here."

"Maybe it's the first thing that popped into his head. You are right though, Golden is very clean. Like, freaky clean."

He glanced up the sidewalk. "One of the reasons we moved here. Dad likes the small town atmosphere and my sister wants a place where she and my nephew can settle down for good."

"And you?"

He shrugged. "I'm good anywhere."

From the reservation in his tone, she wondered if that were true.

They cleaned what little there was, then moved to the next shop.

"Where did you move here from?" she asked.

"Everywhere."

She chuckled. "That narrows it down."

"Sorry." A wry smile curved his lips. "We ran a traveling Wild West Rodeo Show, so we were on the road most of the year."

"It must be strange to be in one place."

"Strange, but good. My family is happy."

She snapped her fingers. "That's right, you were in the Eureka Games this summer."

Was she imagining it or did his chest just puff up?

"You happen to catch my act?"

"No, I was out of town with my sister."

His grin faded. "Then how did you know I was part of the games?"

"My friend told me."

"So, you were talking about me?"

And the charmer was back.

She rolled her eyes. "Actually, I was lamenting your recklessness that got us in hot water."

"I do love the water."

She shook her head and laughed. "Are you this charming with all the girls?"

He rubbed a hand down his face. "Only the ones who get in trouble with me."

Don't blush. Whatever you do, don't blush!

"So, what's a Wild West show?"

"Started out as a rodeo. Dad was a bull rider and my sister a barrel racer."

"What did you do?"

"Trick riding. I was on the professional rodeo circuit for a long time too."

She frowned. "Trick riding?"

"Stunts while seated, standing on the saddle or, sometimes, hanging off a horse."

"Is that safe?"

"If you do it right."

At his confident grin, Juliette didn't doubt his expertise.

"I ride," she blurted.

"Yeah? Do you board a horse?"

"No. When I can get away from the job, I go to a place that offers horseback riding."

He moved the broom around. "I haven't had a chance to really check out the trails around here, but this is some beautiful country."

"But you miss being on the road?"

His brow crinkled and he threw back her words from earlier. "Why would you say that?"

She wasn't trying to read anything into the conversation, but she sensed a longing in Ty.

"The excitement in your eyes when you talked about it."

"Good guess, but I'm okay with being in Golden. The circuit was fun, but we have plans."

Juliette found an actual smudge on the window she was currently examining and sprayed cleaner before applying some elbow grease. Ty brushed the stray leaves scattered about them.

"What about you?" he asked.

"Occupational therapist."

"You help people regain function after injuries?"

She glanced at him in surprise. Most of the time she had to explain her job to people.

"That's one aspect. I work at a rehab facility on a number of different cases."

"Sounds rewarding."

"It is."

She loved her job, had a passion for her career. She thought perhaps it had started as a way of overcompensating after the stroller incident. To make up for going along with the lie. But the work was rewarding to her, not just a means to an end.

Ty's gaze grew cloudy. "My brother has MS."

"That can be scary."

"It has been tough, but he's getting treatment. We're taking it day by day."

Juliette knew it wasn't that simple. Understood the emotional costs. She wanted to sympathize more with Ty, but they moved to the end of Main Street and crossed at the light. As they started on the next storefront, he changed the subject.

"So what does anyone do for fun around here?"

"Define *fun*."

He tilted his head. "If I have to explain, you probably don't know how to do it."

"I have fun," she insisted.

Wait. She did, didn't she? Sure, she'd been working steadily since returning to Golden after college, but she did stuff.

"What's your idea of fun?" he challenged.

"Working out."

"That's a necessity. Try again."

"I hang out with my sister. Sometimes go horseback riding." Although as she thought about it, even that had been a while ago.

"Okay. Do you travel?"

"No."

"Take a vacation?"

"No."

"I heard there's a nice lake in Golden. Do you go boating? Swimming?"

"No."

He sent her a pitying glance. "You need to shake things up in your life."

"And I suppose you think you can show me how?"

His grin widened and his eyes sparkled, as if he was thinking, *Challenge accepted.*

Good grief.

Here was the problem. In a matter of two days, Ty had disturbed her constant, solid life. And to her utter dismay, she found him entertaining. Unexpected. A shake-up she needed.

What did she do now?

They stopped at Blue Ridge Cottage. As Juliette glanced inside, the owner, Serena Stanhope, waved. A huge grin curved her lips when she noticed Ty and she called for someone to join her. Most likely her friend Heidi Welch. News of this community service was going to be all around town before they even finished.

Another story to live down.

"Hiking? Camping?" Ty continued.

"Stop. I live a boring life, okay?"

He leaned a shoulder against a lamppost and crossed his ankles. "This area has a lot to offer. I'd think you'd be off on an adventure every weekend."

Maybe, if she had a person to go on adventures with. Addie was busy with her job and son. Her sister was busy with her own life. Besides her work, what did Juliette do?

In college, she'd been willing to go on an

impromptu shopping trip or to the movies when she should have been studying. Looked at it like a guilty pleasure. When was the last time she'd done something for herself?

"Is that what you enjoy?" she asked him. "Adventures?"

"I don't mind being spontaneous."

"So what would you do?"

"Before buying the farm? Probably would have kept traveling on the circuit. But now? I've got a barn project that keeps me on my toes."

"Is that fun?"

"In a new kind of way. Guess I'm seeing just how far I can push myself. Not resting on my laurels. Seeing what I can accomplish out of my comfort zone."

She couldn't resist asking, "Your laurels being?"

Ty blinked, like he'd said too much. Then his cocky grin reappeared. "Winning competitions."

"Of course."

They ended up at the Nugget B and B.

"This is it. The end of our community service."

"This wasn't so bad, was it?" he asked, handing over her broom.

"Not a chore I'd like to repeat, but it was nice being outside on a beautiful day."

He winked at her. "See. I knew you had it in you."

She felt her face heat. "Maybe, but I still maintain that this was all your fault."

"Guess we'll have to agree to disagree."

"Which is probably every conversation you have with people."

"Are you saying I'm difficult?"

"We wouldn't be in this mess if—"

"Hold on, kids," a voice came from her right. "Don't want another confrontation getting out of control."

Juliette looked over to see Chief Davis walking their way.

"Checking up on us?" she asked.

"Actually, yes. Also, I wanted to make sure you two hadn't gotten into more mischief before your community service was over. I don't like making arrests on sunny days."

She frowned. "That doesn't make sense."

"Doesn't know how to have fun *or* get a joke," Ty muttered under his breath.

She swiveled to him. "I heard that."

"The truth hurts."

Indeed it did. He made her sound like a cold, uptight fish.

He's not wrong.

She would be so happy when this month was over and she could go back to normal.

Until the truth comes out you'll never be normal.

She was about to tell her inner self to keep quiet, but both men were staring at her.

"What?" she demanded.

The chief shook his head. "I said, I have an update on your court-appointed community service."

She didn't want to ask, but did anyway. "What is it?"

"You're to volunteer the hours set by the judge at Crestview Farm. They need some free labor."

"Crestview Farm. I'm not familiar—"

"Wait a minute," Ty cut in. "That's my farm."

"Well, what do you know," the chief said, rocking back on his heels.

"Your farm?" Juliette gasped.

Ty focused on the chief. "How did this happen?"

The chief shrugged. "I don't hand out the assignments."

"But…" Juliette sputtered. "I can't work with him again."

"Maybe I don't want to work with you either," Ty countered.

They stood toe to toe, staring at each other, like it was the scene in the parking lot all over again.

The chief moved closer. "I'm thinking you two should take a step back."

Juliette shook her head. He was so close, she could smell Ty's outdoorsy cologne mixed with hard work and sunshine. She closed her eyes and took in a deep breath of crisp mountain air to clear her mind.

When she looked at Ty again, his facial expression had closed up. Gone was the charmer. She had no idea what he could be thinking.

"You both are free to go home."

Ty glanced at the chief. "Sure it was Crestview Farm you heard?"

"Positive."

He turned back to Juliette. "Seems we'll be seeing each other again."

He turned on his heel and walked in the opposite direction. Juliette swallowed hard.

"You okay?" Brady asked.

"Yes… Just, ah, getting over the shock."

"If this is too much, I could put a word in with the judge. Get you a different assignment."

"No." Just what she needed, more for the judge to be displeased about. "I'll be there."

Could they possibly share the same space without strangling each other? Seems they had no other choice but to find out.

CHAPTER FOUR

"COMMUNITY SERVICE?" Pam Bishop asked in the pointed tone that made Juliette cringe. They were washing the dishes the following Friday night after dinner. Julictte had been running late at work when her mother called and invited her to join them.

Juliette had met with the judge a few days ago but hadn't been able to bring her mother up to speed until tonight. "She upped my community service hours."

Her mother's eye went wide. "Whatever for?"

"To make a point, I'm sure."

Juliette thought about the conversation. Judge Murphy did not hide her disappointment, and that was before she'd learned about the town sign. Since Juliette had been late for the appointment, the judge had to leave to get back to court, so the assignment hadn't been given until her assistant called this morning to confirm that she was indeed to report to Crestview Farm.

"You were just trying to get the town council's attention for a good reason."

"But I did disrupt their scheduled meeting." She heaved out a sigh. "I suppose it could have been worse."

Her mother's eyes went wide. "Worse how?"

"They could have put me in jail and thrown away the key."

"They wouldn't lose it if they had one of my key chains," Ivy piped up.

Juliette glanced over her shoulder and smiled at her sister seated at the table, busy at work. "That's very true."

Her twenty-five-year-old sister had fallen in love with jewelry making after Juliette had discovered and introduced Ivy to the art last summer. Juliette had taken her to Atlanta for a week to learn the trade. She was very detailed-focused, which made this a perfect skill for her. She created key chains—the four-leaf clover ring Juliette proudly carried—along with colorful beaded bracelets and earrings. Ivy worked part-time at a local law firm, doing filing and paperwork, and now on her art, hoping to sell the pieces as her skill level increased.

"But you'll keep out of trouble now?" her mother queried.

Juliette didn't miss the hopeful tone in her

voice. She frowned, thinking about working with Ty again. They'd survived cleaning up Main Street together, hadn't they? And to be honest, a tiny part of her wouldn't mind spending time with him again.

"I'll try," Juliette said as her mother handed her another dish to dry. "Once Ivy makes us rich with her jewelry designs, I'll hire out-of-town agitators."

"Don't bring your sister into it," her mom warned.

Juliette met Ivy's gaze and they shared a secret grin. The sisters were close and no amount of censure from their parents could draw them apart.

"So far I'm assigned to Crestview Farm." Ty's face flashed in her mind, his eyes sparkling with a mischief she couldn't forget. "At least Brady gave me a heads-up before the judge's assistant called."

"The old Perkins farm?" Her mother shook her head. "That's right, there are new owners."

"Remember you told me about the Eureka Games from the summer? The family who once owned a rodeo bought the farm."

"Oh, yes. I watched the daughter showcase a barrel racing event. And the brother—"

"Ty."

"—was seated on his horse, holding up a hoop while Adam Wright shot an arrow straight through." She shuddered. "It was too close for comfort."

Juliette remembered her friend Adam being on the archery team in high school. He'd been good, but aiming at a man on a moving horse? Once she pictured Ty on the horse in her mind, that pirate's smile on his face, it made sense.

"Ty said he was a trick rider."

"Ty, hmm. The man you had community service with on Saturday?"

So she'd heard.

"Juliette, what were you thinking taking Brady's sign?"

That she'd been badgered into her behavior. And that, technically, she'd wanted to put it back.

Unusual, but Ty's charm had struck a chord deep inside her. If he continued smiling at her like he had the other day, well, she wasn't sure how she'd react.

"You had to be there."

"And now you'll be at their farm?"

"After making up for the sign incident, Ty and I know we can work together."

At least she hoped so. Cleaning downtown

was one thing. Working on his farm where he had control was another.

"In any case, I'm hoping I might mention the equine program while I'm there. Get their take on the idea."

"I'm not interested in horseback riding anymore," Ivy announced as she strung together beads. "I prefer spending my time making jewelry."

"It shows, because you've done a beautiful job." Juliette tossed the damp towel on the counter. "But other kids like to ride, so I want to make it happen for them."

"You will," Ivy said as she separated the red beads from the blue. At least her sister had faith in her.

"Do you think this Ty will go along with your goal?"

"I'm sure to find out."

Her mother got a flinty gleam in her eyes. "Why haven't you and Brady ever dated? You'd make a cute couple."

Chief Brady Davis was firmly in the friend zone. They'd known each other forever, which put him squarely out of the dating pool. He didn't make her…jittery. On edge. Waiting for the next shoe to drop. Not like with Ty.

In fact, other than her first real crush, who'd stood her up that day long ago in the park, she'd never had this butterfly-in-the-stomach reaction. Sure, she liked the guys she'd dated, but had never seen any of the relationships as serious. Long-term. It was easier that way. Once any guy started getting too close, she closed down. The belief that she didn't deserve happiness would overwhelm her, things would fall apart and she'd move on.

An image of Ty, his dark hair, sultry eyes and developed muscles, made her catch her breath. What would he think if he learned that she'd never straightened out the truth about stopping the baby stroller? He definitely had an unruly streak, so maybe he'd understand. But who stole a city sign and why did that excite her? And why couldn't she ignore the way he made her feel? Because she didn't want to, much to her chagrin.

Foolhardy? Probably.

Yes, he was handsome, in a rugged way. His eyes sparkled when he ramped up the natural charm, making her insides quake. But was there more to the man? She'd gotten a glimpse of his resolve when he'd mentioned his family and her initial attraction for him intensified. Then the charm started oozing and his smile took her breath away.

Good grief, he got to her every time.

And now she was going to have to see him on a regular basis.

No good deed went unpunished.

Shaking off her thoughts, she said, "But, I do have some good news."

As her mother wiped down the countertop, she sent Juliette a strange look. "Why are you blushing?"

"No reason." Could she be any more obvious? Juliette pulled out a chair across from her softly humming sister, changing the direction of the conversation.

"Ivy, Serena would like to feature some of your work at Blue Ridge Cottage."

Her sister quieted, but kept her head down, hyperfocused.

"That's wonderful," their mother said.

"Ivy? What do you think?"

Head still down, she asked, "How much does she want? Do I have to have to deliver it right away?" She dropped her tool and her fingers fluttered. "I can't make it all tonight."

Juliette reached over to steady her sister's hand. "Of course not. I have a plan."

Ivy's head rose. "A plan?"

"Yes." Juliette kept her tone calm as the panic rose in her sister. "You're right, you can't make an entire collection tonight and Serena doesn't expect you to. Okay?"

Ivy gave her a jerky nod.

Juliette rose and walked to the hook on the wall where she'd hung her sweater and the crammed tote bag she carried to work. She brought it to the table, searched inside and removed a folder.

"I came up with a schedule you could try. Since you still have to go to work at the law office, you can work around it." She slid the paper toward Ivy. "On the mornings you go to the office, you'll work on the jewelry in the afternoon. On your days off, you pick the morning or afternoon to continue creating, leaving us a little sister bonding time.

"You can arrange it any way you like. But no staying up late to work," Juliette teased. "You need a good night's sleep to create your one-of-a-kind pieces."

Pleasure colored her sister's face. "Tell me the truth. Do you think they're pretty? That they'd actually sell?"

Juliette dug out her clover key chain and dangled it from her finger. "Only the very best."

"I promise to keep to a schedule." Ivy glanced at their mother. "And I'll need time with my new dog."

Juliette didn't miss the wrinkles tighten

around her mother's eyes, but she managed a smile. "Yes. It's time."

A huge smile brightened Ivy's lovely face. "I settled on Bruno for a name." She glanced at Juliette. "I found it in the book of names you gave me."

"A very noble name."

Ivy's attention turned back to their mother. "So when can we pick him out?"

"I'll talk to your father. Maybe this weekend when we're both off."

It took everything in Juliette not to intervene and tell Ivy they'd pick out a dog together. This was a promise her parents had yet to fulfill and she wanted them to carry through. Juliette didn't reside here, wouldn't be part of the daily care of a pet, so she didn't have a say. Her folks needed to be on board and part of the process.

The chair legs scratched the floor as Ivy pushed backward. "I'll go ask Dad now."

She took off, leaving Juliette and her mother behind.

"I suppose there's no way out of it," her mom said with a sigh as she joined Juliette at the table. "A dog. What was I thinking?"

"You have been trying to do this for a long time."

"Usually it's a phase with Ivy, but this time

she's determined." Her mother looked everywhere but at Juliette. "Perhaps you could—"

Juliette held up her hand. "No, this has to be you and Dad."

"I suppose that's fair."

"I love every minute with Ivy, but this time…"

"You're right. Your father and I always put a lot of responsibility on you when you were a kid and we worked full-time."

"Which I never minded. You've both been a constant for us." Juliette grinned. "She's the smartest one in the family, if you ask me."

"Mostly because of your nurturing. You helped her find her way in life. Got her the job at the law office."

"We've all had a part."

Her mother shook her head. "I'm suddenly realizing I've missed out on a lot with Ivy."

"And I probably should have pushed you more to be involved."

"I guess we're both guilty of loving her too much?"

This was one area of guilt Juliette would gladly claim. "And lucky to be a part of her life."

The room went silent before her mother said, 'I've been thinking about dropping down to part-time hours at work."

"Really? How will the insurance agency run without you?" Juliette teased.

"We have a hardworking staff and Helen can fill my shoes." She stared down at her hands. "When you called to tell me about Serena offering to feature Ivy's jewelry at the store, I realized here was a chance for me and Ivy to spend more time together, make her dream come true." She looked up and met Juliette's gaze. "You don't mind, do you?"

"Wow. Okay, I guess."

Her mother's gaze grew serious. "It'll mean more time for you to focus on you and your life." She held up a hand when Juliette opened her mouth, effectively silencing her. "Look. I've done the research. There's so much that goes into a business and I'm hoping Ivy will be open to having a partner instead of figuring it out alone. I'll cut down my time at the office. Make it happen."

Something akin to panic tightened in Juliette's chest. "I'm the one who makes it happen," she couldn't help but blurt out. "Ivy and me. We're a team."

Her mother nodded and slipped an arm around Juliette's shoulder. "And you still will be a team, always. But you should be thinking about your future. Dating. Seriously dating. Someday you may want to get married, right? Start a family?"

"Not everyone wants that route, Mom."

"Can you honestly tell me you haven't thought about it?"

Of course she had. A lot. Dale and Pam Bishop had been wonderful role models. But the past still cast a shadow over Juliette. She'd been a fraud all this time and that wouldn't change, no matter her dreams for a future. What man, if he learned the truth about what had happened, wouldn't look at her differently?

Unaware of the turmoil swirling inside her, her mother chuckled.

"The hero of Golden should have her own happy ending."

Juliette swallowed back the shame. "That was a long time ago. Everyone has forgotten."

"Not the Danielsons. I ran into Marie and Ellie going into Tessa's clothing store." She frowned. "At least it's still called Tessa's since the new owner hasn't taken over yet." She waved a hand in the air. "Anyway, Ellie just turned seventeen. Can you believe she's already looking into colleges?"

Juliette unrolled a mint that she quickly chewed, hoping it would settle her stomach.

"Marie was going on and on about how

smart Ellie is and that if it hadn't been for your selfless act that day, the story might have ended differently for their family. She said the mayor has been talking about it a lot recently." He mother patted her hand. "You did a good thing."

Juliette jumped up. "I need to run. I have to get to the farm early tomorrow."

She grabbed her tote and crossed the room to take her sweater from the hook.

"You can't ignore the past."

No truer words had ever been spoken.

"We were so proud of you that day."

"You shouldn't have been," Juliette said with a touch of heat in her tone.

"What? How could we not be?"

"Because it was an accident. I didn't—"

Ivy bopped into the kitchen. "Dad and I looked at the animal rescue website, Juliette." She went up on tiptoe and started bouncing. "I found Bruno!"

Juliette hugged Ivy. "Good for you."

Her smile dimmed. "Are you leaving?"

"Yes. I have to go out to the farm tomorrow."

She kissed her sister and nodded at her mother. Before she could escape out the back door, her mom stopped her. "Accident?"

"Forget it." She'd almost blurted the truth,

not missing her mother's less-than-convinced look. Now she was sick to her stomach over the thought. "I need to get in the right mindset to deal with Ty tomorrow."

She had to be pretty rattled if the thought of spending time with Ty was better than facing her own mother.

Thankfully a knowing grin crossed her mother's lips instead of more questions about that day. "Ty, huh?"

It took all her power not to roll her eyes. "I'll talk to you later."

"I can't wait for a report."

At least Ty was a distraction she could handle. The truth? That was a whole other issue.

TY HEFTED THE saddle up onto the stand in the tack room after taking Juniper out for a morning ride before starting his chores. The air had been crisp, chilling his cheeks. The wind had brushed over his face as he rounded the arena, running through his old tricks. It was second nature to stand and lift one leg over Juniper's head to balance his weight in the stirrup on one side of the black horse. Or to stand on the saddle as the horse raced, then drop down to stroke Juniper's head. They made quite the team.

As always when he rode, he missed his

old life. The thrill of mastering the tricks. The crowds yelling and clapping as he went through his act, the fans waiting to meet him afterward. It had all gone to his head. Here, in Golden, no one really knew him, which was different. Living life out of the spotlight was going to take some getting used to, but with the list of repairs needed around the farm, he pushed the past to the back of his mind.

The morning quiet was broken when his father, Brando, filled the doorway. "Got an interesting proposition to run by you."

"More interesting than the one you sprang on me last weekend?"

Brando didn't bother to look chastened.

After the police chief had dropped the news that Juliette's community service hours were at the farm, Ty had gone right home to confront his father. The old man didn't miss a beat by confirming the news.

"Why didn't you tell me up front?"

"To be fair, I hadn't got the confirmation from the judge yet."

Ty hung the bridle on a hook mounted on the wall. "But you suspected?"

Brando shrugged. "We're pretty new here, but I made it clear we wanted to do our civic duty."

"We?" Ty muttered.

Not that it should have surprised Ty. His dad had always helped down-on-their-luck folks when they owned the traveling rodeo. Why should his actions in Golden be any different?

Ty had had a week to cool his heels. To get ready to face Juliette again. She'd piqued his interest, but that didn't mean he had to be excited about this community service project like the rest of his family.

He lifted his shoulder. "I've got to take care of Juniper." He'd already hosed down the horse, now he made his way to where his horse waited to be groomed, grabbing a brush as he passed by the supply shelf. "What's up?"

His father followed him. "Juliette Bishop is starting her community service here today."

"I'm aware." He rubbed an eyebrow. "Liz is in charge of this, right?"

"Your sister had an appointment with the accountant this morning."

Of course she did.

"Which puts you in charge," his father added.

Truth be told, Ty had woken this morning with Juliette on his mind. As he pictured her smiling face, he'd jumped out of bed, ready to start the day. But as the hours wore on, he remembered how prickly she could be and with all he had going on, supervising her gave him pause.

Brando adjusted his Stetson. "How are the barn repairs going?"

"Finished yesterday. With Colton's help."

"Bad as you expected?"

Ty ran the brush over Juniper's side. The horse danced sideways. "We got it taken care of."

"And Juliette?"

"The building needs to be painted, inside and out."

"Sure that isn't too much for her?"

Ty recognized the gleam in his father's eyes. "Did you have something else in mind?"

"Maybe down the road."

Ty rounded Juniper, stroking his nose, before finishing the job. "What's going on, Dad?"

"We may have a chance to bring more income into the farm."

Ty led Juniper back to his stall, his shoed hooves clip-clopping on the concrete floor. "In what way?"

"Apparently Juliette tried to start an equine rehabilitation program, but the farm she worked with sold and she lost her access. I've gotten to be friends with Harry Carmichael and he told me he knows about a fund that would support the program. We could make a deal where she gets to run her program here as part of her service hours."

Ty knew his dad and asked, "And what do we get in return?"

"In exchange, the fund will cover expenses to board, feed and care for the horses."

"Sounds too good to be true."

"That's what I thought, but Harry assured me it's legit. It'll be a good fit for the farm. Get our name out there. Juliette is certified, but would need to access our facilities before jumping in. Other than that, I don't see a downside."

Neither did Ty. But Juliette had a set number of hours to complete. Question was, if they agreed, would she stick around after her service was completed?

"Does your new friend Harry think Juliette is up to this?"

"She's tried to get the program up and running before." Brando's spine went as stiff as steel. "I want to see where this leads."

Ty recognized the stance and swallowed a groan. His dad was going to be stubborn for sure. "So I take it that you're not interested in my opinion?"

"Just give this a chance and then we'll talk."

Ty ran a hand through his hair. He needed a cut, but when did he have time? Between the chores, the barn, worrying about how to pay if they needed a new well system, he didn't have time to babysit Juliette, good intentions or not.

"We've got to keep the farm in a good light and that stunt you pulled in town didn't boost our reputation."

Ty had managed to dodge this conversation all week, but knew a dressing down was coming. "I did a cleanup day. No big deal."

Brando's face grew red. "You defaced city property."

"Which I fixed and put back in place."

"And you involved that woman."

"To be fair, she got caught just as red-handed as me."

He remembered her face, the shock, then the smile that followed. She might act all buttoned-up, but Juliette had enjoyed the antics until the chief showed up.

"Is this gonna be the last time? 'Cause we've got the farm to worry about."

"I told you I was all in, Dad. I put the rodeo behind me and am ready to make Crestview Farm a moneymaker. I can't promise I might not slip up a time or two, but I'm committed."

He waited for his father to remind him that

he'd said those same words before. Instead, his father muttered something under his breath that sounded like "irresponsible" and "old habits," but to his credit, the old man didn't linger on his frustration for long.

A truck door closed in the distance and soon his sister walked toward the stable office. When she saw them her steps slowed and her somber expression made his heart sink. She tossed her long, light brown braid over her shoulder and headed their way.

"That was a short visit," his father observed.

"Wasn't much to chat about. We're pretty much in the same boat as before." She lifted her chin at Ty. "You selling the old equipment you found in the barn went a long way toward the repairs."

When Ty had enlisted his friends to help him clean out the barn, they'd discovered some outdated farming equipment they'd never use, along with sporting goods. He'd been ready to give the sports gear away to Adam Wright, owner of Deep North Adventures, but Adam insisted on purchasing the inventory. Ty was also able to sell the old farm stuff and bring in enough to cover the lumber and paint needed to finish the barn project.

"So why the long face?" Brando demanded.

Liz's gaze quickly bounced off Ty's before facing her father. "As long as we don't have any major repairs, we should be okay until we bring in more revenue."

Both Ty and Liz had been in agreement about not telling their father how bad the well system might be. He'd taken it hard when he nearly lost the rodeo. They didn't want to burden Brando, who'd tried to put his family first, by worrying him.

Ty had checked into a new pump and everything that went along with a new installation. When he had a service guy come out for an inspection, the man explained that there was a decrease of water making its way to the surface. He suggested they re-dig the well, and then they'd need a new pump. When he mentioned the estimate, Ty had to keep his jaw from dropping. The job would put a sizable dent in what was left of their savings. Liz's horseback riding lessons were increasing, but it wasn't enough to support capital investments around the farm just yet.

Suddenly Juliette's equine program sounded good.

"Don't worry," Brando said. "We Pendergrasses always land on our feet."

A joke going back to the rodeo days. Their

accomplishments had been commendable, until Brando had let the finances get away from him. It had taken a long time to dig out of that hole and they couldn't afford to lose it all now.

So Ty and Liz held back regarding the money situation. Brando would be hurt if he found out they were leery of him being in control. He'd kicked himself over what had happened for long enough. It was time for the siblings to step in.

"We do, Dad," Liz said. "I'll be in the office."

After Liz left, Brando gave Ty the squinty eye. "You be nice to Juliette when she shows up. Bad enough you two got in trouble, but if we want to convince her to run her program here, you need to pull out all the charm."

"What makes you think I haven't already?"

Brando grinned. "Oh, I got no doubt, since you talked her into your mischief. This time, make sure you're on board for a good cause."

With that, Brando strolled away, whistling.

Ty took a deep breath and marched to the office.

Liz sat behind the desk staring at the computer screen.

"Give it to me straight," he said.

Clicking the mouse, Liz leaned back in the

chair. "It's tight, Ty. We've sunk more money into this place than we expected."

He took a seat in the only other chair in the office.

Liz dug through some papers until she extracted one from the pile. "Did you get any more quotes for the well?"

The first estimate to fix the system had made his head ache. He'd almost been afraid to ask any other companies, but did anyway. "They're all pretty much comparable, as in more than we can afford."

"But we can't allow the pump to go out."

Didn't he know it? The knot in his gut kept him awake at night. "The last guy told me we had a few months, max, before time ran out."

Liz dropped the paper. Clicked the mouse. "Are we ready to start the petting zoo?"

"Colton is ready with the goats. I got a good price on some llamas and we have plenty of chickens for now."

"Think we could start selling eggs?"

"Don't see why not. We just need a cohesive program to put it all together."

"I've been working on that."

"Along with the lessons, balancing the books and worrying about Colton?"

Her smile was tight when she said, "Goes with the job."

"Why don't you let me run all this by Adam. He's been advising small businesses in Golden. We could use his insight."

She let out a long sigh. "I'm afraid I have to agree."

"I'll give him a call and set up an appointment."

"Before or after you supervise Juliette's community service?"

"I still don't see why you can't do it," he groused.

"Because I'm busy." A genuine grin returned to her lips, covering the worry Ty read on her face every day. "Besides, you and Juliette have already established a bond, being lawbreakers and all."

"You're never going to let me live that down, are you?"

"Well, you did start your life of crime a long time ago."

"One time," he asserted. "And it wasn't my fault the bull broke out of the rig and raced down the highway."

"Not your fault? You were in charge of keeping the trailer in top shape but you were too busy chatting up the ladies. We're lucky you and Juniper chased the bull down and got him into that field so the team could drive the trailer there and lure him back inside. And,

Scott talked the police out of charging you with reckless endangerment and trespassing. That farmer wasn't happy that you and the bull trampled his cornstalks."

"Which I made up for by letting all my fans know when the farmer brought in the corn harvest, and then I went there to do a guest appearance. Sold most of his crop that day."

Liz chuckled. "You always do manage to work things out."

Maybe in his past life. But now? He couldn't mess up or his family, and their farm, would suffer.

"I've left my wild ways behind. Now I'm mostly an upstanding citizen."

"By that logic, you're right, I should supervise Juliette. No telling what trouble you'll get into next."

The idea didn't sit well with Ty. As much as he'd complained, he wanted more time with Juliette. Forcing a positive expression, he said, "Look at it this way. With my experience walking the line, this'll be a breeze."

Liz shook her head and chuckled. "You sure about this?"

A car door slammed outside. Juliette, right on time. He pictured her red hair pulled back like the other day, her creamy skin kissed by the sun. Darn if his chest didn't hitch a bit.

"Yeah, I'm sure. I want to see how Juliette handles a paintbrush."

"Be nice," Liz warned.

Ty placed a hand over his chest as if wounded. "Please, sis. I'm always nice."

Whether Juliette believed him or not remained to be seen.

CHAPTER FIVE

JULIETTE SHIELDED HER eyes against the strong morning sun as she watched Ty saunter her way. Why did he have to be so handsome? And grab her attention every time she saw him?

Get a grip on yourself.

Her mother asking Juliette what the future looked like had made her think long and hard about her interest in Ty. Did her mom have a point? Should she be looking ahead? She hadn't before meeting him. Being in close proximity with him because of the community service hours was going to make her wonder even more.

"You made it," he said in way of greeting.

His dark hair shone in the bright light, brushing his shirt collar. His tanned skin proved that the man was outdoors a lot. An unbuttoned plaid flannel covered a black T-shirt, pulling tight against his impressive chest and arm muscles. The worn jeans and boots gave credence to the fact that the man wasn't afraid of hard work.

"Did you think I'd find an excuse to dodge my service hours?"

He shrugged.

"Look, I know you weren't thrilled when Brady told us I'd be assigned to your farm, but I'm here, ready to work."

Then she could be on her way and get Ty out of her system.

He looked her over, from her hair pulled back in a ponytail, to her navy T-shirt and denim jeans, to her worn sneakers.

"You dressed appropriately."

She stuffed her hands in the front pockets of her jeans. "Since I wasn't sure what task I'd be performing, I erred on the side of you intentionally giving me a messy job."

Ty grinned, his warm smile making her stomach flip. "Me?"

Juliette snorted.

"You erred correctly, darlin'."

She stared at him. "What did you just call me?"

"Darlin'. Heard that's your title around here."

It was bad enough that folks still considered her a hero and called her the town darling. She didn't want Ty on that bandwagon.

"You can forget about it."

He winked at her. "Don't think I will. The name fits."

She ground her molars together.

"How do you feel about painting?" he asked, seamlessly changing the subject.

She tilted her head, giving her time to deal with the nickname while looking as if she was mulling his question over. "I have nothing against it."

"Great. Let's head to the barn."

He turned with a swagger that had her chuckling under her breath. Was he like this with everyone? She supposed it didn't matter. Doing the job and heading home were her plans.

Not far from the stable stood a tall barn, the doors flung wide open. As they drew closer, she peeked inside. Empty, except for a few sawhorses and a tarp on which sat several five-gallon buckets of paint. Jason Aldean's country music rocked from a Bluetooth speaker.

He waved her inside, then grabbed a screw-driver and knelt on one knee to lift the paint lid. Juliette caught a glimpse of the color choice and laughed.

"Red?"

Ty stood and scratched his head. "What's wrong with red?"

"Kind of cliché, don't you think?"

"I guess, but if you're going to live on a farm, might as well do what's expected and embrace the lifestyle."

She sent him a side glance. "Somehow I don't think you've ever done what's been expected."

A chagrined frown lined his forehead. "I suppose we didn't exactly meet on the best of terms."

"True, but I have to give you props for going after what you wanted. Even if it was only a parking space."

He chuckled. "And you don't go after what you want?"

"Not for me, for other people."

"I suppose that's what makes us different."

"I don't think so. You wouldn't have come here to help your family with the farm if you were only about you."

His expression closed. "Try telling my dad that."

"Family issues?"

"Who doesn't have them? I'm sure you do."

She wasn't going near that topic with a ten-foot pole. "What do you say we get started?"

A slow grin crossed Ty's lips. "Sure thing."

Before long. Juliette stood on a scaffold Ty had erected, a pan of paint beside her so she could start rolling the outside of the barn. He'd left to take care of some other chores, so she breathed in the autumn air and savored the quiet. The wind rustled the leaves in the trees, the scents and sounds of animals surrounded her. Before long she was humming softly with the music, the back and forth of the strokes creating a sense of calm. Once she'd finished a wide swath, she climbed down, hands on hips as she tried to figure out how she was going to move the scaffolding to the next section.

"Need some help?" she heard from behind her.

She swung around to find a lanky teenage boy and a dog seated at his feet.

"I didn't hear you walk up."

He grinned in that charming way that told Juliette he was a Pendergrass.

"Sorry. I'm Colton." He pointed to the dog. "And this is Shep. My uncle Ty sent me over to help you."

"Good timing." She pointed to the scaffolding. "How do we move this thing?"

"It's on wheels," Ty said as she strode around the side of the barn. "Just release the brakes and we can roll it to the next position."

Caught off guard by his sudden appearance, she jerked, then spun around. "I would have figured it out eventually."

"I'm sure you would have, but we Pendergrasses are always a step ahead."

She couldn't argue that point. As the men moved the rig, Juliette hid her smile. They bantered like pros, giving each other a hard time like only family could. Colton gave as good as he got, which impressed Juliette. She did have a hard time staying one step ahead of Ty, not because he was a Pendergrass, but because there was something about him that made her lose her composure. All he had to do was smile, like right now, and her insides went all gooey.

"Shake it off," she whispered to herself.

"You say something?" Ty asked.

"Just wondering when you were going to get out of my way so I can finish the job."

Ty glanced at the partially painted structure. "Hate to break it to you, but you won't finish this job today."

That's what she was afraid of. More hours spent in Ty's company and she might not leave unscathed.

Ty waved his arm out wide toward the scaffold and bowed at the waist. Yeah, this guy was trouble.

She followed Colton up. The two started

the upper half of the barn front while Ty finished the lower.

"So," she said to her coworker, "are you attending Golden High?"

"Yes. I'm a junior this year."

"How do you like it?"

"This'll be the first time I've been at the same school all year."

"Are you getting involved?"

"Some. I'm still figuring it out."

Juliette remembered those days, trying to navigate high school and all the emotions that went with it. Had to be difficult for Colton as the new kid.

He turned her way. "Did you go there?"

"I did. Born and raised in Golden."

"That must be cool."

Maybe, if she hadn't been keeping the truth from the town for as long as she had.

They chatted about the teachers and classes he was taking when Ty chimed in.

"Did you ask Kelsey to homecoming?"

Red crept up Colton's neck. "I'm working on it."

"Don't wait too long," Ty said. "Some other guy might ask her before you do."

"When is the dance?" Juliette asked.

"Friday."

Her eyes went wide. "In a week?"

Colton colored. "Did I mess up?"

Juliette smiled to cover her surprised reaction. "No, but I think maybe the girl in question might like some time, you know, to buy a dress and plan her hairstyle."

Colton groaned. "I was going to do it yesterday, but a bunch of people came up to us and I didn't want to ask in front of them in case she said no."

"Do you have her phone number?" Ty asked.

"Yeah. We exchanged them when we paired up in chem lab."

"Wait." Juliette held up her hand. She wasn't a pro at this, usually going solo or with a group of girlfriends to dances when she was in school, but she knew a woman's thought process. "I'd highly recommend you ask her in person."

"I guess I could do it on Monday."

"Will you run into her this weekend?"

"She said something about going to the library after work today."

"You should meet her there. Surprise her."

Colton perked up. "You think?"

"I do." Juliette swiped her brush along the edge of the building until they ran out of paint. They climbed down, Ty ready to refill the pan.

"Who is the lucky girl?" Juliette asked.

"Kelsey Ryman."

Juliette smiled. "I know Kelsey. The rehab facility where I work is part of the medical program at Golden High. She's doing clinics with us right now."

"She mentioned that but I'm not up to speed on the program."

"It's for students on a medical track. The rehab, the urgent care clinic and a private doctor's office offer a few hours a week for kids to come and see what it's like to be part of the medical field. If I remember correctly, Kelsey is working on getting a certified nursing assistant certificate."

"She said something about going to nursing school."

"It's a good way to get a little practical experience under your belt, especially before going into medical school."

"My uncle—"

Colton sent a glance at Ty.

Ty nodded. "It's okay, Juliette knows about Uncle Scott."

Surprise crossed Colton's face.

Juliette didn't miss the exchange. "Are you interested in the medical field?"

"Sometimes I think about it, especially

when my granddad and mom are talking about my uncle."

"You never mentioned it," Ty said, walking closer to them.

Colton shrugged. "I didn't want to make a big deal. You all have enough going on."

Ty squeezed his shoulder. "If you think you want to go that route, do it. We're proud of you no matter what you decide to do in the future."

"Talk to Kelsey about it," Juliette suggested. "She can give you the details."

"Maybe it's not too late to get into the program." The teen glanced at his uncle. "Do you mind if I take off?"

"To the library?" Ty asked.

Colton's face colored again.

"Go," Ty told him.

"Thanks," Colton said to her before striding back to the farmhouse like a man on a mission, Shep at his heels.

Ty came to stand beside her as they watched the boy's progress, close enough that she felt his body heat, inhaled the citrus scent of his cologne. She should move, but she really didn't want to.

"I had no idea he was interested in medicine."

Juliette turned her head. "Do you think it's because of your brother?"

"What happened with Scott really made an impression on Colton." Ty walked to the bucket, checking the contents inside. "Almost done with this one."

"Hey, if you don't want to talk about it, I get it. But let me just say, it's easier to talk to someone who has walked a similar path."

He ran a hand through his hair, messing it more. He couldn't be any more attractive if he tried.

Ty hadn't agreed to talk about his brother, but he hadn't shot her down either. She decided to start the conversation. "When did it start?"

He hesitated, then began talking.

"About four years ago. First, Scott lost his balance from time to time. We didn't think much of it. He didn't compete like we did, wasn't athletic, had more of a head for numbers. Just before I left to go on a competition circuit, he started experiencing numbness in one hand. My sister made him go to the doctor and after some tests, he was diagnosed with multiple sclerosis." He stared into the distance. "By the time I got back, the balance issues had gotten so much worse, he couldn't walk."

Juliette thought she heard a hint of guilt in his voice. She sensed there was a story there, but now wasn't the time to push. As she'd learned with the families of her patients, it took time to deal with the ups and downs along the way.

"His decline happened over a period of months. We were in shock."

Juliette took his hand in hers. "It's never easy seeing someone we love suffer or struggle."

He gripped her hand tighter. "Especially when you can't do anything to make it better."

She knew that all too well. "That's why there are professionals to work with him."

Ty blew out a breath. "Yeah, he has the best care, but the distance apart is tough on everyone. Once we move him here, we'll have to find new doctors and a place to live and..."

Her heart ached when his voice trailed off.

"It's been a learning curve for all of us. He's still considering some local places to live."

"Where is he, if you don't mind me asking?"

"Texas."

How did they do it? She could never be separated from her sister.

"When can he move?"

"Last time my dad was out there, they thought he might be ready sometime in the beginning of next year. We figured we'd have plenty of time to find an assisted living facility, but we're on waiting lists. FaceTime has come in handy to show Scott his options."

"I'd be happy to help. I know a lot of the doctors and facility directors in the area."

In fact, her mind was already whirling with possibilities. She knew of a newly constructed assisted living facility in Clarkston that was almost ready to take patients. She could make some calls...

He turned his head to give her a soft smile, all cockiness gone. "Thanks. We've been working on it, but any additional advice will help."

"Have you and your family gone to counseling?"

He went stiff. "Us? Why?"

"This is a huge issue your family is dealing with." She lifted her chin toward the farmhouse. "Everyone must have different emotions and ways of dealing with the situation."

"I guess. I mean, we don't try to hide it from each other."

"That's good, but there are always feelings we keep buried, not to hurt anyone, but because we don't know how to process them.

Talking to a professional can open up avenues of conversation."

"Someone like you?"

"I'm not a counselor, but I do know how hard a medical diagnosis can be on a family."

He nodded. "Good to know."

She'd thrown a lot his way. It was clear the Pendergrasses were still struggling and too much information at one time might be overload.

"You'll get your brother's situation settled and Colton will figure out how to deal with it as time goes on."

"That and getting involved with a girl he likes."

She chuckled. "The other reason he would be interested in the medical program?"

When Ty shrugged, his shoulder bumped hers, sending a wave of shivers over her. "At that age, you'd be surprised what a guy will do to get a girl's attention."

"His age?"

He chuckled. "Okay, any age. If a guy was trying to impress a woman, that is."

"From what I've seen, you have confidence in spades. How have you not fallen yet?"

"Who says I haven't?"

Her eyes went wide.

"Just kidding."

Her lips pressed together.

"To answer your question, it's a little hard when you don't date."

"I find that hard to believe."

"It's been a tough couple of years. To be honest, my attention has been elsewhere."

"Still, no dates at all?"

"Okay, maybe here and there, but nothing serious." He turned his gaze to her. "How about you?"

She glanced away and echoed, "Nothing serious."

"Aren't we a pair."

Were they? If there weren't obstacles in the way, if she wasn't always worried about her lie coming to light, she'd be interested in getting to the bottom of this attraction between them.

"So, the farm," she said. "What are your plans?"

"To make it a tourist attraction."

"That's where the barn comes in?"

He glanced at the structure. "After I made repairs, I figured a new coat of paint was needed to show we're serious. If we hold a farmers market or some type of event, the barn is large enough to house vendors."

"Sounds like you want to get moving on

your plans." She brushed her hands together. "Let's finish this up."

He glanced at her cheek.

"What?"

"You have paint on your face."

She swiped a hand over her cheek.

"No, here."

Ty reached out to brush his thumb over her skin. The rough touch sent a current of electricity though her limbs. It took her a minute to realize he was lingering, not in any hurry to remove the smudge. Their gazes met and she held her breath, waiting. For what, she wasn't sure. Her head was muddled by Ty's closeness, and the scent of his cologne, as the space closed in around them.

What was happening to her?

A horse whinnied somewhere in the distance and Ty blinked, breaking the spell between them. Which was good, especially when Juliette noticed a tall woman with a light brown braid and a long-limbed stride coming their way.

When she stopped, Ty cleared the intent scrutiny from his expression and sent the woman a careless grin.

"Juliette, this is my sister, Liz."

Gathering her wayward emotions, Juliette said, "Hi, Liz."

"I'm happy to meet you." Liz glanced at the barn. "You're making progress."

"Juliette could make a career out of painting if she ever wanted to leave her nine-to-five gig."

"Not anytime soon."

Liz sent her a subdued smile. "If you don't mind, I need to speak to my brother."

"Oh. Do you... I can go inside the barn—"

"No." A frown marred Liz's brow.

Ty took a step toward her. "What's wrong?"

"I messed up, Ty. I got my dates mixed up. My trip to visit Scott to see what he thinks about future living accommodations is the same weekend as the homecoming dance."

"Trust me, Colton will understand if you can't be there."

Liz tossed the braid over her shoulder, her voice trembling. "I can't believe I did this."

"It's not like you did it on purpose."

"I know. The doctor wants to talk about Scott moving and he needs to come to some sort of decision."

Ty slung his arm over his sister's shoulders. "Don't stress. We'll figure it out."

"I'm glad you said that, because I need you to go to the dance in my place."

Ty's arm dropped. "You want me to what?"

"Please. Be there for Colton. I know he's nervous about his first dance."

Panic crossed Ty's face. With a slow movement, he nodded.

"Thanks. I knew I could count on you."

Liz shot Juliette a nod and turned on her heel to walk back to the stable. Ty, on the other hand, paced for a moment or two while running a hand through his already tousled hair then stopped directly before Juliette. With desperation in his voice he said, "You have to go with me."

"To a high school dance?" Juliette choked out.

Yeah, his request was out of the blue. Not his most smooth moment. "You gotta help me out here."

Juliette's mouth dropped open. "How did your problem become my problem?"

"It's not," he admitted. But he was desperate.

What did he know about being a chaperone? He hadn't done all the typical high school stuff. He'd been on the road and loving it, without benefit of any chaperones. Who was he to keep the kids in line?

But Juliette had grown up in Golden. She was the town darling. If anyone could keep a bunch of high school kids in line, it was her. Hadn't she managed to get him good a time or two?

"I can't…" He faltered. "What do I know about a school dance?"

"By the horror on your face, I'm guessing nothing?"

She was so right. At this point, he'd offer to complete all of Juliette's service hours on the farm if she'd go with him.

"So what do you say? Help a guy out here?"

The amused sparkle in her pretty green eyes made his hopes sink.

"After you landed me in hot water with the police chief? Why on earth would I agree?"

"You're enjoying this, aren't you."

She crossed her arms over her chest. "Yes. I truly am."

He blew out a frustrated breath. "C'mon. I don't know anyone else in town to ask."

"So you're asking me by default?"

"I didn't mean—" He ran a hand down his face. Pulled himself together. "Are you always this difficult?"

A glimmer of a smile curved her lips. "Not when I'm having a good time."

"Fine. Take pity on me, then. Come with me and I'll…paint the rest of the barn for you."

"You'd really finish my service hours?"

He swallowed hard. "I would."

She tapped a finger on her chin. Was she considering his proposal?

"Tell you what."

At the renewed sparkle in her eyes, he groaned.

"I'll do this, but you'll owe me."

His hand shout out. "Deal."

She eyed his hand, then met his gaze. "Not so quick."

His arm wavered.

"You won't know when, and you won't know where, but when I snap my fingers for the favor to be returned, you'll agree, no questions asked."

"Pretty bossy."

"Take it or leave it."

What was he getting himself into? He didn't really need a date, did he? He was used to being solo. This couldn't be so bad. But then he thought about navigating a school function and his stomach tightened. If this had been a rodeo event he'd know what to do, but normal life? Sometimes he didn't have a clue.

Yeah, he needed her and she knew it.

He straightened his arm. "Agreed."

She paused, then reached out to take his hand. They shook. And if he wanted to keep her hand in his a little longer, he didn't question the motivation.

"We have an hour before lunch," she said. "Let's get more work done."

"You don't want me to finish the job for you?"

"No. I think the ideas you have for the farm will be good for Golden, so I'm willing to slap more paint on the barn for the cause."

At his hesitancy, she laughed. "You don't believe me?"

No, in fact, the opposite. He'd heard that she was up to support a cause, but never thought it would include the farm.

"My dad mentioned something about an equine therapy program you're trying to establish."

"It might be a good fit with what you've already got going on."

"I'll admit, I don't know much about it."

"Since horses have similar temperaments as humans, like social and responsive behaviors, it's easy for the patients to make a connection with the horse. Even if a client never climbs into a saddle, just being in the vicinity might ease anxiety."

Interested, Ty probed further. "Are most clients afraid to get on a horse?"

"Sometimes. The reasons vary, but the results are promising."

"Huh. I've only ever been around folks who are comfortable on a horse. I never thought about riding as a way to help people."

"I have my certification and hope to one day start a program locally."

"How'd you decide you'd like to offer this program?"

"I love to ride. It's so calming and peaceful. I've taken my sister, although it's been years, and realized it could benefit patients. I guess I want to share the experience."

He knew all about the joy that came from being around horses. For a long time it had been his life. Still was, on a different level.

"I hear you. I'm more at home on a horse than anywhere else."

She sent him a sly glance. "I did hear that about you."

"That's a story for another time. For now, we figure out how to make your program work."

She sighed. "We'll just have to see what happens."

"Maybe you just need the right people around."

She narrowed her eyes at him. "You know,

it's annoying that under all that bravado, you're a nice guy."

"Why thank you, darlin'."

Her expression grew dark. "Ixnay on the nickname."

"It fits."

"No. Not now, not ever."

"You know you're making it impossible to stop."

She rolled her eyes, but he didn't miss the twitch of her lips when she looked away.

They moved to the paint bucket together, nearly knocking heads as they leaned in for their brushes. Her ponytail swung over her shoulder, brushing his face. The scent of peppermint tickled his nose and while he could have stared at her pretty face for hours, they had a barn to paint.

His gaze traveled to her lips. The thought of kissing her took hold. They had this strong attraction but, for the life of him, couldn't figure out why. They were so different. She was as by the book as he was easygoing. He might have promised his dad he'd settle down, but that didn't stop him from wanting to jump on his horse and ride with the wind. And when he pictured it, Juliette was right beside him.

He broke the connection and stepped away before he did something stupid. She'd just agreed to be his date, he didn't what to blow it. Not only that, he liked her.

Good grief. How had she managed to captivate him so thoroughly? The woman who had saved a toddler, for Pete's sake. Why had she agreed to go to a dance with a rebel like him?

CHAPTER SIX

ON WEDNESDAY THE following week, Juliette took the morning off to drive to Crestview Farm. After talking to Ty, she'd run the idea of the equine program past Dr. Johnson again. For once, he'd seemed interested. Or was it because she'd nagged him enough? She wasn't sure until he mentioned funding that had come into the clinic, earmarked for the equine program, so he gave her the green light to start a preliminary assessment.

She'd gone back to the farm Sunday to finish painting the barn, but Ty had been busy and wasn't able to spend much time with her. She hoped today would be different.

As she got closer to the stable, she fought a tingle of excitement shooting through her at the thought of running into him, then just as quickly shook it off. She was a professional. She wasn't looking for romance. Then she remembered she'd accepted his invitation to a homecoming dance. Good grief, how had that happened? The panic in his eyes had grabbed something inside her, a shared unwillingness to let anyone see any weakness, a camaraderie of sorts. So she'd said yes before she thought it through. Wouldn't she have felt the same way if someone asked her to chaperone a high school dance last minute? Guess they had more in common than she'd realized.

Taking a breath, she exited her car and grabbed the tablet she'd brought along to take notes. She'd focus on the job at hand, not a mental picture of Ty's dreamy brown eyes and the rogue's smile that never failed to make her stomach pitch with anticipation when he sent a glance her way.

She smoothed the denim skirt she'd paired with a light pink sweater and low boots. She'd been around stables enough to know her work outfit wouldn't be a good choice for riding today. As she walked into the cool breezeway, the nasal snuff from a horse reached her ears, along with the earthy scents that accompanied a trip to the farm.

The sound of hoofs pounding the soil grabbed her attention. Turning around, she exited the stable to see a horse and rider in the large training arena. Curious, she moved closer, making out Ty's intent expression as the horse galloped while he grabbed hold of the straps on the back of the saddle in order to vault himself from one side of the horse to the other. When he dipped low, Juliette let out a gasp. How did he manage such feats without falling off? Then he swung back in the saddle, pulled his feet from the stirrups and stood, all while the black horse kept up his steady speed. If she hadn't been intrigued by the guy beforehand, she certainly was now.

He sat, slowing the horse's pace. She could see him speaking to the animal as they made a final lap around the ring. At one point he noticed her and waved. Even with the distance between them, she didn't miss the charmer's smile, which brightened her entire day.

No romance, remember? To be honest, as she watched his muscles move as he controlled the horse and noticed his dark hair shine in the morning sun, she couldn't recall why having an interest in him was a bad idea.

Ty's horse trotted to the gate. He hopped down to open it and lead the horse through. Juliette went back to the stable. She was here to talk to Liz, not gawk at Ty's unparalleled skills. He finally walked in from the other direction, stopping at the grooming area. When he caught sight of her, those gorgeous eyes lit up. "Did we have another workday lined up?"

"No, I think we finished it all on Sunday.

I'm here to assess the farm for the equine therapy program."

The huge black horse shook his head. Ty rubbed the animal's neck, then tied the lead to the wall. "You got the go-ahead from your boss?"

"More like he sent me on a fact-finding mission."

Ty brushed the dust from his jeans. "So, you're here to do what, exactly?"

"Check out the facility." She glanced back toward the parking lot. "Actually, Liz is supposed to meet me."

"Dad's taking her to the airport in a little while so she's packing. She should be here soon."

"She didn't mention that she was leaving today. I can come back another time if today is inconvenient."

"Let me cool Juniper down and then I can give you a tour while we wait." He eyed her from head to toe. "Hate to make you leave after you got all dressed up."

She contained an eye roll. "Thanks."

As Ty went through the motions of grooming the horse, she noticed his strong arms and broad shoulders tugging against his taut shirt. As much as she'd completed this task many times after riding, it took on a whole new dimension as she watched Ty. Before long he'd brushed and wiped down the horse and led him to a stall. He returned with a glimmer of interest in his eyes.

"What do you need to know first?"

After watching Ty on his horse, she felt secure that he was knowledgeable about their animals. "Can you tell me about the temperaments of your horses?"

He waved her to the stalls, his bootheels echoing on the concrete floor. When they reached the black horse she'd seen him with, he raised a thumb in the animal's direction.

"This is my horse, Juniper. He's used to the trick riding I did in the circuit, so I don't think he'd be a good fit for the program."

"I have to say, your moves in the arena were pretty impressive."

"Years of practice."

"Plus a natural ease on horseback, I'd say."

"That too." He nodded to the horse. "We go back a long way. Been in a lot of shows together. Can't imagine not taking Juniper out every day."

They walked a few feet to the next stall. "This is Maggie," he said. "In her older years, she's gotten docile and good with children. Tri, in the next stall, can be spunky, but she listens to commands. Liz uses both of them when giving lessons, especially for beginners."

Juliette moved closer. A medium-sized, light chestnut–colored horse greeted her with a soft nicker. Juliette reached over to rub her forehead.

"I think she was hoping I'd have snacks," she commented.

"We can give them treats after the tour."

Juliette moved the next stall to see a paint horse, brown with white patches. "I don't think I've ever seen such a distinctive mane. It looks like it's been dyed in blond, copper and brown sections."

"She's a beauty for sure."

Juliette added to her notes. "So these two would be possibilities for the program?"

"Yes. I went online to get more information and figured you can work with these two."

Juliette sent him a surprised glance. "You looked up the program?"

"Sure." He shrugged like it was no big deal. "I wanted to be better informed."

Her heart squeezed. Most people she knew didn't really ask about the programs she headed up. Maybe because of the wall she'd put up long ago, but she had to admit, it was nice.

He listened to her.

With Ty, she didn't feel like a fraud, because he didn't know her history. He had encountered the less buttoned-up side of her, and it made her want to open up to him, be less defensive and guarded when he showed genuine interest in her projects.

She typed in additional notes, then faced him. "We'll also work with the children to teach them to groom the horses to some degree, depending on their ability."

"We?" he asked as one side of his mouth kicked up.

"Okay, mostly me."

He showed her around the rest of the stable. Everything was well maintained, from the tack room to the food storage area. The Pendergrasses took the care and maintenance of their horses seriously.

"Your setup is impressive."

"Thanks. We worked hard to make sure all of our stock has a good place to live."

"Like they're family?"

He rubbed his head. "I guess I consider our animals extended family."

She loved his admission. Yes, he was a charmer. A charmer with a heart of gold.

Their gazes met and held. She found it hard to inhale at this moment. If she blinked, would it break the connection between them?

She didn't have to find out, because approaching voices broke the spell.

Ty shook his head and glanced to his right. When Juliette followed his gaze, she saw Liz and Brando coming their way.

"Good morning," Liz said, sending her brother an amused smile. Ty rolled his eyes.

"I heard you're leaving soon," Juliette said, taking the attention away from what they'd stumbled upon. It also gave her time to pull herself together.

"I am, but I wanted to discuss a few things with you before we head to the airport." Liz motioned toward a closed door. "Do you mind coming to my office?"

"Lead the way."

She glanced at Ty, who was headed to the grooming area with his father.

After getting settled, Liz got right to the point. "I know you're here to assess the stable situation. I want you to know that we'd really like to assist you with the therapy program."

"Ty gave me that impression."

Liz picked up a pen, tapping it on the desk. "I understand he told you about our brother?"

"He did."

"Then you can understand why supporting a program here is near and dear to our hearts. After the Eureka Games last summer,

I made it known that Crestview Farm supports the MS community. I had a parent call to ask about horseback riding lessons for her disabled child. At first I wasn't sure how to respond, and after Dad told me about your wish to implement a program, I got excited. I thought I should talk to you."

"This is the preliminary stage, but I'd love to work here at some point."

"And we'd love to have you." She glanced at Juliette's outfit. "I'm assuming you aren't going to ride today, but please come back anytime."

"Thanks. I'll take you up on that offer."

Liz tidied up some papers on the desk. "When I get back from seeing my brother, I'll admit, I'm going to be busy with the lessons I have lined up."

Juliette grinned. "Ty told me you were a barrel racing champ."

Liz's smile was humble. "I've won my share of competitions."

"So this is really a family business."

"Ty and I grew up around the rodeo. Guess it flows through our blood."

"I saw him on Juniper this morning. I can't even conceive of taking those chances on a horse."

"That's Ty. He was born to be in the limelight. You can imagine how popular he was on the circuit."

"And now he's working on your farm."

"Once we decided to settle here, he was committed." Liz pressed her lips together before saying, "Still is, even though we're in the process of working on the direction for the farm. It's challenging, but Ty is smart. We need him to make this place run efficiently so he's not tempted to go back to the rodeo."

After hearing Ty talk about the farm, she didn't get the impression he would leave. But there was always that possibility. She flashed back to him on the horse and wondered if the pull of performing would lure him back to his roots. Her belly twisted. She wasn't sure how she felt about the possibility of him leaving.

"Liz, let's get a move on," Brando called from outside the doorway.

She checked her watch. "Dad's right. If we don't leave now, I'll miss my flight."

They both rose.

"Have a safe trip," Juliette said as they walked to the door.

They left the office. The family hugged their goodbyes.

"Don't forget about the dance," Liz warned, pointing a finger at her brother.

Ty shot Juliette a quick glance. "I won't."

Before long the two left, leaving Juliette and Ty alone in the stable.

"Get everything figured out?" he asked.

"I think so." She went over what she and Liz had discussed.

He pushed up his shirtsleeves. "So you'll be back to ride?"

"And work. I think I still owe you more service hours." She frowned. "Maybe I'll bring my sister with me. I'd love to get her back on a horse again, but her new passion has her busy."

"What's she into?"

"Making jewelry. She's really quite good at it. My friend Serena has offered to sell her designs at her store."

"So, no horses?"

"Probably not. As she informed me, she isn't into horses right now." She chuckled. "When I do come to ride, I guess I'll be by myself."

He winked at her. "No you won't, darlin'. I'll be here."

Why did he always say things like that to her? And why did it affect her every time?

Her rule of not dating any guy from Golden was in jeopardy. Ty seemed to be unraveling the rules she'd imposed upon herself. It took him to make her aware that she could enjoy a man's attention. Technically, he wasn't from Golden, so did that mean her rule didn't apply? But he was living here now, so was there a difference? She didn't care either way. She liked Ty. Period.

Even though their first meeting hadn't been stellar, it woke something in her. A desire to be free. To spread her wings and be her authentic self. Each time they were together, she wanted to throw caution to the wind and see what surprises were in store for them both.

Her phone beeped with an incoming text. Addie, reminding her they were meeting for lunch then going to the store in order to buy a dress for the dance. "I need to leave, but today was a good start. I think I have enough information to start my proposal."

"Glad we could help."

He walked her to her car. "So, I'll pick you up at seven on Friday night?"

"I'll be ready."

He sent her the grin that made her warm all over, leaving her with that curious twist in her tummy that wouldn't go away.

SEATED AT A table inside A Touch of Tabby café, Juliette pushed her nearly empty plate away. "That salad was huge. I can't believe I ate so much."

Addie finished the last of her sandwich and sent Juliette a hint-hint eyebrow raise. "Being on the farm will do that to a person."

"It's not like I was working. I was there to gather information for the equine program."

Addie leaned back and stretched, her blond ponytail drifting over her shoulder. "I led the advanced aerobics class this morning, so I splurged."

Juliette dabbed her lips and folded her napkin in half. "Have you decided if you're going to open your own fitness center?"

"Still trying to decide. I have money put aside, but I worry since I'm a single mom. What if something happens? It's only Jacob and me so I don't want to blow my nest egg on a gym and then end up broke."

"Did you ever talk to Adam about putting together a business proposal?"

"Yes. He went through the entire gamut of what it takes to start a business." She shook her head. "Now I'm more conflicted than ever."

"Then take your time. You have a good job at the spa. Other than wanting to open a center, it's not a necessity."

"True." She sighed. "I've always dreamed of having my own gym."

"With your illustrious reputation, it would be a hit."

"Illustrious?"

"State track champ."

Addie shrugged. "That was a long time ago."

"If the time isn't right now, it doesn't mean it'll never happen."

The server stopped by the table to remove their plates. Addie asked for more iced tea before the girl returned to the kitchen, then her lips curved in an amused grin. "Now, about the homecoming dance."

"We've been over this. I'm doing Ty a favor."

Addie held her hands up. "I didn't say anything."

"You didn't have to. Your entertainment at my expense is written all over your face."

"Even you have to admit this is strange. If I remember correctly, you didn't enjoy dances when we were in high school."

"Again, a favor."

Addie thanked the server as she filled their glasses. "Remember when Tommy Miller asked me to go to prom senior year?"

"How could I forget? You were on cloud nine for weeks."

"I was. And then Tommy's best friend Zach asked you to go too."

Juliette pressed her lips together. She'd been excited when Zach asked her to the dance, until her mother told her that Zach's mom was announcing that her son was going to prom with the town hero. The local paper caught wind and wanted to publish a story and take pictures. It was all too much and afterward, when he asked her out on a date, she refused. Not her best moment, but she had genuinely been sick over the attention.

"I never understood the big deal. Why you didn't want to go out with Zach."

Juliette had never told Addie why. About a lot of things.

She pushed her glass around. "I guess I thought it wasn't that big a deal."

"He was your prom date!"

"Not everyone thinks prom is a big deal."

"But homecoming all these years later is?"

Juliette allowed a small smile. "Okay, you got me there."

"Ty is a hardworking and very good-looking man." Addie pointed a finger at Juliette. "You better not pull a Zach and dump him afterward."

Juliette cringed, from her previous actions and knowing there was no way she would stop seeing Ty.

"Despite me being less than gracious, I'm sure Zach grew up to be an admirable man."

"He's a surgeon in Atlanta, so I'd say so."

Juliette let out a laugh. "Don't worry. I have no intention of calling things off with Ty."

"Good to hear, because I don't want Ty to have to find a new woman to date like Zach did."

Juliette's heart hurt at that thought, but said, "A girl he ended up dating the remainder of the school year."

"Yeah, but you broke his heart."

"Apparently he got over it."

They both chuckled over the memory. Addie stared out the window, her face growing pensive.

"What's up?" Juliette asked.

Addie frowned as she met Juliette's gaze. "This walk down memory lane has me thinking about Josh and how much I miss him."

"I imagine you always will."

Juliette had been there for her friend after the initial shock of her husband's death, had witnessed her soul-crushing grief. At the time, she hadn't been in a serious relationship. Couldn't conceive of ever loving another person so deeply, then going through the motions after losing that special someone. Since Ty had come into her life, she'd gotten a small inkling of what it was like to be close to someone. If Ty ever left, Juliette wasn't sure how she'd react.

"He was always so careful," Addie went on to say, her tone tight with emotion. "Even though I worried every time he went to work, I thought he was invincible."

"No one is, especially not in a career like law enforcement."

Tears lit Addie's eyes. "Never in a million years did I think I'd be raising Jacob on my own."

Juliette reached across the table to squeeze her friend's hand in sympathy. "You aren't alone. You have me."

"Which I can never repay. Those first days…"

"Hey, don't go there."

Addie shook her head. "You're right. We have more interesting topics to explore, like your date with Ty."

Juliette rolled her eyes.

After a few moments, Addie shook off her funk. "Nothing cures the blues like watching someone else shop and spend their money."

"I'd agree, but I'm the one spending the money."

"For a date," Addie reminded her.

"Then let's go shopping. If any store has the best selection, it's Tessa's."

They settled the bill and walked outside. The cloudless, deep blue sky greeted them. All around them the changing leaves created a kaleidoscope of color. Juliette hugged herself. She loved the mountains this time of year.

Golden was decorated for autumn, with cornstalks and scarecrows, festive wreaths on doors, and fallen leaves dotting the sidewalks. Right now, the annual Oktoberfest revelry was drawing in tourists at the park. Trick-or-treating would soon follow. Once the crowds left, Golden would revert to a small town ready to celebrate Thanksgiving.

As they passed the law office before reaching Tessa's, Ivy exited the front door. Her face lit up when she saw Juliette.

"Did you come to see me after work?" her sister asked.

"Happy coincidence," Juliette told her as she pulled Ivy in for a quick hug. "We're on our way to the clothing store."

Ivy's eyes went wide. "I'm going there too."

"What's the occasion?" Addie asked.

Ivy held out a tote bag. "I brought some of my jewelry samples. I thought since Serena is going to sell them in her store, Tessa might do the same."

Juliette exchanged a quick glance with Addie, then said to Ivy, "You know she's in the middle of selling the store."

"What does that matter? If she likes my bracelets, she can sell them."

"Honey, the new owner might have different plans."

Ivy's brows angled. "Then the new owner can take an order. I bought more supplies and can make more jewelry."

Juliette wasn't sure what to do. She recognized the hopeful expression on Ivy's face and didn't want to ruin the moment by being negative.

Addie placed a hand on Juliette's arm to keep her from saying anything. "We can always ask, Ivy."

Ivy's smile returned and she hurried ahead of them to the store.

"I don't want her to be disappointed," Juliette said in a low voice.

"If she's going to be in business, she has to learn, right?"

"I suppose."

"Let her spread her wings and see what happens."

At this point, it was all Juliette could do.

They followed Ivy into the store, already in a conversation with Tessa.

"Let it be," Addie said as she steered Juliette to the fancy dress section.

Before long, she'd picked out three dresses to try on. Ivy still wasn't back, but Juliette could hear voices at the front of the store.

"Maybe I should—"

"Not interfere." Addie took her by the shoulders, twirled her around and pushed her toward the fitting room.

With a sigh, Juliette pulled the curtain closed and proceeded to try on the garments.

"Well?" came Addie's voice.

"Hold on." Smoothing her hands over the clingy fabric of a jade green sheath dress, Juliette smiled. This was the one. She whipped open the curtain and stepped out. "Ta-da."

Addie blinked. "Holy smokes. Ty isn't going to be able to take his eyes off you."

Juliette went to stand in front of the mirror. Moved one way, then the other, to get a full picture of the fit. "It's not too…much?"

"Yeah, it is, but in a good way. That's what you're going for, isn't it?"

Juliette tilted her head one way then the other as she studied her image in the glass. "It's not a style I'd normally buy, but I like it."

Addie came to stand beside her. "Ty must really be a special guy."

"No more than anyone else."

Addie coughed out, "Right."

Juliette swiveled to playfully shove her friend's shoulder. As she did, Ivy came into the room, her lips curved downward.

"Ivy, what's wrong?"

"Tessa can't buy any of my designs. She said the new owner will be taking over soon."

"Then you can come back and talk to her then."

"Maybe this was a mistake."

"Oh, honey, no. You still have your display at Blue Ridge Cottage to be excited about." Juliette looked around for inspiration to get her sister out of what was fast becoming a full-blown sad moment. She noticed a cute dress hanging on a return rack and walked over to remove it. "What do you think, Ivy? Do you want me to buy this dress for you to wear when Serena showcases your jewelry?"

Ivy's fingers fluttered as she blurted, "You don't always have to take care of me. I'm not a kid."

Juliette lowered the hanger. "I didn't say you were."

Ivy's face grew more distressed. "I don't want a dress. I wanted Tessa to buy my jewelry." She ignored the garment in Juliette's hand. "I don't want to do this anymore," she announced and left the room.

Juliette brushed her hair from her cheek. "She must have missed the cues that Tessa wasn't turning her down personally, just the opportunity to buy her product. Ivy took it to heart."

"It's going to take time, but this jewelry business is going to be good for Ivy. And what about you?"

Addie's words pulled Juliette from her alarm over Ivy. "Me?"

"Come on, Juls." Addie placed the dress back on the rack. "You're always working overtime at the clinic or at home reading up on new ways to interact with your patients. I've often wanted to know more about what moves you or understand the decisions you make, but you shut me out." Her friend frowned. "It's aggravating because you're my best friend."

"I…" What could Juliette say? Addie was right. But how to explain that she was protecting herself against her own past?

"I'm sorry."

Addie waved a hand. "Going to this dance is the first thing I've seen you excited about in a long time. And I have to tell you, I'll be really disappointed if you don't enjoy yourself."

Juliette felt as if the wind had been knocked out of her. "You don't think I enjoy myself?"

"I don't know," Addie shot back. "Do you?"

Did she? She'd been staying ahead of her secret, throwing her life into so many different directions to feel worthy after the big lie, that she didn't take the time to slow down and just be. Could Addie be right? Hadn't her mother been accusing her of the same thing? Yes, Juliette was looking forward to spending the evening with Ty, but she was helping him out of a jam, that was it.

When will you allow yourself to be truly happy?

She didn't want to contemplate that question or risk telling the truth, because it always came back to her being a fraud. She didn't deserve to be happy. She'd boxed herself into a corner a long time ago.

Addie crossed the room. "I don't want you to be mad at me."

Juliette's shoulders dropped. "I'm not. I'm… This has given me a lot to think about."

"Why don't you change out of that dress."

Juliette glanced down. She hadn't realized she was still wearing it.

As she changed, and crunched on another

mint to settle her stomach, Juliette closed off her mind like she did whenever she was overwhelmed. Addie's words hurt, and Ivy's disappointment worried her. Maybe it would be best for everyone if she backed out of the dance.

When she stepped out of the fitting room, Addie's gaze settled on Juliette's face. "Please don't tell me you're going to cancel on Ty."

Juliette glanced away, guilt heating her face. "What are you doing, reading my mind?"

"I don't have to."

When Juliette had her emotions under control, she peeked at her friend. Addie had her arms crossed over her chest, sporting a frown.

"I've known you forever, Juls, even if you do keep a part of yourself closed off to me."

Juliette ran a finger over the soft fabric of the dress draped on her arm. Despite being taken aback by Addie's accusation—and the tiny zing of truth in her friend's words that she was *not* going to consider right now—a little flame of excitement at Ty seeing her in the new dress flared in her belly.

"I won't cancel on Ty," she promised.

Juliette paid for the dress, then the two left each other on the sidewalk to go in different directions. She stopped short when she saw

Ivy crouched down, petting a poodle on a leash while she chatted with the dog mom. It looked like Ivy had moved on already.

Ivy rose and noticed Juliette. With a smile on her face, she waved Juliette over to meet the animal. As she did, Juliette saw Ty and Colton going into the men's store, laughing over something. Probably to get their clothes for the dance. Their good moods made her realize she had a choice, at least in this particular instance. Let fear drag her down or take a chance and truly enjoy her time at the dance.

As the men disappeared into the store, Juliette wondered if she did deserve to be happy, just as Addie advised. Could Ty be the one person to make that possibility come true?

CHAPTER SEVEN

"Tonight is the big night," Gayle Ann announced. She was with the Matchmakers Club in the Golden Community Center after finishing another meeting with townspeople who were planning upcoming Christmas activities. They only had a month or so until everything turned festive, so they'd called the meeting quickly to confirm proposed ideas. Once the others had left, the matchmakers remained to discuss the evening ahead.

Bunny's face lit up. "I heard Juliette bought a pretty dress to bamboozle Ty."

Wanda Sue laughed. "Who uses the word *bamboozle*?"

Bunny's lips turned down. "Someone who heard that the dress will turn heads."

"Ladies," Gayle Ann intervened, "concentrate. Reports, please."

"Since Brando got Liz on board with our mission," Alveda said, "it moved up our timetable."

Brando's chest puffed out. "Didn't even

have to ask her twice to give up her chaperone spot at the dance."

"How'd you manage that?" Alveda asked.

"I confided in her about what we're up to and she loved the idea of matching her brother to Juliette. She's the one who suggested she take a trip out of town that weekend. In a manufactured panic, she talked her brother into taking her place." His pride faded. "Course, she'll hate missing Colton having a good time, but I think he's kinda relieved his mama won't be there."

The women rushed to make him feel better.

"Back to Juliette," Bunny said, her face flushed. "I saw her and Ivy outside of Tessa's and went inside the shop to get the scoop. Tessa was impressed with Juliette's selection and we all know she's got a good eye for fashion."

"And Ty got himself a nice suit," Brando added.

Gayle Ann smiled. It was all coming together.

"The theme of homecoming is Dancing Under the Stars," Alveda informed the group. "Pretty romantic if you ask me."

Wanda Sue let out a sigh. "Oh, to be young again."

Gayle Ann chuckled, then went back to business. "So, all our i's are dotted?"

Alveda, who had been taking notes for the meeting, closed her notebook and said, "Our plan is proceeding. It's been easier than I thought it would be."

"No, no, no," Wanda Sue said in a panic. "Don't say that. You'll jinx them."

Bunny snorted. "Jinx?"

Wanda Sue turned to her friend. "Haven't you watched any romantic movies?"

"You're getting all sappy on us," Bunny said. "This is real work."

"With consequences," Wanda Sue countered.

"Right now, the plan is in motion and going our way," Gayle Ann told the group. "No panicking."

"Gayle Ann is right," Harry added. "Tonight will be a magical night for Juliette and Ty."

"See," Gayle Ann said as she sat back in her chair. "Magic. What could possibly go wrong?"

FRIDAY NIGHT ARRIVED a lot sooner than Ty had anticipated. He stood on Juliette's front porch, wondering if he'd made a mistake. He'd never let Colton down by not showing up to homecoming, but what was he thinking asking Juliette to accompany him? She had this way of getting under his skin and he wanted more. Only way to get more was to spend time with her, despite their rocky beginning.

So here he stood in a new suit and shiny boots, a corsage box in his hand, hesitating to ring the doorbell. When had a woman ever tied him up in knots this way? Never, that's when.

Nerves hadn't been a problem when taking out women before. He wasn't sure why Juliette affected him so, but she was doing a stellar job of staying on his mind. He was pretty good at reading people, and he guessed her reticence made him curious. There were times when her quiet reserve was on full display, but other times she gave as good as she got. Now they were going on an official date. For a guy who wanted to focus on his family and the farm, he was amazed at how Juliette had easily worked her way into his life.

Working out the tension from his shoulders, he finally pressed the bell. A moment later it opened. Juliette stood on the other side, a welcoming smile on her pretty face. His throat went dry. She'd pulled her hair up, with curls escaping around her ears. She wore a stylish dress in a pretty jade that skimmed her figure and brought out the color of her eyes, and suddenly, he realized he was out of his league.

Since his nerves were getting the better of him, he said, "I have something for you."

"You do?"

He shoved the clear plastic box her way.

"A corsage?"

As she opened the box, her face lit up when she glimpsed the white roses nestled in a spray of greenery. The florist had told him this was a classic choice, so he went with the recommendation. When Juliette lifted the flowers to her nose and inhaled, followed by a slow spreading smile, his chest went tight.

Her gaze met his and he read the pleasure there. "Why the flowers?"

"Isn't that what you do when you take someone to a dance?"

"We're really not going to the dance. We're chaperones."

"Doesn't mean I can't get you flowers, darlin'." He took the wristlet from the box and slipped it over her hand, his fingers brushing over her soft skin. Her startled gaze darted to his. He supposed she felt the same jolt, wondering where this simmering attraction came from.

"I can honestly say you're the first woman I've ever done this for."

Her eyebrows rose in question.

"Never went to a school dance."

She choked on a surprised laugh. "Seriously? That can't be right."

"Not everyone is a town darling."

A stricken expression crossed her face. "I didn't mean…"

"I know," he assured her, not taking offense. The fact that he hadn't been interested in high school traditions was pretty ridiculous. "On the bright side, I have a pro to show me the ropes."

She shifted, something in her gaze catching his attention. Pain, maybe? Definitely uncertainty. Why?

His fingers moved one last time over her skin. She shook her head and held the door open. "Let me get my purse and wrap."

As she stepped away, her minty scent lingered, now mingled with the aroma of the roses. Ty's nerves eased at her reaction to his gift and his lingering touch. They might not be going to a rowdy club where he'd once felt comfortable, but he could do this. Taking a beautiful woman to a dance, even if it was for high school students, might be the best thing he'd done in a long time.

Juliette locked the door and tucked the colorful wrap around her shoulders as they walked down the path to the dark sedan parked at the curb. She stopped short.

"Where's your truck?"

"It's not exactly the most date-worthy vehicle for the evening."

She slowly turned her head toward him. "Were you holding out on me?"

"No." His collar suddenly felt tight around his neck. "I rented it for the night."

She blinked. "Rented?"

"Yep." When she continued to stare at the car, he said, "Something wrong?"

Shiny eyes met his. "No, it's just that no one has ever done anything special like this for me."

Hadn't done what? Made her feel exceptional? He couldn't believe it, but her stunned expression said otherwise.

"I don't know what to say," she whispered.

"Don't say anything. We're out for a night on the town. Let's get in this car and go."

When she started walking again, he opened the door and she slipped inside. Once he was behind the wheel, he drove through town toward their destination. The car was quiet until Juliette let out a laugh.

"What's so funny?"

"This might sound silly, but I'm nervous about tonight."

"You are? Why?"

Out of the corner of his eye, he caught her biting her lower lip. The motion, and her sweet uncertainty, got to his heart every time.

"It's been a long time since high school dances, corsages and anticipation," she said.

He cleared this throat. "So tell me what to expect."

She tugged the wrap tighter. "Couples dancing, others nervously standing on the sidelines waiting to be asked to dance. Acknowledging the homecoming court, and revealing the king and queen. The cheerleaders performing a special routine to send the football team off with chants for the final game against their rival."

He sent her an amused glance. "Which were you?"

"I was voted onto the homecoming court my senior year."

"Any other accolades you want to share?"

She squirmed in her seat. "Class president for two years running. I headed up lots of different fundraisers through the four years."

"So your causes started at an early age." He chuckled. "I figured with you being the town darling, you'd be popular."

"No... That whole thing got blown out of

proportion. I'm a plain old person like everyone else."

There was something in her voice. A pain that belied being the purported hero. Now was not the time to delve into her past, so he made a mental checklist to get answers later.

"Not everyone."

She twisted in the seat to face him, her tone wry. "I find that hard to believe. I would think you wouldn't have any shortage of girls lining up to wait and see if you'd ask them to a dance."

"I was more interested in the rodeo. And we traveled, so I never really had any permanent ties. Every weekend I was off with my dad or one of his friends at a show. School events weren't on my list."

"Please tell me you went to your graduation."

He turned to send her a grin. She waved her hands toward the windshield. "Keep your eyes on the road."

He straightened in his seat with a chuckle. "Yeah, got my cap and gown and walked across the stage when they called my name."

"Good, because that's an important milestone."

"Says the woman who aced her high school events."

"That's different."

"Let me guess. Valedictorian?"

"Not quite, but my grades got me into a good college."

"So this homecoming thing is a big deal?"

She shrugged, but he sensed he was right. "Not as big as prom, but still a major dance."

"Were you—"

Her voice grew quiet. "No. Never prom queen, thank goodness."

Ty wasn't quite sure how to unpack that comment, so he moved on. "I'm glad Colton is going, and with a date. After so many years on the road, he's happy to settle down and live a normal life."

"You say that like it's a bad thing."

"Normal wasn't always my goal." He shot her a smile. "It's kinda growing on me now."

They arrived at the high school as students decked out in sparkling dresses and immaculately pressed shirts and pants walked from the parking lot to the building. Exiting the car, Ty came around to open the door and help Juliette out.

"Ready?"

She pressed her lips together, then said, "As I'll ever be."

"Me too."

He held out his hand. She glanced down,

then clasped her fingers in his. Electricity shimmered between them. He watched Juliette fight a shiver in response. Over the years, he'd dated, had fun, but never experienced a unique connection to a woman. Not until now. With Juliette.

Inside the gymnasium, the lights were low and the music loud. Far from the honky-tonks he'd frequented. Sparkly stars hung from the ceiling and glittered in the ambient lighting. The decorations gave a person the impression they were under the stars on a dark night.

Juliette pointed to the principal. "There's Mrs. Rush. Guess we should find out what our duties are." She beelined to a middle-aged woman. As she did, other adults, faculty from the sounds of it, surrounded her. She introduced Ty, then the conversation turned to Juliette's years in school, her accomplishments as class president, her high grades, her popularity with the student body. All the while, he observed her growing unease. It made him wonder why this do-gooder, who never seemed to want the praise, ran from it.

"So, tonight," Juliette said, putting an end to the focus on her. "What do you want us to do?"

The principal gave them the rundown and

ended with, "We want the kids to have a good time, without the mischief."

Said mischief must have been happening because the woman frowned and crossed the room. Ty glanced at Juliette, catching the laughter in her eyes.

"What?" he asked in mock outrage.

"Somehow I think you'll have an easy time sniffing out mischief."

He pointed at himself. "Are you implying that I'm a troublemaker?"

"I'm not implying, I know it."

He laughed. "You aren't wrong."

They found a position on the sidelines to watch the goings-on. Spoke to the other chaperones. Ty wasn't surprised that Juliette knew everyone, started a conversation with each person she knew, asking how they were. It reminded Ty that despite trying to capitalize on tourism, at its core, Golden was still very much a small town.

Colton stopped by to introduce Kelsey. His cheeks were flushed with pride and Kelsey couldn't keep her eyes off him. All in all, not a bad night.

Especially with Juliette by his side.

At one point, the football team lined up at one end of the gym. They were playing their rivals the following weekend, so the crowd clapped and encouraged the players. Juliette leaned close to say, "I'm so glad the school still holds on to its traditions."

He wasn't much of a traditional guy, but he was happy for Colton's sake. The atmosphere went a long way in making him glad his family had chosen to live in Golden. Otherwise, he never would have met Juliette.

As silence fell between them, a romantic ballad played and couples filled the dance floor for a slow Chris Stapleton song. Ty noticed Colton take Kelsey in his arms for the slow dance. He smothered a grimace at the awkward way they moved until they grew comfortable with each other.

Ty turned his head, catching Juliette swaying to the beat. He held out his hand. "May I have the honor?"

Juliette glanced around. "Are we allowed to dance?"

He leaned close and whispered, "I won't tell if you won't."

She grinned that conspirator's grin that hit him straight in the gut. "Why, I think I will."

They stayed on the sidelines. Ty twirled her to him with a flourish, capturing her delighted laugh.

"I'm impressed by your moves."

"Just because I never attended a school

dance doesn't mean I don't know how to dance."

Ty twirled her again, this time sending them into the shadows beside the folded bleachers, removing them from direct line of vision of the rest of the dancers.

He gently tugged her close. Her minty scent enveloped him. They swayed in time to the beat, his arms circling her waist. Juliette looked up and their eyes met and held.

"There's another tradition, you know," he said in a low tone.

Her voice was breathy when she asked, "There is?"

"Yes. Our first kiss."

He lowered his head to brush his lips over hers. She went still at first, but soon softened against him, the kiss going deeper. Within moments it was over. When they parted, the color on her face heightened. She edged back, but not far enough away that he couldn't pull her back into his arms.

Was she as stunned as he was? Felt the kiss to her toes? He wasn't sure how to gauge his reaction to her touch since he'd never felt this way with another woman.

Instead of worrying, he tugged her close again, ready for another kiss, when a commotion sounded from across the gym. Voices grew louder, then came a shout, followed by a scream. Juliette jerked out of his arms as they both squinted into the dimly lit room.

"WHAT'S GOING ON?" Juliette asked, thankful for the distraction after that scorching kiss. *What were they thinking, to steal a kiss like they were teenagers? We're chaperones for Pete's sake.* "And why are people running around?"

"Let's go find out," Ty said over the commotion. He took her hand and led her from the secluded hideaway, heading to the action located in the center of the gymnasium.

She took a few steps, only to have something step on her foot and touch her leg. She shrieked and nearly jumped into Ty's arms. "What was that?"

They moved to a circle of students to find a goat scurrying about, bleating in confusion.

Juliette blinked. "Is that…a goat?"

"A familiar goat."

She glanced at Ty, wondering what he was talking about when Colton ran into the circle and stopped with a skid. He approached the animal and scooped it up, talking softly.

"That's not…" Juliette started to say.

"One of ours?" Ty frowned. "Yeah."

Kelsey hurried behind Colton, her eyebrows angling in confusion. "Colton, why are you holding a goat?"

Colton and Ty's gazes met for a split second. Juliette's stomach sank when she glimpsed the embarrassment on the teen's face.

"Why don't we go out to the lobby," she suggested.

Colton turned on his bootheel to escape all eyes on them. Once the four were alone, Ty jumped in. "Care to explain?"

"I swear, I don't know how he got here. I'm sure I closed the latch tight after I fed the tribe earlier today."

"This is yours?" Kelsey eked out.

Colton nodded miserably. "Even if he did get away from the pen, how'd he get to the school? Into the gymnasium?"

Juliette noticed a trio of boys lingering by the main door, doing a poor job of hiding their hysterics while slapping each other on the back. "I believe they most likely have the answer."

Ty's expression grew grave. With just one footstep in the boys' direction, they scrambled over each other to get out the door. By this time, the principal joined them, not at all happy.

"Do we have a problem, Mr. Pendergrass?"

Colton went from red to white. "No, ma'am."

Juliette stepped into the fray. "I believe this is a misunderstanding, Mrs. Rush. I know Colton and there's no way he would have disrupted this dance with a prank."

Both Ty and Colton sent her a grateful look.

Mrs. Rush crossed her arms over her chest. "And yet here he stands, proof in hand."

The goat let out a loud maa.

"My nephew isn't behind this," Ty said, heat in his tone.

"That remains to be—"

Mrs. Rush was interrupted when the doors opened and the school resource officer dragged in the boys Juliette had pointed out. To a man, they each had guilt written all over their faces. One tried to smother a laugh, but received a stern scowl from the principal for his efforts.

"Found these young men running to a truck. Looked like they were up to no good," the officer informed them.

"Explain," Mrs. Rush demanded, her ire focused in a new direction.

The boys exchanged nervous glances, then one said, "It was a prank." He tilted his chin toward Colton. "We always do it to the new kids."

When Ty made a move, Juliette grabbed his arm.

"So you brought the goat into the building?" Mrs. Rush asked.

They nodded.

"After trespassing on our property," Ty fumed.

"I called the chief," the officer said. 'He'll be here any minute."

"I should take him outside," Colton said, inching away from the crowd, the goat squirming in his arms. Kelsey went with him.

Ty ran a hand through his hair. "I can't believe this," he said for Juliette's ears only.

She leaned in close. "If it makes you feel any better, at least Kelsey is still by his side."

"This night meant so much to him."

Juliette heard the suppressed emotion in his tight tone. She didn't have the words to respond, so she remained quiet.

Moments later, Brady strode into the lobby. When his gaze landed on Ty and Juliette, his eyes narrowed. "Not you two again."

Annoyance shot through Juliette. "Someone played a prank."

At Brady's raised eyebrow she sputtered, "Not us!" She pointed to the boys hovering behind the resource officer.

Once the story was retold, she swallowed hard when Brady asked Ty, "Do you want to press charges?"

In his anger, Juliette wasn't sure what Ty would decide. Maybe in a few hours, when tempers had cooled, it would be a better time to make that call.

Ty stared down the scared boys with a hard glance. "No. Just tell them it better not happen again."

Brady nodded. "I'll go with the boys to make sure they safely return the goat from where they took it."

Ty sent Juliette an "I'm sorry" look. "It's okay. I'll take the goat back to the farm. I'm sure you've got better things to do than head out there tonight."

A slow grin spread over Brady's face. "Nah. You two enjoy the rest of your date."

"Brady…" Juliette said in a warning tone.

"I look forward to your next brush with the law."

Ty muttered under his breath as Brady went to round up the boys and herd them outside. Moments later Colton and Kelsey returned.

"You okay?" Ty asked.

"Not really. I, ah, think I'm going to go home." He turned to Kelsey. "If you want to stay, I'll understand."

"No, I came with you. Just let me get my things."

She hurried off, leaving Colton sagging against the wall. "I didn't have a clue."

"That's usually how a prank works," Ty said as he went to stand beside his nephew. "I'm sorry your night got ruined."

Colton lifted one shoulder toward his ear.

"If it's any consolation," Juliette said, "I know those boys' parents. I could really get them in trouble if I make a few phone calls."

Colton barely smiled. He glanced at Ty. "Is this one of those hold-your-head-up moments?"

"Afraid it is."

"It stinks."

"Indeed it does, but you'll have the high ground. And believe it or not, people will admire you for that."

It was clear Colton didn't believe him.

Kelsey returned and the two left.

"Now what?" Juliette asked. "I don't know the chaperone protocol when a disaster occurs."

"Me either. What do you say we figure it out together."

They went back to the gym where the party carried on as if nothing had happened. A few kids came up to ask Ty how Colton was doing, which warmed Juliette's heart. Yes, when Colton went back to school things would be awkward for a time, but it seemed like he had some true friends.

The cheerleaders performed a cheer routine, minus the athletic moves, because of their fancy dresses. It ended up more of a chant, but the crowd responded with claps. The remainder of the night continued as if the prank hadn't even occurred.

Ty, on the other hand, was quiet until the dance ended. Once the kids left and the cleanup crew arrived, they walked to the car. When they were seated inside, Juliette said, "As a first-time chaperone, I wonder how that dance rated on a scale of one to ten?"

Ty pulled out onto the main road to downtown Golden. "Most of the kids would probably give it a nine or ten. Colton'll probably score it a one."

Juliette shuddered. "I can't believe this happened."

"I wasn't about to say it out loud, but whether Colt likes it or not, it was a learning experience."

"Which are supremely awful."

In the light of the dashboard, Juliette saw Ty smile. "He'll survive."

"How are you?"

"Still pretty steamed." He let out a harsh breath. "Look, I get pranks. We did 'em all the time on the circuit. Knew about it and expected it. But Colton? He's trying to make his mark in a new place. And for a teen? This is his worst nightmare."

"He seems like a tough kid. In a month, he'll forget all about it."

He sent her a sharp glance. "You don't really believe that, do you?"

With the secrets in her past, no, she didn't. But she wanted to desperately believe it for Colton.

Ty scowled, his hands tight on the wheel as he drove. "I'm glad I missed all that stuff by not being a steady student in high school."

"You turned out fine."

After a pause, he said, "Did I? I still think about chucking it all to return to the rodeo. Sometimes I want to jump on Juniper and ride over the mountains and escape. And then I'd leave Colton behind when he needs me. What part of that says I grew up fine?"

The air in the car simmered with his anger.

"I'm not sure I'm up to a normal life."

Juliette's heart sank at his confession. The idea of him leaving was unthinkable. She took his hand in hers as if to hold on for dear life. Like that connection would keep him from riding away from Golden.

"I'd miss you if you weren't around," Juliette finally said when she could find her voice. "Who am I going to get into trouble with if you're gone?"

"I guess we are pretty good at staying on the chief's radar. We'd disappoint him if I took off."

Her too, but she relaxed when his humor returned.

When they arrived at her cottage, he walked her to the door.

"Despite the drama, I had a good time." She tugged the wrap tighter around her shoulders.

"Until the whole goat incident, so did I." His eyes grew dark. He leaned in and whispered, "How about we finish what we started?"

Shivers covered her from head to toe. "I've always been one to keep at a task until it's completed."

He chuckled. "I love the way you talk."

Taking his face between her palms. Juliette whispered, "I love the way you kiss." She tugged him the last inch and they lost themselves in a blinding kiss. When she needed air, she took a step back.

Ty ran a shaky hand through his hair. "I should probably leave."

"Yes. For both our sakes," she managed

to say through her thick throat. "Thanks for tonight."

He shot her one of his pirate smiles, turned on his heel and walked to the car. The car he'd rented for her. Her chest squeezed tight and her eyes went hot with tears. If he really knew her, knew she wasn't who everyone thought she was, would he have asked her to the dance tonight? Want to be in the same room as her? Continue kissing her?

Unless you become the woman he believes you to be.

Could she be that woman? She desperately wanted to, because somehow Ty had breached her defenses.

CHAPTER EIGHT

IT HAD TO have been the stars. Fake sparkly cardboard stars, but still, they'd created a romantic vibe nonetheless and Juliette fell head-first.

The kiss in the gym had been totally unexpected. Not unwelcome, but problematic. What about her resolve to remain unaffected by Ty? That theory went up in smoke the minute his lips claimed hers. High school dances may have been part of the past and she had been kissed since then, but no one had made her heart race more than Ty.

He'd said a quiet good-night after their second explosive kiss, leaving her stunned. She'd watched him drive away, shaking her head, a rebellious smile curving her lips. He'd actually rented a car for their night out. Who did that? Nice guys with a lot of charm, that's who.

And now she couldn't stop thinking about him.

"Juls, did you hear me?"

She shook out of her reverie and glanced at Addie. "What did you say?"

"We were talking about Serena's upcoming wedding."

"And I haven't received the RSVP telling me that you're attending," the bride-to-be admonished.

"Sorry. I meant to get it out to you, but I've been so busy it must have slipped my mind."

Serena sent her a knowing smile. "Because you've been otherwise distracted by the cowboy in town?"

Great, they knew. Juliette eyed her best friend. "Thanks."

Addie shrugged. "I couldn't help it. You going to the dance was too juicy not to share."

The group of women had met to catch up at a new gathering place in town, located on the edge of a fast-moving creek. The Perch offered soft drinks and wine, along with appetizers like charcuterie boards and other savory selections. A wooden deck stretched out from the building, stopping just before reaching the steep bank. Nestled in a cocoon of fully mature trees, it gave folks a fine view of the wide creek and a waterfall located not too far away. String lights crisscrossed overhead. With the weather being nice, the women had pulled together tables and chairs outside to enjoy the cool night and each other.

They'd all dressed up for the occasion. Juliette, in a flowing floral print dress, a denim jacket along with low boots. It wasn't often she splurged by putting on a pretty outfit to go out with friends, but she was glad Addie had insisted. They were all busy and met too infrequently for her liking.

This girls' night out focused on the wedding and their significant others. All were paired up, except for Juliette and Addie. Before tonight Juliette had been okay with it. That is until Ty had blown into town with his whiskey brown eyes, charming smile and a mischievous streak she was drawn to no matter how much she tried to convince herself that upstanding women of a certain age didn't give in to high jinks.

Juliette stared at the smiling faces around the table. Serena, soon-to-be-married owner of Blue Ridge Cottage on Main Street. Heidi was an accountant in town. Sisters, Grace, the attorney Ivy worked for, and Faith, who ran Put Your Feet Up, a vacation service. And then there was Carrie, chamber of commerce director. She and Addie rounded out the table.

"We went to Tessa's and it took Juls forever to pick out a dress. There was a pile of outfits in every color in the dressing room after we left. Glad I didn't have to pick up."

Juliette found herself protesting. "You're exaggerating."

"Maybe, but you were very particular about what you were going to wear."

"Fine. I wanted to look nice when I chaperoned the dance with Ty. His sister was supposed to be there, but had to go out of town. Ty didn't want to let his nephew down by not showing up."

Grace pointed a finger at her. "Is that the excuse the kids are using these days?"

She refused to set Grace straight on that fact, saying, "It was nostalgic to go back to those high school days and watch the kids have fun. Ty's nephew and his date looked like they were having the time of their lives, until the goat incident."

Faith cringed. "Pranking a dance. The worst tradition at Golden High."

"That's because you got caught," Grace informed her sister.

"Not me specifically, the crowd I hung with at the time." Faith groaned. "I still can't believe we thought water balloons at a dance would be funny."

Grace elbowed Heidi. "Remember when Logan and Reid shrink-wrapped the football players' cars outside the gym? Their big mistake was not realizing that the principal at the time had driven his wife's car that night. He was pretty ticked."

Heidi chuckled. "They're lucky they're Mastersons or they'd have been suspended. But no one outdid them for a long time."

"If I remember right," Faith went on to say, "Brady was involved with that stunt too."

Juliette perked up. Good to know, especially if the police chief decided to needle her and Ty again.

"Unfortunately for Colton, it ruined his night." Juliette couldn't get his dejected expression out of her mind. "Thankfully the mess got straightened out. Not for the pranksters, but for the remainder of the dance."

"What about you and Ty?" came Serena's sly question.

"The rest of the night was fine."

Especially the kiss in the gym and at my front door.

She tried to ignore the swirl in her belly, but her emotions decided to be contrary.

"So, is Ty as much of the rebel as we've heard?" Faith asked as she placed a piece of cheese on a cracker. She hesitated before taking a bite, then set it down.

"He was very well-behaved."

Except for only two kisses. Which was a bit of a shame. She liked when he went off script.

"Surprising," Grace piped in, "especially

after we heard about the sign incident in town. As a lawyer, I gotta point out, that was ill-advised."

Juliette glared at Addie, who threw her hands up in defense. "Now, that I did not mention."

"Nope," Grace said. "Heard about it at the courthouse."

"It's unusual. You don't usually date guys from town," Faith added as she studied Juliette.

"I was being a friend," she explained, refusing to squirm in her seat.

Heidi snorted. "Right."

Juliette could have argued her case, but her friends weren't buying it. Better to just keep her mouth shut and let them get the teasing out of their systems.

"I'm happy for you," Carrie said. "I've worked with Ty and he's a nice guy."

"And crazy talented on a horse," Serena said.

"Plus, he's cute," Addie added.

Juliette frowned at her friend.

"Hey, I'm only speaking the truth."

Yes, she knew all these things about Ty, but she still hadn't entirely wrapped her mind around what happened the night before. She didn't want to build up the importance of the kisses, only to be let down if Ty learned the real truth about covering up her bogus hero status and walked away.

Her mind had whirled as she readied for bed after the dance. Mostly about Ty's kisses, but what about the people she'd run into? Would she have made homecoming court if her reputation hadn't secured the privilege? What about class president? Was there a student who had deserved it more but lost out because of her false hero status? She didn't like dwelling on these questions, but they'd bombarded her mind just the same, followed closely by the everlasting guilt she refused to shed.

"Back to the wedding," Serena said, redirecting the conversation. "You are coming, right, Juliette?"

"Yes."

"Good, because I added two to the list."

Juliette's jaw dropped. "Two? I haven't…"

At the amused expressions, Juliette realized she'd walked right into that one. "Thank you," she muttered.

With a drawn-out sigh, Serena leaned back in her chair and glanced up to the inky sky dotted with stars. "I can't believe it's finally here."

"After all the planning," Carrie said, "it's going to be lovely. Mrs. M. is beside herself."

"I couldn't have done half of it without her."

Heidi's forehead wrinkled. "Has anyone noticed she's been spending a lot of time with Judge Carmichael? I asked Alveda about it but she's been annoyingly closemouthed."

Carrie nodded. "Now that you mention it, I saw them at Smitty's Pub recently and they looked rather cozy."

"Are they dating?" Faith asked.

"If they are, it's sweet," Grace said.

Juliette had indeed seen the older couple together. Now that the focus of the conversation had shifted, she was glad to add what she knew. "Just the other day I saw them hand in hand walking down Main Street."

Serena looked around, as if gauging the crowd around them, then leaned in to whisper in a conspiratorial tone, "I can't reveal my source, but yes, they're dating."

"We know your source is Logan," Addie said with a laugh.

"Still, they're slowly getting the news out. Well, as slowly as you can in Golden, because she doesn't want a fuss."

Juliette thought that was the smart attitude. Having the entire town assume they knew what was going on with you was exhausting.

"Anyway, they'll be at the wedding, so we can keep an eye on them," Heidi announced.

"How about we leave them alone?" Juliette suggested, her tone dry. "Privacy is not a bad thing."

She was happy to see her friends married or in relationships, but it was also a reminder of what was missing in her own life. Self-induced, yes. And honestly, until the past week or so, she'd been fine. Her career kept her busy so she didn't dwell on her lack of a romance. Ivy was always front and center, but with her mother's decision to drop to part-time at the office, that was going to change. If Juliette wanted, she could focus on her future. But the idea of the truth being revealed after all this time still scared her.

As the women ordered another round of drinks, Juliette noticed Faith had opted for water again.

"Are you feeling okay?"

Faith glanced at Grace, who grinned. "You might as well tell them."

After taking a sip from her glass, Faith announced, "I'm pregnant."

Squeals of delight came from everyone at the table.

Serena got up to hug Faith. "This is so exciting."

Faith glowed. "We've been keeping it quiet for a while, but I think it's okay to let you all know now."

Carrie asked, "When are you due?"

"End of February."

"Roan must be over the moon," Addie said.

"He's happy, but the kids are happier. They can't wait for a baby."

Juliette thought about their blended family and how hard they worked to make it one. If anyone deserved to be happy, it was Faith.

As if reading her mind, Grace turned to Juliette. "You know we want to see you happy too."

The others at the table nodded. Suddenly tears welled up in her eyes. "Excuse me, I need to go to the ladies' room."

On a shaky breath, Juliette rose, her foot getting tangled between the chair and table leg. She did a little jig, then hurried away before any of the women asked what was wrong. How could she tell them that she felt bad about keeping the truth from them for all these years? She couldn't, so she ran.

After escaping to the bathroom, she splashed water on her face. Looked in the mirror. All she saw reflected in her eyes was guilt. Why didn't anyone else see it? Probably because they had no reason to doubt the story. Juliette had never straightened it out, so she deserved the weight pressing down on her.

You could tell them the truth.

If she was brave enough. But after fifteen

years? All the questions, the looks of disappointment she'd receive. No, it was better to just keep quiet like she had for this long.

She exited the restroom to cut through the busy dining room to join her friends. A group rose from a table and she nearly collided with the mayor as he stood before her.

"Juliette. What a surprise."

Her heart seized. "Mayor Danielson. How are you?"

"Doing fine." He pushed in the chair as his group started toward the door. "I'm glad I ran into you. We're throwing a party for Ellie and we'd love for you to come."

Juliette froze. Why would they include her? She really hadn't been part of their orbit for years. "A party?"

Pride beamed on his face. "She got accepted into her first choice college. We couldn't be more proud, especially after hearing so early in the process."

"That's very nice, but I wouldn't want to intrude on a family celebration."

"Are you kidding? You're family. If you hadn't been so quick to action all those years ago, Ellie might not be with us today. So we want you there. In fact, we insist."

"I… Um…"

Not reading her distress, he went on. "We'll reach out with the details." He squeezed her shoulder as he passed by. Juliette stood there, rubbing her tight chest. The mayor had boxed her in again.

"Hey, are you okay?" Addie asked as she came alongside Juliette.

"Yes." She glanced at her friend who had her purse strap over her shoulder. "Where are you going?"

"The babysitter called. Jacob watched a scary show on television and he's kinda freaking out."

"You'd think after the last movie that kept him up all night he'd pick a different show."

"Apparently it's a popular series with his classmates. So now I have to go home and calm him down."

"Wait. You drove. Let me get my purse and I'll come with you."

"No, go enjoy the rest of your night. It's not like you go out very often. One of the girls will take you home."

"Are you sure?"

"Positive."

"Okay, but call if you need anything."

"I will."

As her friend rushed out the door, Juliette returned to the deck. Her friends were laughing as she sat down.

"What did I miss?"

"Serena was telling us that if she hadn't

picked out the wedding venue when she did," Carrie informed her, "Logan was going to kidnap her and bring her to the county clerk's office."

The bride-to-be grinned. "I know he doesn't care about all the little details for the wedding, but he's been a good sport all along. At the time I thought he was teasing, until I saw the serious look on his face. I shot back, telling him the only way I'd get married without family with us was if we went to Las Vegas. Before I knew it, he was on his phone, checking flights. I grabbed his cell and had to hide it until he got that crazy notion out of his head."

"It wasn't a crazy idea and I still stand by it," a deep voice spoke behind Juliette. She twisted in her seat to see Logan headed their way.

Serena jumped up, her face flushing with pleasure. "What are you doing here?"

"Missing you," her fiancé said as he rounded the table, wrapped an arm around her waist and pulled her in for a kiss. Multiple aahs sounded from the table.

"It really was a close call," Heidi said. "But as usual, Serena talked him down. Now we all get to watch them exchange vows."

Then, the rest of the significant others showed up. Heidi jumped up to hug Reid,

Deke came behind Grace to lean down and kiss his wife's cheek, Carrie reached out to take Adam's hand, and Faith and Roan exchanged content grins.

Juliette rolled her eyes. "I thought this was supposed to be a girls night."

Faith leaned over. "It doesn't have to be. Call Ty."

She bit her lower lip. As much as she loved the idea, it was late. By the time he got to town, if he could even make it, everyone would be heading home. And then they'd be alone and have to discuss the kiss. She wasn't ready for that conversation.

"Stop talking yourself out of it," Faith admonished.

Should she go for it? Was it too weird? She pulled out her phone and stared at the screen, her thumbs hovering over the keyboard. She pulled up his contact when all of a sudden she heard boots echo against the wooden deck. Gooseflesh broke out over her skin. She knew before she turned that it was Ty.

"Heard there's a party," he said to everyone in way of a greeting.

Juliette shot a scowl at Faith. "You knew?"

"Nope. The guys showing up was a complete surprise."

Still, her friend looked guilty. "But?"

"But, we knew Ty met up with the guys tonight."

"And you didn't think to tell me?"

"Why would we? We didn't know they'd crash our party and besides, you didn't tell us you went on a date with Ty until after the fact."

She couldn't argue with that logic. Holding back a sigh, she glanced over her shoulder. Ty sent her that rogue's smile and she lost all coherent thought.

Ty REALIZED BY the look on Juliette's face that his showing up unannounced was a complete surprise. He kept the smile on his face, even though the look he shot Adam promised revenge.

When the guys had found out about his date with Juliette, he should have known they'd set him up, telling him they wanted to stop by the new hangout, conveniently leaving out the fact that the women were there. He'd never admit it, but he was glad they did.

As the group began to mingle, he took a seat beside Juliette. "I think we were set up."

Juliette's gaze passed over each person and she shook her head sorrowfully. "And I thought they were such nice people."

Ty laughed, relieved that she wasn't miffed at him for showing up out of the blue.

"I should have known something was up. Adam was acting weird."

"None of the women were."

He met her gaze. "We must be losing our edge."

She sent him a grin that warmed him from head to toe. "Speak for yourself."

After their date last night, he wasn't sure how she'd respond to him. He didn't know if their kisses had rocked her world, but they'd knocked his on its axis. He couldn't stop thinking about her; her surprise when he gave her the corsage, how lovely she looked in the green dress that reflected the color of her eyes, her hair pulled up, framing her face. Was she as taken by him as he was with her? Surprised by this connection that had linked them together since the first moment they'd met?

He didn't want to push if she wasn't interested, because the unease that flashed in her eyes every now and again made him wary. Was it him? He didn't know how he'd feel if she didn't return the attraction. They'd see each other at the farm and he didn't want things to be awkward between them because he really liked her. This spontaneous meetup was natural, more to his liking. And by her smile, he hoped Juliette thought so too.

"Where were you tonight?" she asked.

"We ran into each other at Smitty's Pub, then Logan wanted me to see the venue where he and Serena are getting married. The next thing I knew, we ended up here. You?"

"A little shopping and then we came here for appetizers."

He glanced around the deck. "Nice place."

"Just opened this summer. It's a great place to hang out with friends."

"You ladies come here often?"

She glanced around the deck. "Not really. I mean, they might, but I'm usually busy with a project."

"So how did they talk you into joining them tonight?"

Her lopsided grin went straight to his heart. "My best friend Addie came by my house and nagged me into getting out for a few hours."

"Let me guess. You had a very important uprising to plot and didn't want to be disturbed?"

Her chuckle lilted in the air. "Not exactly. Honestly, I was going to kick my feet up with a bowl of popcorn and watch a movie."

"I had a similar night lined up. Until Colton ditched me."

"Come again?"

He moved closer, inhaling her minty sweet scent. "Colton and I went to Smitty's to get dinner when Kelsey called. He asked if he could hang out with her, which meant me going solo, but Adam and his crew took pity on me and convinced me to join them."

Juliette angled her head, a strand of hair slipping from behind her ear to brush her cheek. He fisted his fingers to keep from tucking it back into her rich, thick hair.

"I already knew some of the guys when I arrived in town," he explained, "including Adam. Now that I've become part of Golden, I've expanded that circle." He gazed over her shoulder. "To be honest, I've missed the social aspect of being on the rodeo circuit."

"For partners in crime, we sure aren't very dangerous if our friends have to drag us out for a night on the town."

"I spent all day fixing fences, which now that I say it, sounds boring, so yeah, I was up for some action."

Their eyes met and held.

Juliette cleared her voice. "So we were saved by our friends."

"Maybe. Unless you want to go on our own adventure."

She scanned the group as if considering his suggestion. Leaned closer. "Now that they're all paired up, they don't even know we're here," she whispered, her lips close to his ear. "What did you have in mind?"

Her breath, whispering over his skin, had

him shifting in the chair. He cleared his suddenly tight throat. "We could go for a drive."

"Now?"

"You got better plans?"

She hesitated. "As a matter of fact, I don't."

They stood and slipped away from the table without being noticed. He took her hand once they were outside. They were headed to his truck when he detoured.

"What are you doing?"

"Adam mentioned a large boulder on the side of the creek where they used to fish. Let's check it out."

She tugged back on his arm. "We can't go down there. It's dark."

He wiggled his eyebrows in challenge.

She rolled her eyes.

He led her around the building. "What's the big deal? There's a path."

Her tone pitched higher. "A path meant to be used in the daylight."

"C'mon, darlin'," he said as he carefully led her down the uneven ground. "Don't get all prim on me now."

He saw the flame leap into her eyes, knowing she couldn't resist, and carefully led her down on a trail to the edge of the rushing water.

"I'm never going to hear the end of this," he heard her mutter.

He glanced over his shoulder. "We do have a habit of getting people to talk about us."

In the moonlight streaming through the tree branches, he could make out the scowl on her pretty face.

"That's a bad thing?" he asked, thinking he should be asking himself the same question. Having people talk about him didn't exactly make him come off as responsible, and that's what he needed to convince his dad he could take care of the farm.

"I'm uncomfortable with people in my business."

"Says the woman who was ready to steal a city sign with me."

She went to throw up her hands, but one was still connected to his. "Hey, you never said anything about stealing it."

"It was sort of implied."

"Thankfully your poorly thought out plan didn't work."

They drew close to the edge. The rushing water grew louder, drowning out all the other sounds round them. They were hidden from prying eyes on the deck by a thick barrier of tree trunks and natural vegetation. Sure enough, a large boulder sat sentinel on the bank.

"This has to be the spot."

Juliette shivered. A perfect excuse to put an arm around her shoulders. "You okay?"

She snuggled against him. "I am now."

The silver light from the moon tangled in the eddies of the water, splashing over rocks and broken tree branches. Juliette let out a sigh and pointed to the other side.

"I've never told anyone, but I love waterfalls."

Sure enough, water cascaded down two levels of the falls, pouring into the creek.

Ty watched her wistful expression and wondered where it came from. "Why would you keep that a secret?"

She shrugged, but he sensed she was holding back.

He tugged her closer. "Is it a not-liking-anyone-in-your-business thing?"

"I suppose."

"I noticed last night that you were uncomfortable when people kept talking about your past accomplishments."

"Wouldn't you be if the focus was on you? It was a dance, not a reunion."

"Darlin', I lived for the limelight at the rodeo. Not the person to ask that question."

They went quiet for a time, drinking in the beauty. Even in the night shadows, Ty was entranced by their surroundings, more so with the woman beside him. Then he remembered something she'd said to him.

"Does it have anything to do with you being the town hero?"

She went stiff.

"You don't have to talk about it if you don't want to."

"It's just…" He felt her relax. "That day was not a big deal, but became a big deal and I haven't been able to live it down."

"Why would you want to? From what I heard, you saved a little girl."

"She was in a stroller, in the middle of the road."

"And so were you. Timing."

He watched her bite her lower lip.

"It was timing, right?"

"Of course." She ducked from under his arm and stepped away. Not far, since there was only a small open patch to stand in, but far enough that he didn't like the loss of her warmth. She bent down to pick up a stone and toss it in the bubbling water.

"Do you ever regret how certain events shaped your life?" she asked.

"Only too much."

He could understand why that day might not line up with who she was now. He had plenty of regrets about the way he'd treated his family when he'd been on the road with the rodeo. Didn't want to revisit his selfishness.

"I've learned that you have to take a stand," he said. He'd sworn to his family he'd be there and meant to keep that vow.

She ran her hands up and down her arms. Chilled from the cold night air or the direction of the conversation?

"I realize we haven't known each other very long, but you can talk to me."

She turned to him, remorse shining in her eyes. "Thanks, but I'm good."

Somehow, he didn't think she was.

Contrary to her mood, Juliette reached out and grabbed his hand, intertwining her fingers in his. To his surprise, she tugged him closer. Her dress swirled around her legs as he ended up against her. Their gazes met and he waited for her to make the next move. She went on tiptoes and brushed her lips over his. He finally wrapped his arms around her and kissed her back wholeheartedly.

Before long, be broke the kiss and smiled down at her. "I could get used to this."

She sent him a rueful smile. "I wouldn't argue against it."

"Good, because I wasn't sure how you felt after last night."

"Apparently the same as you, so let's not analyze it and just enjoy being together."

"I knew there was a reason I liked you."

She stepped back and playfully tapped his arm.

"Okay, no analyzing. What, then?"

Her playful grin almost had him worried, but he already knew he'd say yes to whatever she asked.

"So, about Serena and Logan's wedding."

He stuffed his hands in his pockets.

"It's been brought to my attention that I haven't sent back the RSVP card."

"And this is important because?"

She cleared her throat. "Serena already added me as a guest."

"So what's the problem?"

He waited for her to continue, pretty sure where this discussion was going, but wanting her to make her move.

She straightened her shoulders. "Remember when I agreed to go to the dance and I said I'd call in my marker when you least expected it?"

"I do."

"I'm calling it in now." She lifted her chin. "Will you attend the wedding with me? Seems I'm a plus-two without a date."

"When you put it so nicely, darlin'."

She got that miffed expression he loved. "I'm serious."

"I'd be honored."

Her smile was bright in the moonlight.

"I have another request."

He winked and removed his hands from his pockets. "Good thing I like you."

She shook her head, then said, "So your truck is here?"

"It is. Why?"

"Seems I also need a ride home."

"Another favor, huh?"

She pointed a finger at him. "You owe me since you got me in trouble with the chief."

"And we both paid the price for that, but yeah, I can give you a lift."

Hand in hand, they made their way up the path. The parking lot had cleared out. He hadn't realized how late it had gotten. Spending time with Juliette had a way of making him forget all about the minutes passing by.

As they drove to her cottage, he said, "Are you free tomorrow?"

"What did you have in mind?"

"Liz won't be back until later in the day, but I thought you might want to come to the farm and ride one of the horses."

"I'd love to. After I take them out, I can address the horses' temperaments in my proposal."

"How about ten o'clock?"

"I'll be there."

He sent her a sidelong glance, catching

her smile, which did crazy things to his gut. For a guy who didn't do steady relationships, he couldn't get enough of her, which would cause a problem if he started to put her before the farm.

CHAPTER NINE

"I SPOKE TO my grandson this morning." Gayle Ann dropped a teaspoon of sugar into her tea with a self-satisfied twist of her wrist after relaying her report. "He told me their group of friends met at The Perch and Ty and Juliette slipped off by themselves. I sense romance in the air."

The matchmakers had gathered at Sit A Spell on Sunday morning after church to compare notes on their latest mission.

Alveda frowned. "Was he curious as to why you were asking?"

"No. I simply asked him about his night and he filled me in from there. All our successful matches were together having a good time. Learning about Ty and Juliette was like icing on the cake."

"She's coming to the farm to ride with Ty." Brando checked his watch. "Should be there now."

Harry smiled. "My anonymous donation to the equine program moved things along."

"Got them in each other's orbit, anyway," Alveda agreed.

"And they went to the dance together at the high school Friday night," Bunny said with a twinkle in her eye. "Things are moving right along. Told you that dress would work."

Brando chuckled. "It was all very, what'd ya call it, organic."

Alveda glanced at him. "Organic?"

"Yeah." Brando's face flushed. "Heard it somewhere."

Alveda patted his hand.

"So," Bunny demanded. "What happened?"

He told them about the goat making a cameo appearance.

The spoon dropped from Alveda's hand. "How did the goat get there?"

"Some boys playing a prank. Colton's been down in the dumps ever since."

"Typical Golden High School tricks," Bunny puffed impatiently. "Seems things haven't changed."

"How did it go with Juliette and Ty?" Wanda Sue asked.

Brando shrugged. "I don't know. They had a good time I guess. Ty didn't say and I didn't ask."

Bunny shook her head. "Why don't men ever get the details?"

Gayle Ann and Alveda swapped glances and chuckled.

"But is it enough?" Wanda Sue arched an eyebrow. "From what I remember, Juliette never had many dates while she was in high school and despite going to a dance now, she seems immune to romance."

"Just needs the right man in her life," Bunny blustered.

Wanda Sue shook her head. "I spoke to Pam Bishop. She doesn't understand why her daughter hasn't found a guy to settle down with. She's worried that Juliette will get too immersed in her work and end up lonely."

"Which is a valid concern." Gayle Ann rubbed her fingers at her temple. "Are you saying you don't think the equine program will bring them together?"

Wanda Sue went quiet before saying, "I'm just not sure it's enough."

Brando nodded his head in agreement. "The program is good for the farm. In fact, Liz has folks calling about it already."

"So that's good, right?" Alveda asked.

"It is for Liz. She's a pro at giving lessons, but it might lead to a different problem."

Gayle Ann didn't like Brando's concerned tone. "In what way?"

"You all know that when we moved here,

we had ideas about making the farm inter-active with public access to our animals. The riding lessons and opening the trails for horseback excursions were our first step to-ward public exposure, but we can't overlook the opportunity of Juliette's therapy program. I'm afraid Ty might think his contribution is getting pushed to the sidelines. Seems all he does around the farm are repairs and man-age the finances."

"Are the original plans make-or-break in Ty's eyes?" the judge asked.

"Can't say for sure. He's behind Liz one hundred percent, but if he gets aimless? I don't know. He might go back to the rodeo."

The room grew quiet at Brando's statement.

"You can do both, can't you?" Gayle Ann asked. "Open up more avenues to the public along with the equine side of things?"

"Sure, but the lessons are the biggest source of income."

Bunny sipped her tea, then said, "How much progress has Ty made toward making the farm more tourist friendly?"

Brando shrugged. "He's been so busy with other repairs, he hasn't done much more."

"You said it would take time to reach those goals," Alveda reminded Brando.

"But we don't want to leave Ty out in the cold," Gayle Ann concluded.

Bunny snapped her fingers. "Got an idea."

Alveda grinned. "This'll be good."

Bunny pouted, then said, "Between all of us, we know folks who sell homemade goods. I've got a friend who makes natural soaps. Wanda Sue, you know the folks who have beehives."

"I do. They recently started selling their honey products at local farmers markets."

"And, Alveda," Bunny said, "You easily could sell your pies. If word got out they were available to the public, we'd have a rush of folks tryin' to get their hands on one."

"And how about that young man who has been trying to sell his barbecue sauces?" Harry piped in. "He's got a few bottles for sale at Smitty's Pub."

Gayle Ann grinned at the group. "I like where this is going."

Bunny looked at Brando. "Once Ty has the farm set up where you can get visitors on the property, you could hold a market once a month."

"That might be enough to keep Ty grounded. I told him he's a great manager of the farm, but I'm not sure that's enough for him."

"Then we need to keep him busy," Gayle Ann said.

"And Juliette?" Wanda Sue asked, returning to the other half of the mission.

"We make sure to bring them together whenever possible," Gayle Ann reasoned. "Let love do the rest."

"Not sure that girl will go for it," Bunny said, doubt loud and clear in her voice.

Gayle Ann reached over and took Harry's hand. "Then we let her see what she's missing."

To which Bunny rolled her eyes, Alveda chuckled and Wanda Sue sighed.

Brando glanced at Harry in confusion. "What'd I miss?"

"The next step in our plan. Love in action."

Alveda got a glint in her eyes as she glanced at Gayle Ann. "You know, Juliette loves to be included in projects."

Gayle Ann sat back with a smile. "Isn't it convenient that we have ideas for the farm market and she's just the person to carry them through?"

The women all beamed at each other.

Brando leaned over to the judge. "They're scary."

"Scary smart."

TY STOOD WITH his hands on his hips, glancing down at the well pump. It had glitched again today, which meant he was going to have to buy a new one, and re-dig the well, sooner rather than later.

He rubbed the grease from his fingers with the rag hanging from his belt loop. He'd been hoping to put the purchase off, but they couldn't go without a well that supplied water to the stable.

He'd been able to get the pump working, but how long would the fix last? Probably not long. When the repairman had come out to the property last week, he'd told Ty that he couldn't keep putting off the replacement of the entire well. But hours spent hunched over the books hadn't changed the bottom line, no matter how much he wanted it to.

He blew out a frustrated breath.

"Hey, Uncle Ty."

Ty glanced over his shoulder. Shook off his bleak mood. "Colt."

"I missed you at breakfast this morning."

When the dog ran up to him, Ty bent over to rub his head. "Yeah, I left the house early. Had some things to do around the stable."

"Anything I can do?"

"It's under control."

No way was Ty going to burden Colton with

his worries. Even though his nephew was a big help around the farm, Ty wanted the teen to be carefree for as long as possible.

"So, how did it go with Kelsey last night?"

Colton's smile dipped at one corner. "Sorry I ditched you."

"If I had a pretty girl waiting for me, I'd probably have done the same thing."

Although he didn't have to, since he'd run into Juliette. Another night to remember with a woman who was hard to forget.

Colton shrugged. "It was okay, I guess."

That didn't sound good. "Trouble?"

"I don't know." He ran the tip of his boot in the grass. Shep ran over to smell the spot. "When she called I thought it was just gonna be the two of us. But there was a group of kids from class already there. One guy kept talking to Kelsey. I barely got a chance to hang with her."

Ty secured the enclosure over the pump motor. "Why were there so many people?"

"Turns out it was a study group for that medical program Juliette was telling us about."

Ty scratched his head. "A study group on a Saturday night?"

Colton nodded. "Yeah, that's what I was thinking, but I did mention to her that I was interested in the program. Maybe that's why she invited me."

Ty closed the door to the pump house. "I know that wasn't what you were expecting."

"Is dating gonna be hard?"

Ty chuckled. "I'm not the guy to ask."

Colt sent him a look that said he didn't believe Ty. "You never had a steady girlfriend?"

He'd known women who were friends, women who were girlfriends and some who were exes, but he'd never been a guy in a serious relationship in all that time. "Afraid not."

"Why?"

"Traveling the rodeo circuit doesn't really lend itself to getting to know a woman. We'd be in cities and towns for a short period of time before we moved on. Nothing ever stuck."

Or grabbed his attention like Juliette had from day one and made him want to stick.

"Kelsey kept looking at me, but she didn't come over to sit by me. Do you think I read more into her call than was there? Think she's still miffed about the goat ruining the dance?"

"From where I was standing, it looked like you two were having a good time, so I can't say."

"That's what I thought." Colton stared over the pasture. His voice was thick when he said, "Do you think I should stay away from her?"

"Nothing that drastic. See what happens at school tomorrow. Maybe she has a reason for the way she was acting."

"I guess."

Now what did Ty say? He was not the go-to guy for relationship advice. "It isn't like she's the only girl at school."

If possible, Colton seemed even more dejected. "Yeah, but I really like her."

Ty could relate. "Just talk to her. I hear women like it when we tell them what we're feeling."

Colton shot him a horrified glance.

"I know. Gives me the willies too."

"C'mon, boy," Colton commanded Shep. "We've got chores."

Ty watched his nephew walk away, hurting for the teen. The one thing Ty didn't tell Colton is that for all the polish you put on to win a woman, guys still managed to mess things up.

Since there wasn't anything Ty could do about the pump on a Sunday morning, he picked up his tools and headed back to the stable. As he entered, he saw Juliette walking in from the parking lot side of the building.

Dressed in a long-sleeved yellow T-shirt, worn jeans and boots, she dangled a straw hat from her fingers. She'd pulled her hair back, revealing her milky complexion. Stunning as always, his chest grew tight as she moved closer.

"Good morning," she called out in a cheery voice that was at odds with his mood.

"Back at ya," he said. Placing the tools in the storage room, he then took a moment to drag a hand through his hair and brush off his clothes. When he backed out, she was waiting.

"It's a lovely morning to ride."

The sun was shining and the temperature had risen from chilly to comfortable, but the weight of the decisions he had to make overshadowed the pleasant weather. Seems only Juliette could lift his spirits.

He looked around her. "Your sister didn't come?"

"Not this time. She has some friends she goes to breakfast with on Sunday mornings. Now that she has a place to sell her jewelry, she wanted to tell them all about it."

"So that left you on your own?"

"Yep, that's me, all alone." She grimaced after she said the words. "So, which horse do you recommend I ride?"

He let the comment pass. "I saddled the paint horse, so she's all ready."

"You didn't have to do that. I'm more than capable."

"I'm sure you are, but I needed to give Juniper a good run this morning, so I just handled it after I groomed him."

Disappointment crossed her features. "You've been out already?"

"On my horse, but I'll ride another with you. We can discuss their temperaments if you want."

She flashed him a big smile. "Thanks."

She got to him, she really did. He thought she'd been pretty before, but in that moment, he was transfixed by the curves of her lips. The sparkle in her eyes and the excitement on her face. He sucked in a breath and knew if he tried to speak at this moment, he'd have no words.

The mares were already in the paddock. Ty opened the gate to lead Juliette toward the animals.

"Anything I should know?" she asked as he centered a mounting block for her to climb onto the animal.

He cleared his throat. "Like I said, they're both good-natured. Maggie is older so she's good with riders. Tri has her days when she wants to do her own thing, but those aren't very frequent."

She nodded, grabbed the reins, placed a foot in the stirrup and pulled herself up on the horse, just like a pro. Tri danced once Juliette was seated, but she calmed the horse right away with soothing words.

Placing a boot in the stirrup, Ty launched himself up on Maggie.

Juliette plunked her hat on her head. "Show off."

"What?"

"You don't need help mounting."

He winked at her. "Wouldn't be much of a cowboy if I did."

She laughed, a welcome balm over his frayed nerves.

"Which area do you recommend taking the kids in the program, here in the paddock or in the ring?"

"Initially, the paddock," he advised. "Smaller space, easier to control the environment. If you have riders who are more independent, we can possibly move to the arena, but the horses do like the freedom of the open space. In here, you can walk beside the horse and assure the rider if they're nervous."

"Makes sense. I thought the same thing."

They discussed the possibility of clients in her program coming to the farm. As they did, he watched her take command of the horse. She had good control, knew how to sit straight in the saddle, heels down in the stirrups and had a good grip on the reins. He hadn't known what to expect, but was surprised.

"What?" she asked when she caught him staring at her.

"You really do know how to ride."

"Did you think I was lying?"

"No, it's just that we get tourists who come here to ride the trails who say they've been on a horse when really they sat on a pony led by a worker at a state fair and don't know the difference between the pommel and reins. We spend more time teaching them than actually riding."

Her tone was dry when she said, "I'm glad I passed your expectations."

"In more ways than one."

She sent him a startled look before nudging the horse around the fence line. Surely, as the town darling, she received complements, but from her reaction now, and other times they were together, he wondered if they might actually be few and far between.

Ty trotted beside her. They rode in silence, the clop of the hooves in the dirt keeping beat. A bird swooped by, and in the distance he could hear one of the other horses whinny, but for the most part, the surroundings were calm.

"You seem distracted," Juliette said after they'd made a few rounds.

"It's nothing."

"Your frown says otherwise."

"That obvious?"

"Usually I get either the serious face or your pirate's smile."

Which he sent her way. "You flatter me."

She snorted. "Tell me what's going on."

"Just farm stuff. Repairs, that sort of thing."

Concern flashed in her eyes. "You finished the barn, right? Do I need to help you paint again?"

"The barn is finished, but there are pieces of equipment that need to be replaced."

"I would imagine with an outfit this size, something is always breaking."

He tried not to be sensitive over her innocent comment, but the reality hit home. "It's challenging, but I'm handling it."

"I didn't say you weren't."

So much for keeping his frustration at bay. Did she think he was annoyed at her? He hoped not, but like it or not, Juliette seemed to be in tune with his mood.

What he hoped she didn't see, and had no desire to tell her, was that he had a lot to prove. To his dad, anyway. Being in the rodeo had been easy compared to managing the family farm. On the circuit, he'd been good at what he did. The crowds loved him and in return he gave them his best in every show. Now, in Golden, he didn't have fans to lift his ego. Spur him on. It was his own desire to show everyone that he wasn't just the guy who charmed his way through life, but a man who took his responsibilities seriously. Even if it meant getting an ulcer in the process.

"Running a farm must be worlds different from a rodeo show."

He smiled, thinking back. When he'd performed with other outfits, he'd had only himself and Juniper to worry about, which was part of his father's complaint. Sure, Ty had chipped in while they were on the road, but now it seemed like he took care of everything from the barns to wonky water pumps.

"In some ways," he finally said. "But we still have to care for the animals, that hasn't changed. There are still the same day-to-day kind of headaches."

"Are you in charge of managing the farm?"

"Overall. Liz is busy with lessons and trail rides, although I take some of the groups out. My dad…"

"Your dad?"

"He put in a lot of years running the rodeo, so he pitches in where needed."

"So, what's the problem?"

She was relentless.

"You don't really want to hear about it."

"I do. And I've even been told I can help in certain situations."

Ty brought the mare to a halt. "Let's say we switch seats. You can get a feel of what riding Maggie is like."

They dismounted and switched places. Ty's fingers lingered on her waist as he gave Juliette a boost to get on the horse. She was warm and soft and he could have stayed here all day holding her. He inhaled her minty scent, then let her go, afraid she might wonder what he was doing. He quickly mounted and they started around the paddock again.

"You realize that switching horses won't stop me from asking questions."

"A guy could hope," he quipped.

She laughed. "I repeat. The origin of the scowl?"

"I'm not happy with how long it's taking to get some of my ideas up and rolling. I thought we'd have more revenue coming into the farm by now."

"In what way?"

"This time of year is perfect for outdoor farmers markets. I was hoping to cash in this season, but with the repairs I had to make on the barn, we're behind. The town is filled with folks here for Oktoberfest and I don't have any plans in the works to get them here to spend their money."

"What about the trail rides?"

"Steady but not a huge moneymaker. Liz has done well scheduling lessons, so there's that."

"It comes down to drawing tourists?"

"Right now, yeah. Advertising the riding trails has been great, but we need to get the other avenues going."

Juliette seemed to get lost in an avalanche of ideas as they circled the paddock a few more times.

"How're you doing?" he finally asked.

She shook off her train of thought. "Both horses seem appropriate for the program. I have an expert I'm in touch with who can advise me from here." She smiled. "If we start this up soon, it's another form of revenue for the farm."

Moving farther away from what he'd originally envisioned. Did it matter as long as they were making money? After all, the well wasn't going to fix itself.

"Let's cool the horses down."

She nodded and after they'd gotten their boots on the ground, Juliette followed him to the grooming area. Again, she knew what to do without having to be instructed. Took a bit of the pressure off him that had been mounting all morning. When they'd completed the task, he took the leads and walked both horses to their stalls before rejoining Juliette, who was staring at a dog sitting at the open door.

"Hey," Ty said. "Where'd he come from?"

She turned to him, her eyes wide. "He's not one of yours?"

"Nope. Never seen him before."

She rubbed her forehead.

"You okay?"

"Yes. I just…" She squinted her eyes. "He reminds me of another dog from another time."

Ty walked toward the shaggy mutt. "Let's get you—"

The dog took off.

Ty shook his head and turned back to Juliette, who had turned pale. Before he could ask what was up, she took a roll from her pocket and placed a mint in her mouth.

"That's why you always smell so good."

Her brow wrinkled. "What?"

Ty held out his hand for the roll. "Peppermint. My new favorite scent."

Her face flushed as she handed it over. "Thanks for today. I can't wait to go home and jot down my impressions."

"I hope the horses can be incorporated in your program."

"Me too," she said as they walked to her car. "What are you doing later?"

"Meeting the guys at Smitty's. There's a football game on this afternoon."

"Fun."

"Said with all the enthusiasm of a person who doesn't watch football games." He paused. "Did you want to get together?"

"Thanks, but I have a date with a good book. I'm going to curl up in a comfy chair to read." She lifted a shoulder in the direction of her car. "I should get going."

He tossed the roll of mints her way. "Let me know what your boss thinks about using the farm."

"I will." She caught the volley. "And, Ty?"

"Yeah?"

"Try not to worry about the farm so much."

If only he could. The smile on her face was meant to inspire confidence, but instead it brought deeper dread. To get his mind off the fate of the farm, he leaned over and tipped her hat back from her face. He ran a finger over her silky skin, holding back a whoop when she swayed closer. He tugged a stray curl around his finger, then, moving in, gave her a kiss he'd been dreaming about since she'd first arrived this morning. She placed her hands on his shoulders to steady herself and he swore he heard her sigh. He smiled against her lips and felt her smile back.

A horse whinnied and Juliette stepped back, the tip of her tongue touching her upper lip. He groaned, then pulled her against him again. She ran her fingers through his hair, messing up his already unruly tangles. This time he ended the kiss.

"I could do that all day," he said as he loosely wrapped his arms around her waist, wondering if he was building expectations, for both of them. Was being with Juliette too good to be true?

"And I'd gladly let you, but you have things to do, as do I."

He sent her a mock frown. "Are you always this practical?"

"Are you always this charming?"

The frown turned to a grin. "All day long, darlin'."

Over her shoulder Ty saw Colton headed in their direction.

"How about we finish this another time?"

"You're so sure there will be another time?"

He sent her a smile sure to curl her toes. "Oh, yeah, I'd take that bet."

With a laugh, she turned and walked to her car, leaving him with a strange longing in his chest.

CHAPTER TEN

TY STARED AT the television screen mounted on the wall in Smitty's Pub, so lost in thought, he didn't notice the quarterback pass the ball or hear the referee's whistle blow on the play. He kept thinking about the farm, a possible solution to re-digging the well and how he had to decide where the money should go. The money he could only get if he sold the one possession that meant the world to him.

No, he couldn't think about that right now. Not until he absolutely had no other option available.

With a sigh, he took a sip from the iced tea glass at his elbow. After Juliette had left the stable, he'd spent his time before coming to the pub crunching numbers and they still hadn't added up to any solution.

"You see that play?" Adam asked, then tossed a handful of peanuts into his mouth.

"What play?"

"That's what I thought." Adam's laser-focused gaze aimed straight at him. "Got something on your mind?"

Nothing Ty was going to talk about right now.

"Anything to do with a pretty redhead you've been spending time with?"

Ty narrowed his eyes. "Just come out with it."

"What's up with you and Juliette?"

"We're friends."

"Really." Adam seemed to mull that over. "Friends who just happened to sneak out of The Perch last night? Without saying goodbye?"

"We didn't sneak."

"Good, because if you thought you had, you did a poor job."

With a shrug Ty said, "I gave her a ride home."

"So why was your truck still in the parking lot when I left?"

Ty held back his temper. "Since when did you become my father?"

"Since I've known Juliette for a long time." Adam held up a hand when Ty wanted to argue. "Bottom line? I think you two together works."

He leaned back in surprise. "You do?"

The problem of never having experienced a serious relationship made Ty question if he had what it took to give a woman as amazing as Juliette the kind of commitment she deserved.

"Sure." Confusion wrinkled Adam's forehead. "Don't you?"

"I…" What did he think? That Juliette was on his mind 24/7? That he wanted to see where this attraction was going? Was his interest in Juliette written all over his face? "I've never been in a serious relationship."

"The love 'em and leave 'em type, huh?"

Ty wasn't sure he liked that conclusion. "Not in a bad way. I never made promises I wouldn't keep. Everything was always very casual."

"Juliette's the one to make you change your mind?"

Was she? Yes, he liked her more than any other woman he'd ever dated. Liked how they clicked every day as he learned more about her. But was he feeling this way because he'd promised his dad to be responsible? Did that include a woman to settle down with? A lifetime of kisses in the moonlight?

He rubbed his forehead. The farm weighed heavily on his shoulders, and Juliette was the one area of his life that felt carefree, even with his struggles to understand what was happening to the guy who loved being single.

Ty blew out a frustrated breath. "She might be, but Juliette isn't what's bugging me."

"The farm?"

Ty met Adam's astute gaze.

"It's more than I expected, but I can handle it."

Adam hesitated before saying, "You know it's okay to ask for help."

He knew that. He'd known Adam long enough to see how the man had expanded his already thriving business to make it even more successful. He trusted Adam, but didn't like anyone thinking he couldn't carry the load. Still, he was new at this game and really needed to put aside his pride to make sure his family put their mark on the town.

"Do you remember when I talked about the farm when I first moved here? My idea of drawing tourist traffic?"

Interest gleamed in his friend's eyes. "Sure. A common conversation among Golden residents."

Okay, here came the tough question. "How do you handle change in plans?"

Adam leaned forward, resting his forearms on the table. "In what way?"

"Liz is handling the horseback riding lessons and trail rides, which is the lion's share of our revenue."

"And that's a problem?"

"No. The problem is, how do I incorporate other ideas and make them equally successful? Shouldn't I be focusing on one or the other?"

"It isn't a matter of one or the other. Both will benefit the farm."

"Okay, but my part isn't panning out."

"You expected it to happen overnight?" Adam smiled. "This isn't like your rodeo career, Ty. You're a natural on a horse. Have the personality to engage the fans. Those skills aren't easily going to translate to a new skill set, like building from the ground up. Most businesses take three to five years to start making a profit. You have to be realistic."

That's what he knew deep down inside, but he couldn't wait out the needed repairs. "So what do you suggest?"

"Patience."

"Not in my vocabulary."

Adam shrugged. "You want the farm to become a go-to destination? You're going to have to learn to slow down. Take things a step at a time."

Ty ground his molars.

"I get this is going to be difficult for you, but look at it like a new challenge."

"Says the successful businessman. It's like everything you touch makes money."

"Because I know going into a project that it'll take time to gain traction. The farm will produce revenue, Ty. You might have to re-adjust ideas. Give up old plans for new plans that are more advantageous at the moment. It's not a one-size-fits-all perspective."

"It has only been four months," Ty conceded.

"Don't look at it as a setback."

He didn't, but now he had a decision to make; how to pay for the new well without significantly reducing the remainder of their contingency fund. The only idea he'd been able to come up with to accomplish both nearly broke his spirit.

A cheer went up as the favorite team scored a goal.

"We're missing the game," Adam said.

Ty glanced around the room, finding all eyes on the television. "Go enjoy. I'll be with you guys in a minute."

Adam slapped him on the back, a nod to their camaraderie. "Give it time."

If only he had more time.

With a sigh, he shook off the funk and ordered another drink, then sat back to watch the remainder of the game. A nearby table had ordered ribs and the tangy scent had his mouth watering. He grabbed some peanuts, debating if he should order food, but was caught up in the action on the screen. By the time he was finally immersed, his mind off his problems, someone sat down at his table. He glanced over to see Juliette's smiling face.

He blinked. "Where did you come from?"

She pointed across the room. "The door."

"No, I..." He shook his head. "Never mind. What are you doing here? I thought you were sticking close to home this afternoon."

"I couldn't get our conversation out of my head."

A slow smile spread across his lips. "Which conversation?"

She ignored the bait. Smart woman.

"About how you want to speed up business at the farm." She opened a screen on the tablet for him to view. "I made a list."

A list? Why would she? Because she helped everyone in Golden, apparently, whether they asked or not.

He read over her bullet points. She'd put some thought into her ideas. He looked up to tell her so. As if out of the blue, his father and his new friends had pulled up chairs to the table. He glanced at Juliette and raised an eyebrow. "You recruited a committee?"

Her face turned an appealing shade of pink. "Not on purpose."

"We ran into Juliette when we were sitting outside Sit A Spell," his father cut in. "She stopped to visit and before we knew it, we were making a list of vendors to support a market at the farm."

"And as luck would have it, Juliette was already thinking in that direction," Bunny said.

Juliette scooted to the end of her seat, excitement lighting her pretty eyes. Her arm casually brushed his, bringing with it a jolt of awareness that kicked up when she was close by. Instead of the sensation settling down, it seemed to grow by leaps and bounds every time he was with her. He sucked in a breath and focused on what she was saying.

"Everyone knows different vendors who might be interested in a partnership with the farm. We'll agree with the vendors up front that the farm gets a cut of the revenue for letting them use the space."

Wanda Sue grinned at him. "If you want, we can set up a trial run next weekend."

That soon? When he'd just been complaining to Adam that he didn't know what to do next? This was too good to be true.

He held up his hand. "Is that enough time to get the word out?"

Mrs. M. leaned forward. "You do know

who you're speaking to, right?" She pointed to the seniors. "We are the heartbeat of Golden."

He glanced at a grinning Juliette. "Actually, I didn't know that, although, I know my dad likes you."

"We get the job done," boasted Adam's aunt Bunny.

"Ty," Juliette continued. "They have access to soap makers, honey products, the family who has a produce stand on Saturdays—who are looking for a permanent home, by the way. Plus, through the clinic, I know people who sell homeopathic products and Ivy will need a place to sell her jewelry soon. It's a good time to jump on board."

"But this weekend?"

"It's not a big deal," Judge Carmichael said. "We'll spread flyers around town. We might get folks visiting Golden for the last two weekends of Oktoberfest to stop by, plus, our own townsfolk with be interested to see what you've done with the farm, so they will certainly show up."

"And we have word of mouth," Alveda said.

Juliette caught his gaze. "Plus, I did a little research before stopping for coffee and discovered another way to incorporate the animals on the farm."

A little overwhelmed, Ty nodded for her to elaborate.

"This is an idea for down the road, but what about school tours during the week so students can go horseback riding? You can have goat races, which the kids will love. And if you get more livestock, like a cow for instance, you can show the kids how to milk." The excitement rolling off her was contagious. "Ooh, and you can add a playground and maybe even a maze on the property."

"A maze?"

"Especially in the fall. Kids love harvest festivals, but then in the springtime you could grow sunflowers and have an entirely different kind of maze. That will take more planning to implement, but it's a goal to strive toward. What do you think?"

That Adam had pointed out Ty's lack of patience. In order for the business to grow, it was going to take trial and error, and he had to be okay with that. "It sounds like a lot of work," he warned his new associates.

Mrs. M. waved her hand. "Not to worry. We'll lend a hand and what we can't do, we know others who are capable."

Isn't this why they'd moved to Golden? For the small town support and friendships? Here it was, in play in real time. While the idea was intriguing, all Ty could see were dollar signs, and not in a good way.

"And if I get the therapy program up and running, you can have the proceeds."

He reared back in his chair. "No, you'll be doing the work."

"But you're giving me a place to bring the clients. You know I've been searching for a long time to find a home. Crestview Farm is it."

A home. When Juliette said those words, it went beyond the business of the farm. It struck right to the heart. Would she ever consider living on a farm? Being a part of his family?

Whoa, getting ahead of yourself.

He faced the group. Tamped down his eagerness. He wanted this to work. *Needed* it to work. "You think we can put this together so soon?"

The group exchanged glances. "It's the best shot we've got," Mrs. M. said.

This wouldn't be without sacrifice, Ty knew that. But he'd promised his dad.

"So, what do you say?" his father asked.

Time to be responsible, son, echoed in his ears.

Ty glimpsed the eager faces around the table. How could he turn them down? How could he ignore his own dream, even though he knew the next steps he'd have to take would cost him something very important?

Finally he said, "If you think you can get people to the farm on Saturday, let's give it a try."

Juliette squealed and smiles broke out on the faces of the seniors.

The enthusiasm was infectious. Maybe if they started the weekend market right away, it would ease their financial burden. He could hold off on the unthinkable option. But could they do it all? There was only one way to find out.

He took in Juliette's flushed face, her happy smile. All because she couldn't help but make Ty one of her causes.

He should be flattered, right?

Glancing her way, his heart turned heavy in his chest. When had she become so important to him?

He wanted to be a man worthy of Juliette, and in order to do that, he had to prove he could stand on his own two feet, something he couldn't do if she was always helping him. He didn't want to be relegated to a project, he wanted a romance with the beautiful woman. Could they move in that direction without the farm or her therapy program being the reasons they were always together?

On the heels of those thoughts came a bigger question. After all was said and done, would he let everyone down, including Juliette?

THE NEXT EVENING Juliette stopped by her parents' house after work. She found Ivy hard at work at one end of the kitchen table, her teeth pressing into her lower lip as she threaded the beads into a design. Her mother sat at the other end, papers spread out before her.

"Don't you both look busy," she said as she removed her jacket.

Ivy raised her head and smiled. "Juls, what are you doing here?"

"I thought I might find the members of Team Ivy here." She looked over her mother's shoulder. "What's all that?"

"Business forms. Ivy and I had a long chat about officially starting her business."

Juliette tried to ignore the pang of envy that they hadn't included her.

"We're going to call it Ivy's Creations," her sister announced, pride in her eyes.

Her mother nodded. "We have a meeting set up with Adam Wright to advise us, since finance is his profession. He will make sure we file all the correct paperwork." Her mother beamed. "It's a lot, but we love it."

Clamping down on her back teeth, Juliette sat down. Isn't this what she'd wanted? To have her mother be more involved in Ivy's life? To have Ivy's business grow? So why did her chest ache? She brushed it aside and pasted on a sunny smile. She'd always been, and would continue to be, her sister's biggest cheerleader.

"Well, Ivy's Creations, I have a business proposition for you."

Ivy and their mom exchanged glances.

"Don't leave us in suspense," her mom teased.

She explained about the vendors at Crestview Farm. "It'll be a sort of soft launch to showcase how talented you are. Ivy, you can have your own table. Design the table setup any way you like."

Ivy's hands fluttered. "So soon?"

Juliette kept her voice even and calm. "You were trying to get Tessa to take an order just the other day. This is a sure thing."

Ivy pointed to her pile of completed bracelets and in the process overturned her box with compartments filled with various colored beads. "I can't make enough bracelets before then."

Her mother straightened the box and she and Juliette began replacing the beads. "Ivy, we set up an entire storage area in the spare bedroom. You have more than enough inventory for both Serena's store and the farm market."

"I do?"

"Yes. And at the rate you're going, you'll have made more than enough to replace what we sell over the weekend."

"Mom's right," Juliette added. "You've always had a keen eye in picking out uncommon beads. I've never seen colors like the ones you're using."

Ivy had spent hours online picking out just the right beads. Unusual colors, and the way some beads sparkled, made each piece unique. Her creations didn't look like a craft project made by a kid, rather, they were very professional. Ivy's attention to detail made the jewelry and key chains a perfect gift, one Juliette hoped they could capitalize on.

Ivy jumped up, nearly knocking over her chair, and paced the room. "I need to count how many we have bagged up already."

"Honey, all the bagged items are in the box in the spare room."

As Ivy left the room, Juliette clasped her

hands together. "I didn't mean to get her all worked up."

Her mother laid down her pen. "On the one hand, she's enjoyed the repetition of making the jewelry. On the other, the idea of a business based on her inventory has been stressful. She's been falling back into old patterns a lot lately, like repeating numbers."

"It's not like this is the first time she's reacted to stress. She had a difficult time adapting in school when she moved from one grade to another. It's the unknown she can't handle. But as in all the events in her life, once she sees how smoothly the process goes, she'll settle down and it'll be easier with each new opportunity to sell her creations."

Her mother glanced down at the papers, then up again. "Did I bite off more than I can chew?"

"No, you actually stepped up." Juliette worried her lip, wondering if she should say anything, then decided to plow ahead. "I was jealous when you told me you wanted to help run Ivy's business."

Her mother's mouth fell open. "You were?"

Juliette picked at the hem of her blouse. "Silly really, since you know more about business than I do."

"Perhaps, but you've always been there for

Ivy. You're the one who got her interested in making jewelry." Her eyes clouded. "I can see how you would feel left out."

"But this is good." Juliette met her mom's gaze. "I'm busy at the clinic and it looks like my equine therapy program has a second chance." She took her mother's hand in hers. "I could never devote the amount of time to this business as you can."

"You know we need your input."

"Do you? It sounds to me like Ivy's Creations is in the right hands to make it flourish."

A small grin curved her mother's lips. "So I have your blessing?"

A wave of love caused Juliette's eyes to well up. "Oh, Mom, you're going to be great. You and Ivy will be first-rate partners."

Her mother angled her head and grinned. "Does this new you have anything to do with the handsome young man you went to homecoming with?"

Here they go.

"How did you hear about that?"

"Ivy told me you were dress shopping."

"Hmm. The answer is that I don't know yet, but I'm eager to find out."

The night she'd pulled Ty in for a kiss under the stars, all she'd been thinking was that she'd kissed him because she'd felt so close to him, so grateful he listened to her, even if she hadn't been ready to open up about her past. It was a big step for her, one that scared and excited her simultaneously.

This time her mother squeezed Juliette's hand.

Ivy came back, the stress on her face gone. "I counted all the pieces. Three times. I think you're right, Mom."

"Imagine that. Mom being right."

They all laughed.

Juliette pushed her chair out and rose. "On that note, I should get home."

"Hold on," her mother said as she gathered the papers together to form a tidy pile. "Did the mayor contact you about Ellie's party?"

Juliette's stomach did a flip. "Actually, I saw him the other night and he mentioned it."

"Are you going?"

"I...ah... He didn't give me a date."

Her mother got up to walk over to the calendar hanging on the wall. "Looks like... Oh, no, it's the same night as Serena's wedding."

Relief flowed through Juliette like a flash flood. "I already told Serena I'd be there."

"Juliette doesn't like to see Ellie," Ivy piped up.

Her mother turned, surprise on her face. "Ivy, why would you say that?"

"Because of the dog."

Juliette closed her eyes, willing her sister not to say anything more.

"What dog?" her mother asked.

"The dog on the street."

Her mother glanced at Juliette.

"The day of the stroller incident. Ivy remembers a dog we saw in the park."

"The dog that made you save Ellie."

Her mother sent Juliette a confused look.

"It was a long time ago." Juliette hurried to kiss her mother's cheek, then moved to do the same for her sister. "I'll text you the time for the event on Saturday, Mom." She turned and pointed to her sister. "And you keep making those beautiful pieces."

"I will," Ivy said, then her head went down as she got back to work.

Her mother walked her to the door. "Are you okay?"

She'd really hoped her mom hadn't picked up on her nervousness. "Sure. Why wouldn't I be?"

"You got a bit pale when Ivy mentioned that day."

Juliette waved her hand, noticing it was a tad shaky. "I'm just thinking ahead to the millions you and Ivy are going to make."

Her mother chuckled.

"I'll see you Saturday," she said, then went out the door to her car.

Once inside, she blew out a breath and slammed the steering wheel with the palm of her hand. It seemed Ivy still remembered that day. Would she blow Juliette's cover?

For a fleeting moment, she thought it might be a relief to have the truth finally come out if Ivy inadvertently spilled the beans. But on the heels of that thought came the idea that she would have to face everyone's disappointment. Unable to handle that outcome, she did what she always did, tucked the truth away and hoped that day never came.

CHAPTER ELEVEN

EARLY TUESDAY MORNING Ty met with Liz in the stable office. She'd gotten home late Sunday night after visiting their brother and this was the first time they had a chance to talk privately. He took a seat on the opposite side of her desk.

"How was the visit with Scott?"

"Good. He's doing well, actually. When we're ready to move him closer, the doctor thinks it will be good for him."

Ty nodded. "And you? How are you handling all the changes?"

Liz shot him a surprised glance, but said, "Hanging in there. It helps that Scott's sense of humor hasn't changed at all. He can make me laugh over the silliest things."

"I'm glad to hear that."

She seemed to consider her words before saying, "You've never asked how I'm doing before. I mean, we don't get all sappy, and we are sensitive to the shift in the family dynamics, but we sort of keep it to ourselves."

Leaning back in the chair, Ty studied his sister. "The distance from Scott is hard. You sacrificed being a chaperone at the dance to take care of family business. I guess the least I can do is ask how you're doing."

Liz picked up a pen and tapped it on the desktop. "Why now?"

"Why not now?"

"Don't answer my question with a question."

He allowed a small smile. "Why not?"

"Because it's annoying," she huffed. "You just do that to get a rise out of me."

"It's working."

"It is." She grinned back. "Seriously, why now?"

Ty rolled his shoulders. "I was talking to Juliette about how our family deals with the changes we've made. She was very insightful. Made the point that we need to listen to each other, be open. This is my way of doing just that."

"Hmm. Juliette, huh?"

Yes, apparently he was totally into her. And that was putting it mildly. Just hearing Juliette's name made his chest grow tight with longing.

"She has experience with families in our type of situation because of her career."

"And that's it?"

He narrowed his eyes. "What more would it be?"

"Oh, I don't know, that you like hanging out with her?"

"And if I did?"

"Then I'd be happy for you."

He stared across the room. His gaze halted on a family photo Liz had hung on the wall. It showed a group of smiling Pendergrasses before Scott's health issues and Liz's husband left. "A lot has changed in our lives."

Liz followed the direction of his gaze and sighed. "It has."

He cleared his throat. "Do you think we have what it takes to make the farm a go?"

"I'll admit, when we didn't have Scott at the helm, I was worried." She frowned. "Obviously not as worried as when I didn't check in with Dad to see the muddle he'd made with the rodeo finances."

Ty ran a hand through his hair when he thought about those days. "Thankfully it wasn't as bad as it could have been."

"We made the decision and I, for one, am happy to be in Golden." She paused. "Are you second-guessing things?"

"Not exactly. Which leads me to the reason for this meeting. I've been doing some thinking."

Liz tossed the pen to the desk and crossed her arms over her chest. "Did something happen while I was gone?"

"Nothing that wasn't here when you left."

"The well situation?"

"I've been over the numbers every way I can, Liz. Re-digging the well is going to come close to tapping us out."

"What about a loan?"

"I've applied. We've been turned down because of losing the rodeo. Our credit is still shaky."

"Where did you—"

"Everywhere."

Liz went silent for a moment. He could see the gears in her head turning.

"Doors are opening in the equestrian end of our business," he said. "We need the investment."

"What about your plans for the interactive farm?"

"That can move at a slower pace. Juliette came up with some ideas we can certainly incorporate—"

"Juliette again?" she asked, her tone dry.

"The woman makes a mean list."

"Which happens to include Ty Pendergrass?"

How could he explain what Juliette did to him when he was still trying to figure out this attraction on a daily basis?

With a threat in his tone, he said, "Liz…"

"Fine, I won't interfere. So, what do you suggest?"

"First, I'd like you to run the equestrian side of things. You already do all the lessons and trail rides. Keep the books on this part and I'll focus on the farm."

Worry creased her brow. "Do you think that's a good idea? To separate the two?"

"I do." He'd given this new tactic a lot of thought and decided it was the best way forward. "We'll have weekly meetings. Stay in touch day-to-day."

"Are you sure managing the farm is enough for you?"

"I told you and Dad that I'm all in."

She didn't looked convinced.

"And speaking of that, I have an idea to replace the well."

Liz's eyebrow rose. "Which is?"

It took him a few seconds to actually say the words out loud. When he did, his gut twisted. "I sell Juniper."

Liz jumped up from her chair. "What? No!"

His throat was tight when he said, "It makes sense, Liz."

"But you've had him for years."

He shrugged as if the ache in his chest didn't exist. As if selling Juniper didn't tear his heart out.

She lowered herself. "Ty…"

"I've thought about this long and hard, Liz. It's either that or I go back on the rodeo circuit."

"You promised you'd stay."

"I did, but the revenue to run the farm isn't where we need it to be. For us to succeed, I have to take these measures."

A ferocious frown crossed Liz's forehead. "I don't like either of these options."

"We knew going into this venture that it would be a tough start. I didn't expect as many repairs as we've come across. We have to do all we can to make it successful."

"But sell Juniper? That seems like too much of a sacrifice to me."

"It's my choice, Liz."

She opened her mouth, then closed it.

"I'm going to put out some feelers in the rodeo community."

A mutinous pout puffed out her lips. "I don't like this and I'm going on record as opposing this move. But I also know you enough that if you have your mind set on selling Juniper, nothing I can say will stop you."

He tried for a little humor. "Guess you've been paying attention all these years."

"This isn't funny, Ty."

No, it wasn't. But Liz was right. He'd made up his mind.

"Anything else we need to discuss?" he asked, his tone making it plain that he wasn't up for any more discussion on the matter.

"No. Scott looked at all the literature for the living facilities located here, so now we wait for his input. Also, I need to call Juliette to give her the contact info for the mother who inquired into lessons for her daughter with special needs. The sooner that program gets underway, the better." She eyed Ty. "When are you going forward with the market?"

"Now that the barn is refreshed, the farmers market is going to launch this weekend. I already have folks lined up to sell their goods. We'll see how it goes and reassess afterward."

"This weekend? Isn't that quick?"

"Not with the folks helping get the word out."

"Do I want to know?"

He grinned. "Dad's new friends."

Liz's brows pinched together.

"Don't worry, I've got this covered." He

snapped his fingers as a thought hit him. "We can sell our eggs and see if it's profitable."

"Then let me know what I can do."

"I will." He rose, as ready as he'd ever be to start the search to sell Juniper. He'd gotten as far as the door when Liz called his name. He turned to see that her eyes were bright with unshed tears.

"I don't think I've thanked you."

"For what?"

"Putting the rodeo behind you. Putting your time and focus on the family and making the farm a home. Being there for Colton." He watched her throat move as she swallowed. "It's a lot."

What did he say to that? He'd vowed to prove to his father that he could be responsible, but never in a million years considered what it might cost him.

"I'm here, aren't I?"

The phone rang. Liz wiped her eyes and Ty escaped the office, heading to Juniper's stall, his throat tight. The black horse leaned his head over the half door, snorting as Ty approached. Ty stroked the horse's neck, swallowing hard. He leaned in close to whisper, "It's for the best, bud."

Juniper lifted his head, as if to argue.

"I've made up my mind."

Didn't mean he couldn't hate his decision.

SATURDAY MORNING ROLLED around more quickly than Juliette anticipated. Inside the barn, there was a flurry of activity. She smiled, watching the vendors get ready for a new day, her sister included.

According to their mother, Ivy had been up bright and early, packing and repacking the boxes until it was time to drive out to the farm. Both of their parents had come today, her mother to handle the transactions, their father to carry boxes from the car. Juliette noticed fear, but also excitement, on her sister's face and had to admit, she felt the same way. Today meant a lot to Ivy and their family.

And Ty.

She'd seen him earlier this morning, going through his morning practice on Juniper. He'd sat straight in the saddle, then suddenly lifted a leg, twisted position, and the next thing she knew, he was on his back arched across the saddle, arms stretched out as his fingers brushed the ground below. Her heart was in her throat as she watched him pull himself upright and then drop his body to one side of the horse, his hands on the pommel for support, Juniper galloping full speed. No wonder he'd been a hit at the rodeo.

He was a hit with her too.

The other vendors were busy setting up as

well. There were plenty of soap and honey samples, the scents lingering in the air. The produce tables were overflowing with ripe vegetables. A table featured natural remedies. The last-minute additions of folks selling sauces, jams and cheeses, along with Colton on hand to sell farm fresh eggs, filled out the room. Juliette couldn't miss Mrs. M. and her gang setting out Alveda's pies for sale. The poor woman must have been busy in the kitchen for a week, but the effort was spot-on. Once word got out that Alveda's pies were for sale, there would be a crowd.

Juliette checked the list on her clipboard, playing the organizer. Once the customers arrived she'd fill in wherever necessary, but for now, she made sure each table was ready when the doors opened in—she peeked at her watch—fifteen minutes.

She glanced around the buzz of activity, looking for Ty. She'd stopped to pick up a cup of coffee for both of them and if he didn't show soon, his would get cold. His tardiness bothered her.

He'd been quiet last night. The usual charmer gone, when his friends had hauled tables they'd borrowed from the community center to the barn. She'd been decorating the inside with fall decor of wreaths, gourds and pumpkins, strings of colored leaves, as well as setting up a beverage area where Addie was going to sell cider with her son's baseball team.

Serena had said something that made her laugh when she'd caught Ty's gaze from across the room. He'd sent her a half smile, then looked away. Her stomach dipped, and she wondered if she'd been wrong to push the market. But as she thought back, he'd been on board. Their previous encounters had been teasing, fun and, yes, sometimes serious, but nothing to make him send her mixed signals. Where was her charming pirate?

The concrete floor had been swept clean, the inside walls gleamed a stark white, a contrast to the welcoming red paint on the outside of the building. She tamped down her alarm, expecting him any moment. He wouldn't miss the big day, would he?

Her mother chose that moment to join her.

"Everything okay?"

"Yes." She glanced at her list and back up. "Are you ready for the soft launch of Ivy's Creations?"

"As ready as we'll ever be."

"This is going to be a success, Mom."

Her mother rubbed her hands together. A sign of nerves, for sure.

"I told you that you and Ivy make a strong team," Juliette said. "You're going to do great."

Her mother didn't seem convinced, but turned her attention to Juliette and asked, "And your young man? I was hoping to meet him."

"Ty should be here soon." She met her mom's gaze. "And he's not my young man."

"Then why do you keep peeking at the door?"

"I'm not…"

Her gaze strayed to the barn opening. Still no Ty. Her stomach pitched. Where was he?

Her mother grinned. "You are peeking."

"Okay, I'm peeking. Happy?"

"That you're actually interested in someone? Yes."

Ty arrived at that moment. Her face must have lit up, because her mother turned her head to see what had caught Juliette's attention.

"I take it that's Ty?"

"It is. I'll be right back."

Hearting beating wildly, Juliette picked up Ty's cup and crossed the expanse of the room to meet him. "You're late," she said, adding a teasing note to her voice, as she held out the cup.

The frown knitting his brow grew. "For coffee?"

"No, for your expertise."

"Did something happen?" Ty took the cup and sipped.

"Not exactly. We needed more access to electricity, but your father took care of it."

"Sorry. I had some...business to take care of this morning."

She didn't like the serious tone, hoping that whatever was bothering him last night would be gone today. From the blank expression on his face, she thought better than to meddle.

"More important than the kickoff of your first farmers market?"

He glanced around the barn. "Looks like everyone is ready."

Hmm. He hadn't answered her question. "They are." She wrapped her hand around his bicep and tugged him toward his sister's table. "Someone wants to meet you."

She stopped just as her sister finished with a display of her bracelets. Juliette had bought her a miniature bronze tree from which Ivy could hang earrings and key chains, the tiny limbs now full with sparkly designs.

"Ivy. Can you take a minute to meet my friend?"

Interest on her face, Ivy walked to Ty. "Are you my sister's boyfriend?"

"Ivy!"

"Well that's what I've heard."

Ty chuckled, made a big bow and said, "I'm Ty." He held out his hand to shake. "And you must be the talented Ivy." He leaned down to Ivy's height, placed his hand at an angle beside his mouth and said in a stage whisper, "I've heard you're going to sell out today."

"You did?"

"I did." He made a show of checking her inventory. "Nice."

Ivy beamed. "I'm glad you think so, because I'm nervous."

"Don't be. And besides, I'll be here all day. If you need anything, just wave to get my attention."

Juliette's heart squeezed at his words.

Ivy's shoulders straightened and she returned to her task.

Not to be left out, her parents made sure to get an introduction.

"Juliette's talked about you. I'm glad to finally meet you."

"Mom…"

Ty shook her mother's hand. "You have a very caring daughter."

The corners of her mom's lips tipped up. "We think so."

Her father took Ty's outstretched hand, sizing him up. "Dale Bishop."

"Mr. Bishop, you have two wonderful daughters."

Her dad seemed to relax at the comment.

"Okay," Juliette cut in. "Back to work, everyone."

Once all the awkwardness was over, Juliette said, "That was nice of you to say to Ivy."

"She's got nothing more than the jitters."

"Somehow I doubt you've ever experienced those."

His gaze locked with hers. "You'd be surprised."

Heat washed over her at the intent glimmer in his eyes. She hid it as the first group of shoppers came through the door.

Ty noticed and said, "Guess I should make the rounds."

And like that, he was gone.

Had she missed something?

Before she knew it, the barn was full of curious folks checking out the products. She wandered around, eavesdropping on conversations, happy to hear that purchases were being made. At one point she glanced at Ivy's table to find her deep in conversation with Ty. Her chest went tight. He was so good with people. If for no other reason than he was a good guy, she wanted to make sure this day went well for his future.

When she felt a tap on her shoulder, she dragged her gaze away from Ty and turned to find Liz smiling at her.

"Got a minute?"

She hoped Liz hadn't seen her mooning over Ty. "Sure. What's up?"

"Let's go outside where it's less noisy."

The two moved to the side of the barn, out of the way of shoppers. Liz tossed her braid over her shoulder. "I was giving lessons this morning, but I wanted to talk to you while you were on the property. I haven't had a chance to connect since I got back to town."

"How was your trip?"

"Promising. It's up to Scott now to decide where he lives."

"That's wonderful. I told Ty to let me know if I can help in any way." What she didn't say was that she'd already been in touch with an ALF and her contact there was pretty certain Scott could get a place there once the building passed inspection.

"Thanks. I may take you up on that, but I wanted to talk about your therapy program. Has your specialist given the green light on using our horses?"

"He finally read my report and said to try it on a limited basis."

"Great, because that mother with the special needs childI told you about? She called again, very interested in getting her daughter enrolled."

Joy swept through Juliette. She was finally making progress on her dream to get the program running.

Liz reached into her back jeans pocket and removed a folded piece of paper. "This is the contact information. I told Mrs. Brighton that you'd get a hold of her."

"Thanks, Liz. I can't tell you how much I appreciate it."

Liz clapped a hand on Juliette's shoulder. "Hey, it's good for both of us. You get a client and the farm gets some revenue."

Juliette didn't want to read anything into the program helping the farm, but the way Ty had been vague about the finances, she couldn't help but wonder what was going on.

"I'm going inside to check on the progress," Liz said.

Just as they went back inside, Mrs. M. walked up to Juliette, a big smile on her face.

"We did it."

"It?"

"Sold all of Alveda's pies."

Juliette checked her watch. "In an hour? That must be a record."

"Told you her pies would draw the people out."

"Have you ever been wrong?"

Mrs. M. pretended to think about it. "No, I don't believe I have."

Juliette laughed at the woman's honesty. "Thank you for all your help. You and your friends pulled this off."

"Our pleasure. And before you leave, there's a special pie Alveda put to the side for Ty. Make sure he gets it."

With a wink she took off.

Juliette made the rounds, pleased to see a lot of empty space at Ivy's table. The hours since they'd opened the doors had flown by, but everyone looked happy with their sales.

As she moved away, Wanda Sue came up to her with two cups of cider. "The team's about to sell out. Addie let me grab the last cups." She nodded her head toward Ty, who was standing near the doorway. "Can you bring one to Ty?"

"Sure." She took both cups and walked his way.

His eyebrows rose. "More coffee?"

"Cider."

He took a sip. "Not bad."

"You also have an Alveda pie with your name on it hidden away. I'm to deliver it to you after the market closes down."

"Heard they're pretty famous."

"Keep your fingers crossed that it's a peach pie. They're the best."

He nodded, his eyes focused across the room.

"What's up?"

"My dad."

She followed his gaze. "You're going to have to explain."

"I can't put my finger on it, but I swear he's up to something."

She turned back to him. "At a farmers market?"

"You don't know my father."

"All I see is a man enjoying his friends." She frowned. "Are you always suspicious?"

"Sorry." He shook his head as if to clear it. "It's a long story."

"Better saved for another time?"

"Oh, like you're that forthcoming?"

He was right, but the accusation stung.

"I didn't mean to overstep."

He blew out a breath. "And I shouldn't be a jerk. Sorry."

"I could tell last night that something is bothering you."

"I've got it under control."

"So there is a problem?"

His gaze narrowed. "You can't solve everything, Juliette."

Had she made him angry by setting up the market? Or was it something else? Before she could ask, he walked away.

She'd only wanted to move things along so he'd be settled here in Golden and not thinking about leaving. But had she pushed too far? It wasn't like this was the first time she pushed and paid the consequences. Her community service hours proved his point.

She set out to follow him and apologize when Mayor Danielson and his wife arrived. Juliette tried to lose herself among the shoppers, but the barn had cleared out compared to earlier in the morning. She watched as he stopped to talk to Ivy and her parents, then make the rounds of the room. She was about to slip away when he noticed her and strode over.

"Juliette. Just the woman I wanted to see."

"Mayor."

"I wanted to speak to you about a pet project I've been thinking about. Is there any chance you can stop by my office one day next week?"

Eyes were on them, so she said, "I'll have to check my work schedule."

He nodded. "Call my office and set up a time."

Not that he gave her much choice. "I will."

When he left, she wished she had a roll of mints on hand.

By early afternoon, the crowd had left and everyone was pitching in to clean up. Mrs. M. clapped her hands to get the attention of the room.

"Well, everyone, was today a success?"

The vendors clapped and shouted yes.

"How about we all meet at Smitty's Pub later for a celebration dinner?"

The group as a whole agreed and picked a time to gather. Juliette glanced around to find Ty, but he was missing.

Brando came her way. "Lookin' for my son?"

"Yes. I want to make sure he knows about dinner."

"He's probably in the stable. I asked him to check out the west side of the property for new riding trails."

"Oh, well then could you make sure he knows?"

Brando's gaze shuttered. "I'm leaving for a while. Mind going over to tell him for me?"

Juliette tilted her head, seeing now what Ty was talking about. Brando was up to something.

"I will, if you make sure the peach pie Alveda promised Ty gets to your kitchen. Uneaten."

"Deal," Brando said, then went to join the seniors as they left the barn.

Juliette went to tell her family she'd see them later.

"I'll close up," Liz told Juliette as folks were leaving the barn. "You've been here all day."

"Thanks."

As she walked to her car, she couldn't ignore her worry about Ty. Maybe no one else read the pensive expression he tried to hide, but she saw it. Saw him.

Today was supposed to prove that his idea for the farm could work, yet he wasn't here to see how successful it had been. He might try to elude her, but she was determined to get to the bottom of what was bothering him. Even if it made her a hypocrite.

Turning on her heels, she switched direction and strode into the stable just as Ty was leading Juniper out.

"Ty."

He glanced over his shoulder and stopped as she approached. The horse shook his head and snorted.

"Your father told me you were going out to find new riding trails."

"I am."

"Can't it wait? The vendors are going to get together for dinner at Smitty's later."

"Maybe another time."

She planted her hands on her hips. "You're really going to work now?"

"No time better than the present."

Seems she had no choice but to force the issue with this stubborn man.

"I'm coming with you."

CHAPTER TWELVE

"I DON'T NEED a babysitter."

Ty didn't need Juliette to tag along, but realized his feelings on the matter weren't going to fly when she saddled Tri herself and mounted the horse. They didn't speak as they trotted out past the paddock, harnesses jingling, their destination the undeveloped side of the property.

"How about a friend?"

He really couldn't argue when she was being so nice. He reeled in his mood.

"I'm not sure how long we'll be gone."

"It's okay. Any excuse to go for a ride is fine by me."

He tossed her what he hoped passed as a carefree grin. "Try to keep up."

With that, he squeezed Juniper's sides with his legs and they were off. The wind brushed his cheeks, tousled his hair. This was what he needed, the freedom to race against the wind. To stay ahead of the problems that dogged him, even if escaping wouldn't change his reality.

At the steady rhythm of hoofbeats behind him, Ty glanced over his shoulder. Juliette's huge smile radiated pure joy, lifting his own spirits. She'd pulled her hair into a ponytail, and it bumped over her shoulder as her horse raced. With the sunlight on her face and the sound of laughter on her lips, she was beautiful. She had the biggest heart of anyone he'd ever met and he couldn't deny that her generosity drew him to her. Every day she surprised him, with her humility and caring soul. He had to admit, he'd never experienced anything like it before. He was finding it impossible to live without her, even though it couldn't last. Not with what he had to do for the farm. For his family.

Her laughter drifted through the air again and he decided that for a while he'd forget about his responsibilities and take pleasure in the day and the woman with him.

Before long, they slowed to a walk where the tree line grew thick. Ty reached over to pat Juniper's neck. Tall, mature trees showcased multicolored leaves, shades of yellow, orange and red, found only in autumn and blazing in these mountains. The crisp air and the scent of burning wood filled his senses. Or maybe it was simply being with Juliette.

Ty met Juliette's gaze as she came to his side, a tight grip on the reins to keep from wandering.

"That was fun."

"I always aim to please, darlin'."

She brushed the stray hair from her eyes. "Just like you to make work an adventure."

He chuckled. "That's pretty much the story of my life."

He watched her gaze take in the property around them, undeveloped and pristine. He hated that they'd have to clear out some of the woods to create a new trail.

She sighed. "I envy you."

"I can't imagine that."

She spoke softly to Tri, then to him. "You know what you want and go after it."

Was that longing in her voice?

He shifted in the saddle. "This coming from the woman who set up the market in just a few days?"

"Helping others comes easy for me." She huffed out a breath. "It's the other parts of life that I stumble over."

He made a clicking sound to move Juniper as close to Juliette as possible. "I appreciate your faith in my abilities, but no one escapes life's challenges."

A leaf drifted through the air. Juliette reached out and caught it. Twirled it in her fingers. "I know that. I just wish..."

The gusty breeze whistled as it moved between swaying branches.

"Wish?" he prodded.

She shook off whatever she was going to say. "How do you know where you're going? The trees are pretty thick out here."

Okay, he'd play along. For now. But he'd get to the bottom of her wistfulness before they returned home.

"Dad and I scouted this area last week. He already gave me a general idea of where to stake out new trails. It'll take a little manual labor, but it's better than working out at the gym."

She glanced at his biceps. He wanted to flex, to make her laugh, but when her face grew red, he decided to have mercy. Still, Juliette noticing anything about him created an odd sensation in his chest.

She pointed to an opening. "Is that it?"

He nodded as they steered the horses in that direction. "We found a barely used trail when we came exploring. I think we can widen the path that's already there, clear out some of the brush and have a prime tourist spot." He jutted his chin in that direction. "Want to check it out?"

"I believe I do."

"Follow me."

The steady wind rustled the leaves in the overhead canopy. Other than that, there was a tentative quiet, the only sound coming from the clip-clop of hooves on the packed dirt, along with the occasional snort from one of the animals. The path was narrow, littered with fallen branches and rocks, but the horses were adept at navigating rough terrain. The scent of pine needles and decayed logs hung heavy in the air. The light dimmed under the tree cover, and the temperature grew chilly.

Juliette's sigh carried with the breeze. "This part of your property is beautiful."

He slowed. Turned in the saddle. "Tourists will like the fact that it's untouched."

"It's a shame you have to use this area."

"Part of our business model."

"Still, I hate that in order to make Golden a tourist destination, we have to disturb nature in the process."

"If it makes you feel any better, we're only using this land for trails. Otherwise it'll stay as close to the way you see it today as possible." He rested one hand on the pommel, then swung from the horse. At her raised eyebrow he said, "It'll be easier to talk to you and lead Juniper at the same time."

"Should I dismount?"

"No, you're fine."

And she was. She managed the path like a pro, speaking softly, making sure the horse didn't get hung up on the exposed tree roots. The dressed-up professional Juliette was so different than the jean-clad woman who navigated the woods with ease. How many more layers were there to this woman? And why the urgency to peel away each and every one until he got to the truth?

"I'm glad to hear that you aren't going to make big changes."

Ty paced himself with the movement of the horse, the stress of running the farm slowly dissipating. If only he could be this relaxed all the time.

"Once we get on the other side of the trees, there's a big payoff coming," he told her.

She perked up. "There is? I'll admit, I've never been out here."

He shot her a smile. "Just wait for it."

Silence descended again. The brush around them shook as small animals scurried by, probably alarmed at the big horses passing by.

"In the meantime?" Juliette asked.

He let out a long sigh. "I suppose you want to talk."

"Not necessarily. I can be as quiet as the next person."

He laughed, reading her posture, which said the exact opposite. "Really? You look like you're about to burst with questions."

"Nope." She adjusted the reins in her hand. "Just enjoying the ride."

They meandered for a few more minutes before Ty couldn't stand it any longer. "Spit it out."

"What?" She sent him an intentionally innocent look.

"You invited yourself along."

"You looked like you needed a friend."

What he needed was a financial windfall, but that wasn't happening.

He shouldn't confide in her, but there was no doubt he was going to. He needed to ease into a topic he hadn't yet discussed with anyone but Liz.

"It's the farm."

"Aren't you happy about the market today?" She frowned. "Mrs. M. has the tally of the farm's cut from the vendors. After the crowd that showed up today, I'd imagine it will be put to good use."

"It will. I appreciate the way you all pulled it together."

She leaned back in the saddle. "But…"

He mulled over his thoughts, then said, "I think I need to give you some history."

Juliette steered Tri around a fallen tree limb and nodded.

"The years I was away, working in the rodeo, our business started falling apart," he began. "It wasn't until I came back, after Scott could no longer work and my dad had taken over, that I discovered we were in real financial danger."

"Why wouldn't Brando tell you?"

"You have to understand, my dad and I had a rough relationship. On one hand, he saw my skill with horses when I was young and encouraged it, but when I went out on the circuit, he was ticked. Thought I'd abandoned him by not sticking with our traveling rodeo." He gazed at the hazy light streaming through the tree branches. "To be fair, our family show didn't do much of the tricks and skills I was known for. In order to compete or entertain, I had to go with another outfit. So there was always this…underlying tension between us."

Juniper shook his head and snorted. Ty adjusted the lead.

"When it became clear Scott couldn't run the show, Dad demanded I come home. In a way, he blamed the financial trouble on me because I'd taken off. Left the family." He glanced at her. "He wasn't wrong."

"Ty, how could you know if he didn't tell you?"

"We'd had arguments over less. He's made it clear he thinks I'm irresponsible."

Her ponytail drifted over her shoulder when she tilted her head. "Maybe before, but not now."

"Dad did his best, but it wasn't until Liz called to tell me about Scott that I actually left the circuit."

"Did Liz have a clue about the finances?"

"Not really, she just knew something was off." He threaded the leather rein through his fingers. "I wasn't looking for problems in the business either, but after I'd been back a while, I needed to get a truck fixed. When I went to pay the bill, there was no money. I went home and had it out with Dad."

"That's when you took over?"

He nodded. "And eventually straightened things out. By the time I sold off parts of our rodeo; livestock, equipment and trailers, there really wasn't much of a rodeo left. I had to put my pride aside and work with my father.

That's when we decided to take what we had, what I contributed of my own money, and buy Crestview Farm."

"Which is working out so far."

Not as smoothly as he'd like.

"I have to admit, putting aside my rodeo days was hard at first, but being here on this land? It's vastly fulfilling."

He wasn't sugarcoating it. Surprisingly enough, he really did love this land. Hadn't expected to, didn't want to, but all the same, it was part of Ty's blood now. And because of that, he'd do what was necessary to hold on to it.

Birds chirped and flitted overhead. After a long moment, Juliette asked, "Then what's wrong?"

"My dad is always on me about my old reputation." He chuckled. "He wasn't happy when we got into trouble with the chief."

"I can't imagine why." She tried to keep a serious expression, but a smile broke through. "I have to admit, that day was unexpected."

"But fun?"

She went sober as she met his gaze. "More fun than I've had in a long time."

There was a truth to her words he related to. But as much as he wanted what was happening between them to grow, he had to put his family first.

"We do tend to bring out that side of each other," he said instead of revealing his true feelings on the matter, like how she'd become as vital to him as breathing. "Good or bad."

"I think I'll take them both."

He watched as her smile faded, directing her attention to the trail before them. What caused her to get sad like that? He didn't flatter himself enough to think it had anything to do with him, they hadn't moved that far into a relationship, even though he was ready. But he remembered the way she'd downplayed the town hero status, the way she was surprised when he gave her praise, especially when she put others first, even at her expense.

And since they hadn't made any declarations toward each other, he had to let her know where he stood. "So you see why I have to take our family business seriously."

Something flashed quickly in her eyes. Disappointment? Understanding?

"I do." She lifted one shoulder in a carefree movement. "But since meeting you, I've discovered that we all need to let our hair down once in a while."

Curls framed the creamy skin of her face. He imagined her letting her hair loose, how the auburn curls would float around her shoulders. How the sun might catch different shades of red. How it would feel to twine a soft curl around his finger.

She disrupted his thoughts. "So the real problem is?"

He shook himself and brought Juniper to a halt.

"We need a well that supplies water to the stable re-dug. I've kept Dad out of the loop because he shouldered so much of the burden for so long. Now I need to make sacrifices for the family."

Concern crossed her face. "What does that mean?"

"I've looked into selling Juniper."

Her mouth fell open. She turned her head to look at the black horse nibbling at a small patch of grass, then back to him. He read the shock on her face, her anguish for him written on her lovely features.

"Oh, Ty."

He shrugged, a gesture that was not as casual as it appeared. "It's not ideal, but it was all I could come up with."

"Have you had an offer?"

"Yes, but oddly enough, not for the horse."

Her brows angled.

"Here's where it get tricky."

"Go on."

"One of the promoters I used to work with heard that I was looking to sell Juniper. He called me and suggested another solution that will solve our problems in the short term."

"Which is?"

"I go back on the rodeo circuit to earn the extra money."

JULIETTE'S MIND WENT blank when Ty told her the solution to his dilemma. She swallowed a gasp, then stuttered, "You'd leave Golden?"

"Not for good. Just long enough to perform and earn the extra money we need."

Her heart pounded. Not from the beauty of the day or the serenity of the walk through the woods. Not from the pronouncement that Ty might leave and how the idea hurt her deep inside. No, by the fact that she had no claim on the man. He had to protect his family and she couldn't tell him not to leave just because she'd desperately miss him.

"I know that look," he drawled. "You have an opinion."

She had lots of them, just none she could express. "Are things really that dire?"

"They will be." He lifted one shoulder. "The expense is more than we want to spend right now. The timing however..."

"There's no other way?"

"Not that I've come up with. Trust me, I've looked at this from all angles."

She believed him. He might be a charmer, but he was serious about the farm and taking care of his family. She was halfway in love with him because he was willing to give up Juniper for those he cared about.

As she absorbed the gravity of his decision, the light slowly grew brighter as they moved to the edge of the woods. Tri picked up the pace, ready to be on steady ground.

"I don't have to do this," Ty went on to say. "I could simply sell Juniper and our immediate problems would be solved. But what about new problems that arise in the future? Will I always be looking for something of value to sell? If I go back to the rodeo, I can earn the money and not worry about dipping into our contingency fund or worse, wiping out our savings."

But it could also mean he'd return to a world he loved and not come back.

Her lips turned downward. "What will your dad think?"

"I'll hear about how irresponsible I am, for sure."

But he wasn't. He saw a need and found

the best solution to take care of it. Surely his father would see that.

"This is a good solution, Ty. You can keep Juniper, because I can see it's killing you at the idea of selling him."

His eyes went dark. "It is."

"But you can earn extra income even if your father doesn't like it."

He rubbed Juniper's neck. "Feels like a lose-lose either way."

"Maybe your father won't be as hard on you as you think."

The doubt in his eyes proved he wasn't convinced. Surely his father wouldn't think his proposal was selfish?

"It's hard living down a reputation," he said in a quiet tone.

Juliette swallowed hard. She knew that only too well. Before she had a chance to continue the conversation, they moved out of the woods and into a meadow of faded grass that spread out along a narrow stream. The water sparkled as it splashed over rocks, creating a natural symphony.

"This is like out of a fairy tale," she whispered, but Ty heard her.

"That wasn't my initial observation. I figured it's a great place to have tourists dismount, maybe provide a lunch with the ride.

Let them explore and stretch their legs for a while."

Juliette grabbed hold of the pommel and swung her leg over the horse to slide to the ground. Ty took the reins from her and led the horses to a nearby tree where he wound the reins around a low branch.

Juliette followed a gurgling sound to the bank of the shallow stream, shading her eyes as the sunlight reflected off the water. Again, she hated that this beautiful spot had to be given over to tourists. If she had her way, this would be her secret hideaway. A special place only she and Ty knew about.

When he came to her side, she shook off her fantasy.

"Do you think this place will be popular?" he asked.

"Are you kidding? I'd live here if I could."

"Keeping it natural, remember?"

Still, she could picture a small cottage, a flower garden and children running around in the grass. Yes, a fantasy indeed.

"Once the secret gets out, you'll have riding excursions booked like crazy."

Ty held out his hand. She took hold, reveling in the warmth. His rough skin spoke of his hard work and responsibility. Right then and there, she lost more of her heart to him.

He led her to the bank where they sat. "I'd say let's take our boots off and stick our feet in the water, but it's probably cold."

"Hey, Mr. Adventure, don't chicken out."

"You check it out," he dared her.

Juliette reached out, the water skimming over her fingers. She shivered, wishing for Ty's warm touch again. "You'd be right."

He leaned back, resting his hands palm down behind him. He angled his head toward the sun. "I'm glad to see someone recognizes the truth of those words."

She nudged his shoulder with hers. "You kid, but you're doing an amazing job with the farm."

A frown creased his brow. "Just not fast enough."

"I doubt your father expects an overnight success."

"Just being able to take care of the bills would be nice."

"So…" She didn't want to go there, but asked anyway. "The rodeo?"

He sat up. "I can't see any other way."

To be honest, the more she thought about it, neither could she. When she'd looked him up online after they first met, she'd learned he had a large fan base who missed him. Mostly women—she didn't blame them—but he was a popular draw.

"You'd be gone a lot?"

He grinned. "Missing me already?"

She picked a blade of grass and twirled it in her fingers. "If I am?"

"Aw, darlin', that's the sweetest thing you've said to me."

He reached over to run his thumb across her chin. She shivered again, this time for a different reason. Her eyes met his. He glanced at her lips and she sighed. After a beat, he lowered his head to brush his lips over hers. It was a leisurely exploration, their breaths mingling as one. She could stay here like this forever and still not get enough of him.

She eventually tore herself away, running a finger over her lips, hiding a satisfied smile.

"Gets easier and easier to kiss you," he commented.

"You won't get any argument from me."

He brushed her hair from her cheek and smiled at her. "Enough of my woes. Tell me what's going on with you."

"Same old."

"Liz told me she has a client for your therapy program."

"Yes. She gave me the mom's number earlier today. I'll get in touch with her and set up an appointment."

"Excited?"

"I've waited so long to get the program going, it seems surreal that it's actually going to happen."

"I'm not surprised. You do have a way of getting the job done."

She did, but he had no clue to her motivation. What would he think of her if he knew? That the single most important act in her life had been blown out of proportion and she'd perpetuated the lie? She grew quiet, wishing her achievements hadn't been based on that one day. That one incident. That everything she did was to make up for that one lapse in time.

"You should be proud."

She bit her lip. Snuck a glance out of the corner of her eye. Ty's profile, so strong, so sure, had her wondering if she could confide in him.

"Do you think anyone can really put the past behind them?" she finally asked.

"Interesting question."

She waited a beat. "Have an interesting answer?"

Ty drew one knee up and rested an arm over it. "Coming from a guy who's made a few mistakes in the past, I'd like to think you can."

More often lately, she thought so too. But it had been so long ago. The years had flown by and she hadn't corrected the story. What would happen if she did now, with so many programs and projects she believed in, moving forward? Would it all come to a crashing end?

He turned to look at her. "What's up, Juliette?"

When he said her name like that, all caring and concerned, her heart squeezed so tight she could barely breathe. She reached up to press a hand over her chest.

"I know you think I'm special. The town hero." She paused. "I don't feel that way."

"I get it. You did your good deed and want to leave it at that."

"If I could. But people are always reminding me, bringing it up. Calling me hero. Trust me, I am no hero."

His eyes twinkled. "Modest instead?"

"Not even that." Anger aimed at herself, at the situation, besieged her. "If I'd done something out of the ordinary, I would be proud of myself. But the reputation has carried on for far too long. It's too much."

"If you aren't a hero, then who are you?"

A question she'd been asking herself for years and only came up with one answer. A fraud.

When she didn't say a word, Ty spoke. "Juliette, the important thing in life is being honest with yourself and others. Hoping that things have a way of working out."

Just as he was doing. His father might not like his decision, but Ty saw the big picture and would do what was necessary to fix matters. A choice she'd never come close to making.

"If only that were so easy."

"Trust me, I had to rethink my life when I came back to the family show. It wasn't overnight, but I'm happy where I am most of the time."

"Only most of the time?"

"I do miss performing, but I love the farm more, so I'll do what I have to to keep it ours."

Just like she did what she'd had to do. Make up for the lie that had defined her entire life while keeping it a secret.

The sun was sinking lower in the sky and with it, Juliette's hopes and dreams.

Ty lowered his leg and glanced around. "We should get going. Don't want to be stuck in the woods when it gets dark."

They walked to the horses and started the

trek back. Before leaving the meadow, Juliette took one last longing look. If she'd been able to tell Ty the truth, this would have been the ideal place. But she'd put her fear first, like she'd always done, and wanted to kick herself for it.

Once they had gotten through the woods and emerged on the other side, their horses walked at a leisurely pace. Ty didn't seem ready to give up this wonderful day. Neither did she, but thoughts of her busy life filled her head as they returned to reality.

"Ty, I forgot to tell you. Your sister was filling me in on her visit to see your brother."

He tugged on the reins to slow Juniper. "We're still waiting to hear back from him."

Juliette knew the pressure. Finding that place, along with a hundred other decisions, had become his daily routine.

"Luckily you have a friend who can assist you in the hunt."

He glanced at her and she caught a glimmer of a smile. She calmly led the horse through the grass.

With a dry tone he asked, "What has my friend done?"

"When you told me that you were on a waiting list for Scott, I put out some feelers. There's a new ALF in Clarkston almost ready for residents. An ex coworker of mine is managing the staff, so I can arrange to get your family's name on the list for a tour as soon as they open. I didn't want to say for sure until you knew your brother was coming home."

Confusion, and something else, etched his face. Pain? "Didn't you think we could find a place on our own?"

"You're new to the area and have so much going on with the farm and the horses, I thought reaching out to my contacts would narrow the search for you. Keep you from taking the time to make calls and do research when I work with people who know which facilities are the best."

"Because that's what you do," he muttered.

She glanced his way. "My contact let me know that construction is nearly completed. Since Scott hasn't made a decision yet, I'd suggest you set up an appointment to tour the facility once they have the go-ahead to move in. You can FaceTime with him when you visit. If he doesn't think it's a fit for him, that's fine, he can keep looking elsewhere, but this residence is filling up fast and I used my connections to make sure he has a shot at getting in."

This was one less thing on his plate, but

by his reaction, she'd clearly overstepped. "I wanted to tell you first."

"Juliette, I appreciate the effort, but you didn't have to get involved."

"I know."

The annoyance on his face remained.

"Are you angry?"

Ty ran a hand through his hair. "I'm not sure."

"There I am. Doing it again. Thinking I have all the answers."

"It's okay." He hefted out a breath. "You were just looking out for us, like you do with everyone."

"I was out of line. I apologize."

"No, I should have been more gracious. It's just that…" His expression gentled. "My dad always said we take care of our own. I guess I don't know how to reach out when it comes to Scott."

There he was, being honest with her. *And here I go, trying to be the hero when it's not my place.* Her stomach twisted.

"How about we start over." She stopped Tri, nearly bumping into Juniper as the mare danced to a halt. "So, Ty, tell me, can I use my contacts to find your brother a place to live?"

His expression lightened when he laughed. "How can I refuse?"

She let out a slow, relieved breath.

They picked up the pace to get the horses back to the stables. After they'd been groomed, Ty stopped her outside of Tri's stall. The quickly approaching evening cast shades in the dim corners.

His hand moved around her neck, buried under her ponytail. "Thanks for today. I know I was a bit touchy about Scott's housing, but I enjoyed every minute."

Before she could respond, his lips claimed hers. She leaned in, grabbing hold of his shirt to steady herself. His other hand lifted to palm her cheek and the kiss went deeper.

There was no doubt that Juliette was losing a part of herself to this man each time they were together.

Ty lifted his mouth, meeting her gaze. When he spoke, his voice was husky. "I gotta say, you make living in Golden worthwhile."

She could say the same about him. She was close to giving her heart to this man, a man who had no idea of her past. Could she stop herself?

She couldn't. Not even when he'd been more than honest about his own failings while she'd kept quiet about hers.

Her resolve wavered at the smile in his eyes. The way he gently captured a curl and twined it around his finger. He wanted her to be open, like he had been today; she could read it in his eyes. But she'd held on to her story for so long, never telling another soul. If she told him, would it ruin what was happening between them? Could she take that chance?

And if she did? Her heart nearly split in two over the fear and longing rising in her chest.

CHAPTER THIRTEEN

BY MIDMORNING ON WEDNESDAY, Juliette was running to keep up with her schedule. She'd taken the day off from work because of all the events lined up; the first equine therapy session since she'd made it official, Ivy's jewelry reveal launch at Blue Ridge Cottage, then her meeting with Mayor Danielson. Her stomach turned thinking about what he might want. Instead of dwelling on the unknown, she focused on her client for the therapy session.

After speaking to Mrs. Brighton, she'd made an appointment for early in the morning to meet her daughter. Tilly was a bright-eyed ten-year-old with a congenital musculoskeletal defect that made her left leg shorter than her right.

"Ready to get started?" she asked the little girl, who had her arms wrapped around her mother's waist.

"It's okay, honey," Mrs. Brighton said.

When consulting with Liz, they'd decided the gentle chestnut horse would be the best choice to introduce Tilly to horseback riding since she'd initially be sitting on the horse while Juliette led them around the paddock.

"Maggie's all ready for you," Juliette urged.

"What about my leg?" Tilly looked skeptical. "Will this hurt?"

Juliette had learned that Tilly found it challenging to participate in sports or any activity that required her to run or jump. She'd shown an interest in horses and her mother thought this might be a good way for Tilly to be outdoors more.

"You look like you were born to sit on a horse," Juliette encouraged the little girl.

"Do you really think I could ride?"

"There's only one way to find out."

After her mother untangled herself from her daughter's arms, Tilly shuffled to the horse. Juliette secured her helmet, then helped her up the block and onto Maggie.

The little girl refused to let go of Juliette's hand, so with the other, Juliette held the reins and led the horse around the paddock.

"Are you okay?" she asked.

Tilly nodded, her grip tighter.

"When I was a little girl I used to love horseback riding."

Tilly glanced down at her. "Did it take you a long time to learn?"

"It did. I wasn't very sure of my abilities, but the more I practiced, the easier it became."

"Do you still ride?"

"As often as I can." Juliette glanced around, then leaned closer to Tilly. "Can I tell you a secret?"

Tilly's eyes went wide with interest. "What is it?"

"The more time you spend on a horse, the more you come to love them."

This brought a small smile to Tilly's face.

The girl soaked up all the instructions and by the time they'd gone around the paddock a few more times, Tilly's grip loosened. As Juliette helped her down when they were finished, Tilly wrapped her arms around Juliette in a hug.

"Thank you, Miss Juliette. This was better than I thought it would be."

A slow beginning, but happiness swelled in Juliette.

Tilly hung around to watch the grooming process, still at a distance, but interested just the same, then she and her mother took off. Liz joined her as she closed Maggie in the stall.

"Good job, this morning. I scheduled Tilly for another date in the schedule you left me."

"Thanks, Liz. Tilly was an awesome first

client." She brushed the dust from her jeans, glancing around. "Is Ty here?"

"No, he had to go out of town for a few days."

She'd missed a call from him and had to wonder, had he gone to perform in a rodeo? She didn't ask, not sure she wanted the answer.

Liz's lips trembled as if holding back a grin. "Can I give him a message?"

"I'll text him, but don't let him forget he promised to go with me to Serena and Logan's wedding on Saturday night."

"Ah, the wedding of the century, I hear."

Juliette put away the grooming supplies. "It feels that way after the lengthy planning."

"She must have wanted it to be just right."

Juliette walked with Liz to the office and hefted her purse strap over her shoulder. "We'll find out on Saturday."

"I'm glad you invited Ty."

Juliette tried to brush it off, like her asking Ty to accompany her was no big deal. "He owes me."

Liz chuckled. "Maybe, but I'm still happy he's going." She tilted her head and seemed to measure Juliette. "You're good for him."

Was she? She sure spent enough time wondering. Worrying over how he might react if he learned the truth about her not exactly saving a toddler. Would he think she was good for him then?

Juliette's voice grew thick. "We have fun hanging out."

"Seems like more to me. I've never seen Ty so settled."

"This new life must appeal to him."

"And you. I'd say you definitely appeal to him."

Heat crept up Juliette's neck. "The feeling is mutual."

"I knew it!"

Juliette let out a laugh. "He's cocky enough as it is, so we'll keep this between us."

"You're right." Liz pointed her finger at Juliette. "I want details after the wedding."

"You got it. Now I have to run off to my sister's special event."

"Say hi to Ivy. She's such a sweetie."

"That she is, unless I'm late. Then I'll never hear the end of it."

On the drive home, a warmth spread through Juliette when she thought about Liz's words. Did Ty consider her special? She hoped so, because he was fast becoming the one for her. Yes, they had to deal with her past, but she'd tell him. She would.

Juliette had enough time to change out of

her jeans and T-shirt, shower and dress in a rust-colored sweater dress, with a colorful scarf draped over her shoulders and low suede boots. She arrived at Blue Ridge Cottage with seconds to spare.

Remnants of the Halloween celebration scattered about her; candy wrappers and black and orange streamers rolling end over end down the sidewalk in the wind.

As soon as she entered the lavender-scented store, she was pleased to see a crowd milling about the sales floor. Friends and tourists alike had come out for Ivy's big day. She weaved through the women to find the display table she and her parents had set up the night before. Her mother held a conversation with a potential customer. Ivy, on the other hand, was nowhere to be found.

Juliette glimpsed Serena and hurried over to her friend. "Have you seen my sister?"

"In the back," Serena replied, pointing. "I believe she has a case of the nerves."

Not surprising. Ivy did much better one-on-one, not with crowds. "Thanks."

Hurrying to the back room, Juliette found Ivy pacing, her hands fluttering before her.

"Ivy, what are you doing back here?"

The pacing stopped and tears filled Ivy's

eyes. "There are too many people. I can't make enough jewelry for everyone."

Juliette placed a hand on her sister's shoulder. "No one expects you to. You and Mom have brought more than enough inventory. If you run out, we'll take orders."

"People won't be mad at me?"

Hugging her sister, Juliette said, "Of course not. In fact, not all the big-name designers bring their entire inventory with them to a show. When people can't purchase an item immediately, it makes them want to buy what they can't have. If you run out, that's a win."

Ivy didn't look convinced.

"All you have to do is stand at the table and smile. If you want, I can talk to the customers."

After a long moment, Ivy shook her head. "No, I just needed a minute." She straightened her shoulders. "I can do this."

Juliette brushed her sister's hair over her shoulder. Ivy's uncertainty made her heart ache, but her turnabout in spite of her nerves also made Juliette proud.

Taking a deep breath, Ivy smoothed her hands over the skirt of her dress. Juliette did a double take.

"Is that…?"

Ivy looked down. "Yes, it's the dress you

picked out the day we were at Tessa's. I really did like it, so I went back and bought it." She met Juliette with a shy gaze. "Sorry I got mad at you, but you were right. I should have gotten it that day."

A surprised laugh escaped Juliette.

Ivy twirled in a circle. "Does it look good?"

"Beautiful." Juliette hooked her arm through her sister's. "Now, let's go sell your creations."

As they walked back into the storefront, their mother waved them over. "Here are both my girls." Pleasure glistened in her eyes. "Are you ready, Ivy?"

Ivy cast her eyes downward. "Yes."

"And, Juliette, don't forget your appointment with the mayor."

Juliette stiffened at her mother's casual comment. How did her mother know about the meeting? She hadn't said a word. Besides, ever since she'd set up a date and time with Mayor Danielson's secretary, she'd been on pins and needles, and didn't willingly bring it up.

From across the room, Serena winked at the three Bishop women standing together, then clapped her hands to get everyone's attention.

"Thank you for coming out this morning.

I'm pleased to feature our very own Ivy Bishop and her handmade jewelry collection from Ivy's Creations. Please, enjoy browsing and help yourself to a beverage or cookie as you shop." She pointed to an orange bowl. "And enjoy some leftover Halloween candy."

Juliette stepped to the side, waiting to see what her sister would do. An older lady started asking Ivy how she began her interest in making jewelry and, as Ivy focused on the woman, Juliette could see the tension drain from her sister. Ivy's shoulders relaxed as she started talking about the pieces she'd made. Juliette watched her grow more comfortable in the process. Between their mother ringing up sales and Ivy growing more animated, the pang Juliette had experienced when her mother discussed running the business with Ivy returned with a vengeance.

Serena sidled up to her. "You okay?"

"Thrilled to see Ivy so happy."

"She's quite talented. And once word of mouth gets out about her beautiful pieces, she'll be busy too."

"That's all I wanted."

Serena moved her gaze from the activity around the table to look at Juliette. "But?"

Juliette's hair brushed her cheek as she

turned her head. She tucked it away and said, "Why does there have to be a but?"

"There doesn't, but I sense there is one."

Juliette blew out a breath. "Sorry. It's just that up until now, it's always been Ivy and me."

"And now it's not?"

"Something like that."

Serena hooked her arm through Juliette's. "Look at it this way, now you have more time for other projects."

When she looked at it that way, Juliette realized her friend was right. She could slow down and spend more time with Ty. The idea appealed to her.

"I had my first equine therapy appointment this morning," she said.

Serena pulled back. "Juliette, that's great. How did it go?"

"For the first one, very well."

Serena nudged Juliette with her elbow. "You're bringing new clients to the farm *and* have time to hang out with hunky Ty."

Not ready to share what was happening between them, she got a bit territorial. Right now, Juliette wanted to keep her feelings close, especially since she and Ty hadn't spoken about where the relationship was headed.

She didn't want to jinx it by getting ahead of herself.

"Who said anything about Ty?"

Serena rolled her eyes and ignored her. "How's that going?"

"Fine," Juliette huffed.

"That's a disappointing answer."

Juliette couldn't help it, but the pout on her friend's face made her laugh. "Not everyone is over the moon with their significant other like you and Logan."

"True, but I saw you with Ty that night at The Perch. There were definitely sparks between you two."

She shrugged, even though she wouldn't deny the claim. She had kissed him, after all. "Maybe. We'll see how it goes.

"Are you bringing him to the wedding?"

Juliette sent Serena a sly look. "Do you want me to?"

"I want everyone there, but that's beside the point. Do you want him there?"

Juliette didn't have to think twice about it. "Yes."

Serena clasped her hands over her heart. "Awesome. I have a good feeling about you two."

"I'm not looking—"

"That's what I said until Logan completely

captured my every thinking moment. It seemed like there weren't enough hours in the day to be together and when we did say goodbye after a date, I couldn't wait to see him again. Are you experiencing the same symptoms?"

She was, but said, "Symptoms? How romantic."

"Hey, I'm getting married this weekend so I think I'm allowed my observations."

"Don't rub it in."

Serena's face grew serious. "Then enjoy Ty and let romance take its course."

Would it? Because after he learned the truth... She shook off her apprehension. "I have to say, the man does fill out a suit."

Serena laughed.

"Who fills out a suit?"

Juliette turned to find Addie beside her, holding a cup of lemonade and taking a bite of a cookie.

"Ty," Serena said.

Addie's eyes went wide. "Why are we talking about Ty? Did something happen? Are you still seeing each other?"

Yes, something had happened. Ty had kissed her several times and she couldn't think of anything else. Which should have bothered Juliette because she always put her career and everyone else first, but found she liked thinking about him. Besides, she'd told Addie she wouldn't unceremoniously dump Ty. Didn't her friend believe her?

Juliette hefted her purse strap over her shoulder. "We're talking about the wedding."

"I didn't think this weekend would ever get here," Serena said with a sigh. "But it's going to be a perfect November day and we'll be husband and wife."

Juliette turned to Serena. "Why are you working? Not that I don't appreciate you scheduling this gathering for Ivy's Creations, but don't you have wedding-y things to do?"

"Nope. Everything is in order."

Juliette and Addie exchanged amused glances.

"What?" Serena demanded after noticing.

"Nothing." Juliette patted her arm. "Your day will be perfect."

"Of course it will. Why wouldn't it?" Serena's voice rose. "What are you not telling me?"

"Calm down," Addie said and patted her arm as well. "It'll be perfect."

Juliette jumped in. "It'll be—"

"Everything I imagined," Serena said in a firm tone. "Now, I have to get back to work."

As Serena morphed back to store owner, Juliette's phone dinged an incoming text. She pulled the device from her purse and read the message, pain shooting across her forehead. A reminder about her appointment. Like she needed a text when she'd been fretting over it all morning.

"Everything okay?" Addie asked.

"Yes." She held up her phone. "I have another appointment."

"What's going on?"

"Nothing much," she hedged.

"It has to be more," Addie insisted. "You don't usually take a full day off from work."

"Too much going on."

Addie's gaze pierced hers. "Are you sure? You look overwhelmed."

"Just a busy patch. You know how that goes. It'll be over soon."

Addie frowned. "Is it Ty?"

She flung up her hands. "Why does everyone think everything is about Ty?"

"Whoa, don't get upset, just asking." Addie's face softened. "We haven't talked much lately and you've been wound tighter than usual.

She reined in her apprehension. "I'm fine. Ty is wonderful."

Too wonderful. He made her forget her past, forget her obligations, forget that she lived a lie. No one had ever had the power to make her feel like she didn't have to be the hero. With Ty, she could be herself, whoever that was. The person she needed to become.

Addie still looked worried. "Okay, but you know you can talk to me."

"I do, but right now I need to say goodbye to Ivy and Mom and scoot."

She hugged her good friend, sorry she couldn't confide in Addie and wished the mounting pressure wasn't making her so nervous. As much as she tried, she couldn't control her trepidation at seeing the mayor.

After she spoke to her family, Juliette walked the few blocks off Main to get to the mayor's office. She tried to enjoy the sunny autumn day, but with each step, her stomach twisted in knots. What did he want? And why did she feel her past was teetering on the edge of collapsing around her?

She entered the courthouse. Dragged her feet as she climbed the stairs to the mayor's office. She gave her name to the receptionist and took a seat, jiggling in place as she waited. She smoothed her skirt and cleared her throat. Finally, an inner door opened.

"Miss Bishop?"

Juliette stood.

"This way."

She followed the woman down a hallway to another office. "The mayor is waiting," the young woman said as she opened the door and waved Juliette inside.

She glanced around the very masculine room: dark furniture, large ornately framed paintings, thick carpet her heels sank into. Big windows gave a perfect view of the surrounding mountains, but all Juliette focused on was the gray-haired man finishing a phone call.

"Juliette," Mayor Danielson said, rising from behind his impressive desk. "I'm so glad you could make it."

She stepped farther into the room. "I have to admit, I am curious why you wanted to see me."

"Please." He gestured to a grouping of chairs. "Take a seat."

She sat across from him, purse on her lap, as she fiddled with the strap.

"I'll get right to the point."

Please. She couldn't take the suspense any longer.

"The annual Veterans Day parade is fast approaching. I'm scheduled to speak afterward at Gold Dust Park and since it's a tradition, I'm hoping you'll be there."

"I hadn't thought that far ahead."

Mr. Danielson chuckled. "Just like you to be so busy." He clapped his hands together once so loudly, she jumped. "This year you'll have to make time to attend because I have a special commemoration lined up."

Her stomach dipped. Her life was coming together, she had hope for the future. Was close to confiding the truth to Ty. Why did the mayor have to complicate matters now?

"It's been fifteen years since you saved our dear Ellie. I want to honor you during my speech."

She swallowed hard. "Mayor Danielson, you don't have to do that."

"I insist. You made a big impact on our family, on this town. It's time we recognize just that."

Juliette stood on shaky legs. "I don't need the recognition."

"But you'll get it," he said, a big smile on his face. "I've already told your parents, but asked them not to reveal the surprise until I told you myself."

She closed her eyes. No wonder her mother was so giddy about Juliette's meeting with the mayor. And if her family knew, there would be no way to wiggle out of the commemoration. They'd insist they were proud and if she tried to convince them otherwise, she'd have to explain. She glanced at the mayor.

By the determined expression on his face, he wouldn't let her out of it either.

"So, you'll be there that Friday morning about eleven?"

"I may not be able to get the day off from work."

"No problem. I called your boss and the staff has rearranged your schedule."

Hadn't anyone thought to ask her what she wanted? Or what she had to say, just like fifteen years ago? Only now she was an adult and should put her foot down, but old habits were so hard to change. That, and fear of what others would say.

"Invite your friends to the big day," the mayor continued.

"Are you sure—"

"My family and I look forward to this, Juliette. Don't let me down."

Don't let me down. Four words she truly hated.

With a nod, Juliette turned on her heel and fled the room. As she rushed outside, she gulped huge gusts of the cool air scented with burning leaves and the change of season, hoping to compose herself.

Why hadn't she said anything? Why hadn't she put her foot down?

Like years ago when no one listened to you?

It was all crashing down. She'd waited too long.

Her day of reckoning was upon her.

"YOU'VE BEEN AWFULLY QUIET," Ty said as he and Juliette sat at a table decorated with a floral arrangement of orange roses, yellow sunflowers and rust mums, enjoying the reception at Sever House, where Serena and Logan had exchanged vows thirty minutes earlier.

"It was a lovely ceremony. Serena looked beautiful in her bridal gown."

"I'm not a fashion expert. Dresses all look the same to me."

She shot him an amused glance. "Not everyone wears a lacy full-length gown with a train while sporting a veil in everyday life," she countered.

"I'll give you that." He glanced over the crowed room. "As far as weddings go, this one is pretty nice."

"I'm sure Serena would take that as a ringing endorsement."

He chuckled at her dry tone. A far as he was concerned, he only had eyes for Juliette.

She wore a plum-colored dress with a flowing skirt that twirled around her legs, her hair pulled up in some complicated design. He'd thought her gorgeous from day one, but now, knowing the woman behind the sassy smile, his chest ached with wanting.

As the guests mingled, Ty moved closer. "So, I'll take it that so far this wedding is a success?"

"After all her planning, worrying and making Logan wait, yeah, this is a complete victory for Serena."

The happy couple laughed over something the groom's brother said to the group gathered around them. Ty caught a glimpse of his dad, in conversation with Alveda. He'd never seen the old man as content with life until they moved to Golden.

As much as finances at the farm were up in the air, Ty didn't mind putting the demands of the business aside to spend the evening with Juliette. Actually, he could picture himself doing it every night. They were growing closer, yes, but he still sensed her holding back. He couldn't put his finger on what bothered her. Did she think he was a bad bet? That he couldn't manage the farm, so he would be trouble as a boyfriend? Or that he might be traveling more than he was at home in Golden if he joined the rodeo circuit again?

Guess he still had some soul-searching himself, thinking that he might not measure up to this remarkable woman.

A few couples joined the table and dinner was served. Everyone chatted about the wedding and soon the DJ had the dance floor rocking.

Ty placed his napkin on the table, stood and held out his hand. "Care to dance?"

Juliette took his hand and rose. "I think that can be arranged."

They moved to the floor, swaying to a ballad professing everlasting love.

Ty jutted his chin at the happy couples dancing around them. "Ever think about what those couples have?"

Juliette pulled back to glance at the people on the dance floor. "I don't know." She bit her lower lip. "I've never been in a serious relationship."

"Me either," he admitted, wondering what everlasting love would look like with Juliette.

She hesitated. "Do you want what they have?"

He met her gaze and held it. "I'm beginning to."

She blinked, then turned away. Had he upset her? Or worse, scared her off? No wonder he'd never had a serious girlfriend. He was bad at this.

"Ty, there's something—"

He stepped back, a frown on his face.

"What's wrong?"

"My dad. He's glaring at me."

Juliette twisted to look over her shoulder at Brando. "I'm guessing the news about going back to the rodeo didn't go over well?"

He pulled her back into his arms, not letting his father's expectations ruin this special time with Juliette. Instead, he inhaled her scent, keeping his hands on her waist as they resumed moving with the music.

"He wasn't happy, but I decided to lay it all out for him. He agreed that this was a good way to raise the funds we need."

Her eyebrows rose. "Then why do you think he's upset?"

"Probably because he sees us together and thinks I'm going to blow it with you." Ty held in a sigh. "I can tell he thinks I'm shirking my duties again."

She ran a hand over his shoulder and asked, "When do you head out?"

"Tuesday morning. I signed up for two shows at a fairgrounds, about two hours from here."

"How long will you be gone?"

"I'll be back on Thursday." Why did she look so disheartened? Was it more than his short absence? He had to admit, the idea of leaving her didn't sit well.

He deciding teasing might just get the weight of the world off her, and his own, shoulders. "Are you going to miss me, darlin'?"

"No, I mean, yes, I will, but I wanted to make sure you'd be home on Friday."

"Because we have another market scheduled this weekend? The barn is in good shape, unless you want to change the decorations you put up last time."

"It's not that." She hesitated. Ty had gotten good at reading her moods and sensed there was more going on under the surface than she was saying. "The mayor wants to honor me at the annual parade and I'd really like you to be there."

"Oh, yeah?" He sent a big grin her way. "Well, now, I'll make sure to be home in plenty of time."

She waved a hand. "It's not a big deal and I really wish the mayor wouldn't do this."

Honestly, she did so much for others, she should be honored for all of it, not just one event many years ago. The way she always deflected from being a hero was one of the many things he found appealing about her. He liked Juliette just the way she was right now, hero or not, it didn't matter to him.

"Face it, everyone in Golden loves you. There's no way you can get out of it."

"What if I want to?" she whispered as she rested her head on his chest. "Get out of it, that is."

Once again she was shying away from any acclaim. Now was probably not the best time, but he really wanted to understand her resistance. "Is there a reason you don't want the honor?"

She didn't glance up, speaking to his chest as if she couldn't meet his gaze.

"Look, Ty, if I'd changed my life for a good cause, like you did, giving up what you loved to take care of your family, then I could see the big deal. But I'm not doing anything differently than I have my entire life."

"It's okay to be recognized for the good work you do."

When their eyes did meet, he saw the sorrow there. Why would she be sad about doing a good deed?

"But what if it's not what it seems? What if the mayor blew it all out of proportion?"

"I don't think saving a little girl is blowing things out of proportion."

She shook her head, loosening some of the curls that tumbled to her cheek, frustration evident on her face.

After a long moment and a change of song, he said, "Can I offer some advice?"

"Please."

"Just be a good sport, show up and it'll be over before you know it." He smiled. "If I can go back to the rodeo for a few nights, you can do this."

Her face closed off and again he wondered what he'd said wrong. When the song ended, Juliette stepped back and said, "I need to visit the ladies' room."

She went to the table to collect her small bag and disappeared. As he stood watching her, Adam ambled over.

"Having fun?"

Ty shook off the foreboding that came with Juliette walking away. "Yeah. Nice shindig."

Adam laughed.

"I'll admit, I don't get to many weddings."

Adam lifted his chin in Juliette's direction. "Looks like you and Juliette are becoming a couple."

He'd thought so until she closed down again. He didn't know what to make of her mood or if he had anything to do with it. Was she second-guessing getting involved with a rodeo man?

He glanced at Adam. "Can I ask you a question?"

"Sure."

He led Adam away from nearby folks who might overhear the conversation. "What do you know about the story behind Juliette saving the little girl in the stroller?"

Adam's eyebrows angled. "I wasn't there that day, but the story is legend in Golden. Pretty much what you've probably heard. The stroller drifted into the street and Juliette stopped it before it could get hit by a car."

"Nothing else?"

Adam shrugged. "She's never liked all the attention that goes with it, but that's Juliette."

"Would there be a reason she didn't want to be reminded of that day?"

"Not that I've ever heard."

Ty couldn't shake the feeling that there was more to the story.

Juliette returned, still subdued. Ty tried to enjoy the remainder of the reception. After the final dance, Juliette asked to go home.

They walked outside into the chilly star-filled night. October had swiftly spilled into November. The air carried the woodsmoke from the bonfire lit behind Sever House for the wedding guests to enjoy. In the distance, the sound of merry voices rose from the reception. Juliette wrapped her thick shawl closer around her shoulders before Ty had a chance to place his arm around her and pull her close to his body heat. They approached the parking lot, stopping beside a row of cars.

Once he'd had his fill of looking at the stars, he reached into his pocket to remove a beaded bracelet. "I got this for you."

Her face lit up. "It's one of Ivy's."

"I bought it at the market. Meant to give it to you before now, but, I don't know, between the stars and the wedding…"

Juliette clutched it to her chest. "How sweet."

She moved under the streetlight to get a better view and lost her footing in the loose gravel drive. Before Ty could protect her, she reached out to steady herself on the hood of the closest car, setting off a blaring alarm.

Ty jerked at the sound piercing the night. "What the—?"

The noise went on for what seemed like a long time, then bleeped and shut off.

"Finally, quiet," Ty muttered.

"Something you two want to tell me?" came an amused voice from the darkness.

Ty swung around to see the police chief headed their way, holding up a key fob.

"First the sign, now a car? Seems you two can't stay out of trouble."

Juliette stepped beside Ty. "It was an accident. I stumbled and the car stopped my fall."

"My car."

Ty held in a groan.

The chief just smiled. "Since I'm not on duty and you don't really look like hardened criminals, I'll let it go." He stopped. "What is this, the third time I've caught you two in some kind of mischief?"

The chief knew exactly how many times it had been, but the sparkle in his eyes revealed that he was messing with them, and enjoying it, much to Ty's chagrin.

Juliette laid a hand on Ty's arm, her warmth sinking through the jacket and shirt beneath. "Thanks, Brady."

He nodded. "I'll see you Friday morning, Juliette. The mayor's put out word that he wants the entire town there." He glanced at Ty. "Evening."

Brady got into the car. Ty led Juliette out of the way so the chief could back out.

"He's got it out for us," Ty griped. When

Juliette didn't respond, he turned to see her staring after the chief.

"You okay?"

She shook her head. "Don't mind Brady. He's always had a good sense of humor."

"But you aren't smiling."

She pulled the shawl tighter around herself.

"You seem worried about this honor on Friday."

She shook her head. "Guess I want to be sure you'll be home in time."

"Juliette, that bracelet is a reminder that I promise to be there for you."

A promise that he wasn't the irresponsible kid he'd once been.

Her eyes went bright with tears as she viewed the jewelry in her hand. "Ty…"

"It's clear that the idea of standing before the town isn't something you want, but I can also see you don't want to go into why."

She sighed. "It's such a long story."

"Which I'll have plenty of time to listen to once you're ready."

"No matter what it means between us?"

He heard the misery in her tone. Took hold of her hands and grasped them tightly in his. "I meant what I said earlier. I'm beginning to see my future, our future, differently. What's in the past can't change that, can it?"

She opened her mouth as if to say more, but abruptly closed it like she'd changed her mind.

"When you get back," she whispered.

"I'll always come back to you, Juliette."

CHAPTER FOURTEEN

"HOW MUCH LONGER?" Ty asked for what felt like the fiftieth time.

"Just a few more minutes," came the muffled response from the mechanic under the horse trailer.

Ty tried to rein in his frustration. "That's what you said fifteen minutes ago."

Fred, the mechanic, rolled out from under the trailer. His graying hair was rumpled, along with his wrinkled shirt and stained pants, but the frown on his face was crystal clear. "You want it fast or you want it right?"

"Right," Ty mumbled. He pulled out his phone to call Juliette. The ceremony in Gold Dust Park started in just over two hours and he was running late. If he left now, he might make it.

The call went to voice mail. Again. He hung up, muttering a few choice words under his breath.

Yesterday afternoon, he'd pulled out of the fairgrounds where he'd performed in the rodeo the night before. It was just after noon and he had plenty of time to get back home before the ceremony the next day. Until he heard a loud clunk and the trailer shifted. He stopped immediately and jumped out of his truck to inspect the noise. To his disbelief, the axle on the trailer had broken.

Not taking any chances, he'd unloaded Juniper to return him to the stall he'd been using earlier and had one of his buddies at the stable confirm the damage. Ty had been directed to Fred, who took care of many of the local vehicles and came highly recommended.

"How long will it take to fix?" he'd asked Fred when the man drove out to the fairgrounds to take a look at the damage.

"Probably two hours."

At the moment, that news hadn't been so bad. Worst-case scenario, he'd be home late Thursday night, but he'd still be there for Juliette on Friday morning.

"Can you fit me in now?"

The older guy, in oil stained coveralls shrugged. "Could, but I gotta find the part. Don't have it in stock."

Great. "Think any other garages around here might have the part?" Ty asked.

"Doubt it. Let me make some calls and see what I can do." Fred nodded toward the trailer.

"In the meantime, have the trailer towed to my shop."

The trailer had been delivered, ready to be worked on. Six hours later, the mechanic had found the part, which he'd located at a warehouse a few hours away. He made arrangements for the part to be shipped overnight.

It wasn't a great option, but what choice did Ty have? He couldn't leave Juniper at the fairgrounds now that everyone was packing up to leave, which meant he couldn't drive home and after the ceremony, come back for the horse and trailer. Of all the bad luck. Talk about being between a rock and a hard place.

While waiting, Ty had called Liz to tell her he'd contacted the service company to come out on Monday to start re-digging the well near the stable. Thankfully after the sold-out performances, he'd had enough money left over for the trailer repair as well.

And while he should be happy, the fact that he couldn't get home was killing him. He couldn't abandon Juniper or leave their rolling stock behind, so he had to stay overnight in the small town until the work was completed. He'd tried calling Juliette to explain, but kept getting the option to leave her a message, which made him worry even more. Why wasn't she answering her phone? After leaving a few messages, he finally asked Liz to get ahold of Juliette, but hadn't heard back from either woman.

So now he paced, waiting for the work to be completed so he could get on the road and be with Juliette like he'd promised.

Five minutes, later, Fred rolled out from under the trailer, stood and wiped his hands with a red rag. "All finished."

Ty nearly sagged in relief. "I can't thank you enough."

"Got the impression you're in an all fire hurry to get somewhere important."

He'd already paid the bill, so Ty pulled the truck keys from his pocket. "I am."

"Bet it's got something to do with a lady."

"Why would you say that?"

"Got that look about ya."

He shook Fred's hand. "You'd win that bet."

Then Ty sprinted to the truck to hook up the trailer. After collecting Juniper and getting on the road, he made his way to Juliette, hoping he arrived on time.

"TY'S NOT HERE." Juliette scanned the crowd, her stomach pitching. The antacid she'd chewed earlier wasn't working. "He said he'd be here."

"I'm sure he has a good reason for being late," Addie tried to assure her.

It wasn't working.

Juliette had arrived at the park a little before eleven to find a large crowd already assembled. It was a cold morning, so she'd dressed in black slacks, a gray-and-white-striped sweater and solid jacket. Her parents, along with Ivy, had dressed for the low temperature as well, their beaming faces making Juliette feel worse. Ivy, to be fair, was more interested in the folks who had brought their dogs to the event than her big sister's honor. Juliette wished she could be that preoccupied.

"Did he call?" Addie asked.

"I don't know. I've been so distracted lately, I misplaced my phone."

Addie frowned. "That doesn't sound like you."

No, it didn't, but for the past few days, Juliette hadn't been herself. She'd searched her house, but came up empty. She couldn't decide if she'd left her phone at the stables after her second therapy session, or on her desk at her office, and had no idea if Ty had called her. She hadn't memorized his number and was out of luck without her contact list.

She'd made the decision to come clean with Ty before the parade. If she could admit her mistake to Ty, and he didn't look at her with disgust, then perhaps it wouldn't be so hard to tell everyone else. Especially with him by her side. But her big plan to talk to him when he got home from the rodeo had failed, leaving her sick with worry.

Since meeting Ty, more than once she'd almost told him the truth. Old habits had stopped her, but she'd thought about it more than she ever had before. The need to keep the secret had pressed deep inside her, but now it wanted out. Was it Ty's story about overcoming his reputation that had lit a spark in her? He'd worked hard to gain the confidence of his family. If he could do it, couldn't Juliette?

Not without him by her side. She scanned the park again.

"He promised," Juliette whispered in a barely there voice, fingering the bracelet that he'd given her, along with his promise, circling her wrist.

"Maybe he just got hung up. He'll be here as soon as he can."

Juliette paced. Her heart felt like it was lodged in her throat. She couldn't eat a thing this morning and her stomach was definitely revolting. Suddenly Juliette couldn't breathe.

Her past roared up on her and she had no-where to hide.

"I can't do this," she said.

"Juls, I know you hate the attention," Addie said, "but it's nice that the mayor thinks that much of you."

"He's got it all wrong. He always has."

With a determination she hadn't allowed herself to have before now, she took Addie's hand and dragged her friend over to her parents so she didn't have to say what was coming twice. Ty wasn't here as she'd hoped—she ignored the aching disappointment from his no-show—but just as he'd made peace with his past reputation, it was time she told the truth before the mayor showed up and she let the lie continue any longer.

"Is everything all right?" her father asked. Behind his glasses, his eyes, so much like hers, gleamed with worry.

"I need to tell you all something. Something I should have been truthful about a long time ago."

"Juliette," her mother said with a question in her tone. "What's going on?"

She met Ivy's eyes when her sister joined them. "Me being a hero? This has all been a lie."

Ivy frowned before Juliette turned back to her parents.

"What are you talking about?" her father asked.

"You weren't there that day." She tried to meet her parents' gazes, but couldn't do it. She turned to Addie. "You don't know what really happened."

"You saved Ellie?" her friend asked, her expression unsure.

"I did, but I didn't mean to. It was a lie."

Before she could reveal the truth, the Danielson family joined the group.

"Are you ready to get started?" the mayor asked.

"Can you hold off a few minutes?" Dale Bishop asked. It was then that the mayor noticed the tension with her family.

Juliette's father had moved next to her mother, taking her hand in his. Addie was scowling. Ivy finally had her attention on the scene before her.

The mayor waved to one of the soundmen, his gesture indicating they wait, then said, "What's going on?"

Pam Bishop gazed at her daughter. "We were just going to find out."

Juliette opened her mouth, but nothing came out. Now that the time had come to reveal her secret, she froze. Why wasn't Ty here like he'd promised?

Her mother moved closer and grasped Juliette's arm. "Honey, you're scaring me."

Her father removed his glasses. "Your mother is right. You're usually so even-keeled."

At that moment, calm had deserted her, replaced by a full-blown panic attack. She was tired of hiding the truth. Exhausted that she'd been put in the situation to begin with. Didn't want any kind of honorary title from anyone.

But mostly, she was disappointed that Ty wasn't here. That he hadn't kept his word. Now she was on her own, as she had been all along. She supposed it was better this way.

With all eyes on her, she lifted her chin. Linked her fingers together so hard it hurt.

"I didn't mean to save Ellie. It happened by mistake."

Silence.

Addie shook her head, as if trying to get the words to make sense. "What are you saying?"

Juliette barreled on. She couldn't stop now. "The parade that day didn't turn out like I'd thought. I was supposed to meet a friend, but he didn't show. I was watching over Ivy and she didn't want to leave the park, until she noticed a stray dog. She chased after it and I followed her." She unlinked her fingers and began to wave her hands. "While we were all on the sidewalk, some people came up to talk to Mr. and Mrs. Danielson. They must have thought the other was watching Ellie, but suddenly the stroller hopped over the curb and glided into the street."

She stopped to catch her breath, noticing the wide eyes around her. When no one spoke, she filled the terrible silence.

"I had to stop Ivy from running into the traffic because she was determined to get to the dog. As I did, Ivy pulled away. I lost my balance and fell into the street at the same time the stroller rolled my way, which banged into my leg and stopped in front of me."

No one said a word, identical looks of shock on each face.

"Ellie was crying." Her voice trailed off. "And the dog ran away."

After finally telling the real story, why wasn't anyone talking?

"I never intentionally meant to stop the stroller," Juliette finished.

Ivy came to her and took her hand. "But you did. You saved Ellie."

"I don't understand," her mother said. "Why didn't you tell us what really happened?"

"I think I was initially in shock afterward and couldn't stop the mayor's account of the incident. Then, over time, it was hard to break everyone's belief that I was a hero when no one listened to my side of the story. It went on for too long and what could I say?" She turned back to her parents. "I tried to tell you, but you were so happy about the story you made such a big fuss. Pretty soon the story had grown and everyone was proud of me and if I'd admitted what happened…"

She tried to swallow but her mouth was dry.

Addie's face turned pale. "Why didn't you tell me? After all these years, you never said a word."

Juliette panicked at Addie's blank expression. "I couldn't."

"I told you all about my life. Losing Josh, and the pain that came with it, and you never said a word." Addie's face started to flush with color now. "You lied to me, Juliette. To all of us."

Juliette thought she might vomit.

"I didn't tell anyone. And after a while, it was easier to go along with it than try and explain." Shame slithered through her. "I'm sorry I let it get so out of hand."

Just as she feared, Addie was unreadable and her parents were a mixture of shock and worry. Displeasure etched Mr. and Mrs. Danielson's face. If she looked out to the crowd, would she see the same? She didn't dare turn around.

"What now?" her father asked.

The red-faced mayor finally found his voice. "We can't give an honor right now, not the way things stand."

Just what she'd been telling herself for years.

Unsurprisingly, murmurs rose from the crowd who was now aware of the situation.

"I knew this would happen," Juliette whispered.

A frown knit her mother's forehead. "Juliette, you should have come to us."

Tears blurred her vision. "And say what? That I let the events of that day build up to this moment all these years later?"

"We could have straightened it out..." her mother started to say, but her words trailed off.

"This is a hurdle," her father said, "but we can overcome it."

One tear rolled down Juliette's cheek. "I don't think so, Dad. It was only going to end one way." She swallowed over the lump in her throat. "Badly."

She turned to Addie. "Please say you forgive me."

Addie's mouth stayed sealed shut.

"Mom? Dad?"

Her mother glanced at her father, but both sported helpless expressions.

"I need to leave," Juliette said, rushing around the side of the platform to run toward the park exit.

Her mind whirled. What would happen now? What would Ty say when he learned the ugly truth? She'd admired the way he'd turned his life around, despite the reputation he'd worked hard to overcome. It had given her the confidence to finally admit the truth. But now?

She'd just made it under the stone arch when she ran into the man walking her way.

"THANK GOODNESS, JULIETTE. I thought I was late."

He caught Juliette in his arms to steady her. She pulled back and it was then that he noticed the tears streaking her face.

Fear filled him and he gripped her arms tighter. "What happened?"

"The truth came out." She shook off his hands and swiped at her cheeks. "Where were you?"

The truth? What was she talking about? He shook his head in confusion.

"I've been trying to call you since yesterday."

"I lost my phone."

That explained the silence, but didn't sound like the always prepared Juliette.

"I waited, Ty, but you broke your promise."

Her tone made him nervous. "What's going on?"

"You promised you'd be here."

"The horse trailer broke. I had to wait for the repair before I could head back to Golden." He ran a hand through his hair. Juliette was clearly agitated and accusatory, and he had no clue why. "You're mad at me?"

"I waited."

"But I'm here. Maybe a few minutes late, but it doesn't look like the ceremony has started." He nodded his head toward the platform. "Let's go to the—"

"It's too late."

It was then that he noticed eyes on them. Sensing there was something bigger going on, Ty pulled Juliette from the sidewalk to stop under the heavy limbs of a nearby tree. "Talk to me."

She wiped her cheeks, her face desolate. "I didn't save the little girl in the stroller, Ty. Not really. The story got out of control and I let it. I'm a fraud and now you know the truth about me."

Ty ran a hand over his forehead. There were deeper layers to this story, just as he'd suspected, but had no idea where to start untangling it.

"Everyone is disappointed in me. Addie will probably never speak to me again." Her eyes went wide. "What if I lose my job?"

"Slow down. You're getting ahead of yourself."

"I should have been honest years ago."

"I'm confused. Why weren't you?"

Juliette wouldn't meet his gaze. "It's complicated."

He placed his palm on her cheek, turning her head so their eyes met. "From what I've heard, it wasn't just the stroller incident that made you a hero. You've always put Golden first. And from what I've seen, you've been a hero to this town for years."

She shook her head, her curly hair swinging over her shoulders. "No."

He glanced over her shoulder to see the crowd facing them, like they were performing a drama onstage for all to see. He tugged her arm and walked out of the park to get them away from prying eyes.

"Juliette, it sounds like a big misunderstanding. I'm sure once everyone calms down, you can straighten it out."

"You didn't see their faces."

"That's true."

She glanced up at him, her face awash in misery. "Don't you get it, Ty? I lied to you too."

"Maybe you did and I'll deal with that later, but right now I'm worried about you."

"You deserve better."

He took her chin between his fingers and lifted her face. "No, Juliette. You're the best person I know."

"That's all fiction." Tears welled and slipped down her cheeks. He thumbed the moisture away.

He frowned. "I never pegged you as a coward."

Her body went stiff. "I guess you don't really know me."

She moved around him and fled down the sidewalk, leaving him stunned. Had Juliette just walked out of his life?

By the time she disappeared, he'd pulled himself together and walked to the truck. He drove back to the farm in a haze, unloaded Juniper, and made sure he had plenty of clean hay and food in the stall, functioning like he was sleepwalking.

Juliette had lied to him. Now that he thought back, he'd sensed something was off, but never had he imagined this. All the times she'd deflected praise over her good deeds made sense. She'd felt guilty.

Walking to the paddock, he stopped by the fence, hooking his bootheel on the lower rung and resting his forearms on top, his hands dangling over the wood.

Why hadn't she just been honest with him? He'd talked about the mistakes he'd made in his life. Gave her plenty of openings to reveal the truth. Why didn't she trust him with this big secret like he'd trusted her?

And to accuse his running late as breaking his promise? Like he was still the irresponsible guy he'd worked so hard to change. If he was honest, that hurt more than Juliette keeping her secrets to herself.

He wasn't sure how long he stood there, trying to fit all the puzzle pieces together, when his dad joined him.

"Didn't expect that kind of drama today."

Ty stared over the muddy paddock and up at the mountains in the distance. It was all he could do to keep from jumping on Juniper and escaping right now.

His feet stayed planted on the ground.

"You okay, son?"

"Not sure."

Brando nodded. "That was some big news Juliette dropped."

"Which I'd rather not talk about."

"It might affect her therapy program."

He couldn't go there right now. "We'll deal with that if it becomes an issue."

Silence filtered around them, except for the horses stirring in the stable and the goats bleating from their pen.

Brando cleared his throat. "Seems I owe you an apology."

Ty turned his head to find his father staring straight ahead.

"You do?"

His father cleared his throat. "I was so quick to blame you for all the mistakes I made. Called you all kinds of irresponsible. It was wrong of me."

Ty didn't know what to say.

"When you told me you were going to the rodeo this week, I thought, *Here he goes again. Abandoning us.* Said as much to Liz and she sat me down and read me the riot act. Told me how you were thinkin' about sellin' Juniper, but instead did these shows to get the money for the well." His eyes narrowed in a glare. "Which you kept me in the dark about."

Ty pressed his lips together, then muttered, "Guilty."

Brando let out a gusty sigh. "I don't blame you. I didn't do a good job with our finances for a long time and yet you came home and cleaned things up."

Ty pulled back and gripped the weathered fence between his fingers. "Ever since I've been managing the farm, I've done a good job, Dad. I might have kept some of the decision-making from you, but you gave me the responsibility when we moved here and I willingly accepted."

"You did. Full measure. And that's where I was wrong." Brando placed his elbow on the fence top and angled himself to face Ty. "Liz told me you earned the money for the well and more. And still, you came home instead of giving in to the call of the rodeo. To the excitement you always thrived on. I couldn't be prouder of you, son."

Ty swallowed hard.

"Can you forgive an old coot like me for jumping to conclusions and not seeing what a good man you've become?"

It took a moment for Ty to process the words. Words he'd waited what felt like a lifetime to hear.

"We're family, Dad. We've had our ups and

downs, but we stick together. You taught me that. So, yeah, I can forgive you."

Brando nodded and gazed out over the property. After a few moments, he asked, "What are you gonna do about Juliette?"

"I don't know if there's anything I can do."

She'd walked away before they had a chance to discuss the matter. He didn't know what that meant for them, but knew his chest ached at the thought of losing her over a misunderstanding. "She didn't confide in me, so I don't know where we stand."

"But she's the one, isn't she?"

Ty closed his eyes as a wave of pain swept over him. "Yeah. She's the one."

"Then you gotta fight."

Which made sense in theory, but from the way Juliette looked at the park earlier, he thought it might be a one-sided battle.

You don't know me.

Did he? In this instance, she might be right. She'd kept the truth from him and others. How could they fix the problem if Juliette didn't accept that her self-worth did not begin and end with this hero myth? She was a good person who made a mistake, just like he had. If she didn't make peace with her past and the fallout, where did it leave them?

"It's got to be up to Juliette," Ty said, stepping back from the fence and shoving his hands in his front pockets as a gust of cold wind made him shiver. "She's got to make the first move."

"You sure?"

He knew it in his bones. "I am."

Sadness crossed his father's face. With a hearty pat on Ty's shoulder, the older man walked away.

Ty gazed over the mountains again, wishing for some kind of inspiration on how to deal with the situation. Hoping that he and Juliette would figure things out, but not ignoring his gut feeling that things might never be okay with Juliette again.

CHAPTER FIFTEEN

"I HATE TO SAY IT," Gayle Ann said to the match-makers who were getting ready for the market at Crestview Farm the next morning, each sporting a glum expression. "We failed."

In the early morning light, other vendors were setting up tables to sell their products. Many of the merchants from the last market were there, along with a few new folks who decided to take advantage of the initial success. Between the horseback riding and the fun atmosphere of the market, the farm would quickly become a town favorite.

Colton acted as a runner this morning, helping the vendors out by going back and forth to cars to carry in merchandise or just to answer any logistical questions. Brando had pointed out his crush, Kelsey, who had showed up to sell the farm eggs with his grandson. If the smitten smile on his face was any indication, Colton was happy she'd arrived. Liz strode in a few minutes later, glancing around the barn to make sure everything was in order.

The only missing Pendergrass was Ty.

"I can't believe Juliette kept the truth from everyone for all these years," Wanda Sue said, with a sad shake of her head.

"Gotta admire her resolve," Alveda added as she stacked the pie boxes on the table, the fragrant peach and spices filling the air.

"If we'd had all the information, things would have gone differently in our matching scheme," Bunny said.

Gayle Ann straightened the tablecloth. "We can't be sure."

Wanda Sue's mouth gapped. "You're really admitting defeat? Doesn't sound like you."

She uttered the words she never thought she'd say. "Maybe we pushed things too far."

The matchmakers stood around the table, each lost in thought.

"Now what?" Wanda Sue asked.

Gayle Ann sighed. "This isn't as easy as throwing Juliette and Ty together to make them see how good they are together. While we had challenges with the other couples, this time is different."

"I have to agree," Brando said. "I might not have been around for your other matches, but I know my son. Ty isn't going to force the

issue with Juliette. He'll give her time to figure out next steps, without interfering."

"Which makes time our enemy," Gayle
Ann said.

"Is it?" Judge Carmichael asked.

Gayle Ann raised an eyebrow. "What are
you thinking, Harry?"

"From what we heard yesterday, Juliette
was waiting for Ty to arrive at the park. Do
you think her need to be honest about what
happened came from spending time with Ty?
That their relationship was important enough
for her to finally admit the truth?"

Brando frowned. "What does Ty have to
do with it?"

"In fifteen years, she never once confessed
her secret. Why now?"

The group stopped to think this over.

Bunny pointed to Harry. "Are you saying
the common denominator is Ty? If he hadn't
arrived, Juliette would never have confessed?"

Harry lifted one shoulder. "I can't say that
for sure. It's obvious that hiding the truth has
taken a toll on Juliette. But what I do know is
that Ty is the only outside force to come into
her life, and now she makes the decision."

"And he's been committed to managing
the farm instead of craving the limelight of
the rodeo circuit." Brando rubbed his jaw. "I

didn't tell ya'll, but he took a rodeo performance because we needed to fix a well on the property. And he came right back like he said he would."

"So, if I'm hearing this properly," Gayle Ann said with surprise, "we don't necessarily have to meddle further?"

"There's no guarantee," said the judge. "But if we look at Juliette's track record, she's no quitter."

"The judge makes sense," Bunny said.

"So back to my question," Wanda Sue said. "What's next?"

"We wait," Gayle Ann replied.

"With our fingers crossed," Bunny added.

There was a beat, then they all started chuckling.

"Yeah, like that's gonna happen," Alveda said.

The other vendors had finished setting up and as the doors opened, early morning shoppers streamed into the barn. Alveda moved to Gayle Ann's side and whispered, "Time to hang up this matchmaking business?"

"Do I look like I'm giving in to defeat?"

Alveda chuckled. "Didn't think so."

Gale Ann patted her longtime friend's arm. "Let's sell some pies.

"Along with a little hope."

JULIETTE DRAGGED HERSELF out of bed, showered, and dressed in jeans and an old University of Georgia sweatshirt before heading over to her parents' house. She didn't bother with makeup or running a brush through her hair. What did it matter? She wasn't planning on seeing anyone else today.

When she let herself in, an eerie silence filled the usually noisy home. The scent of freshly brewed coffee guided her to the back of the house. She found her mother in the kitchen, seated at the table, staring into the coffee cup she held between two hands.

"Mom?"

Her mother jumped, spilling coffee over the rim. She set down the cup and placed a hand over her heart. "You scared me. I didn't hear you come in."

Juliette hovered in the doorway. "Can I sit?"

Her mother got up to grab a dishcloth to wipe up the liquid. "What? Of course."

Juliette took a seat on the other side of the table as her mother joined her. Filtered through her thoughts before simply saying, "I'm sorry."

Her mother pushed the cup away. "As you can imagine, the truth came as a surprise."

Juliette looked down to trace a finger over the tabletop. "I was wrong not to tell you."

"Maybe not entirely."

Her head jerked up. "What do you mean?"

"Yes, you carried the truth around when you should have told us," her mother said. "But last night I kept going over the past. No matter what you think, your father and I were proud of you saving Ellie from what might have been a terrible outcome, unintended or not. But I can also recall now that you were unhappy. I'd hate to think we ignored the signs, but can admit it was probably more like we were preoccupied with work and family and life, than picking up on the signals." She frowned. "At that time, you were looking after Ivy while we worked. You rescuing Ellie was a pleasant event that we could celebrate as a family."

"I should have been honest."

"And we shouldn't have put so much pressure on you. You were a child yourself."

Juliette tilted her head. "What about when I got older? When I could have told you everything?"

Her mother's smile was sad. "Seems like we all bear some guilt in this scenario."

"But I have no excuse for lying."

Or placing the blame elsewhere.

Juliette closed her eyes, remembering how she'd accused Ty of breaking his promise. Like he'd arrived late on purpose instead of having a legit emergency. He'd worked hard to turn his reputation around and he'd never forgive her for carelessly tossing those words at him. She couldn't forgive herself.

The back door opened and Ivy rushed in, a barking dog at her heels.

"Juls! You're here. You get to meet Bruno."

Her father entered the kitchen, but Juliette couldn't read his expression as he turned his back to close the door.

"Dad and I went to the rescue shelter. Isn't he beautiful?"

Ivy beamed at Bruno, a light brown cocker spaniel. Realizing he was the star, he pranced around the kitchen, barking, sniffing and jumping on Ivy as if he couldn't believe his good luck at getting a forever home.

"The lady at the shelter said he would be easygoing and affectionate," her father said as he set a big bag with the name of the local pet store on the counter.

Ivy plopped down in a chair and watched Bruno make himself at home. "He's going to be my best friend." Her eyes went wide. "I mean after you, Juls."

"I don't really deserve to be a friend right now," Juliette said, her throat tight.

This was harder than she'd imagined, and she'd imagined the worst.

"That's silly. Of course we're friends. And sisters."

"But I lied, Ivy."

"About the stroller?" Ivy sent her an innocent gaze. "No, you didn't."

Their mother leaned forward. "What are you talking about, Ivy?"

"You were going after the dog, but instead made sure the stroller didn't roll any further into the street. You saved Ellie, Juls. You are a hero."

Her father came behind Ivy to place his hands on her shoulders. "Even if it wasn't intentional, Juliette, the fact is, you saved Ellie."

"And Mayor Danielson did make a big deal about it," her mother said. "As I recall, the story got bigger every time he told it."

"Until I believed the lie I kept telling myself; that I had to keep the truth a secret."

Her mother reached across the table to take her hands. "And carried this around for far too long. We didn't listen to you, honey, and that's on us."

Juliette shook her head. The bottom line was that Ellie hadn't gotten hurt. Why had she never looked at it from that perspective before?

She glanced at her sister. "You're sure, Ivy?"

Ivy nodded. "I remember because I wanted to get the dog. I saw him three times, Juls. Three times." Ivy's face clouded and her hands fluttered as Bruno came over. "I thought you didn't ever want to talk about it because the dog got away. I didn't want you to blame yourself that I didn't get my pet that day."

Juliette jumped up and hurried over to hug her sister. "It's not your fault."

"And not yours," her mother said.

After coming clean with the truth yesterday, was forgiveness going to be within reach?

Before she knew it, the entire Bishop family was in a group hug with Bruno sticking his wet nose into the fray, trying to get in on the loving.

Her mother placed her hands on either side of her daughter's face. "You aren't defined by this one event, Juliette, but by all the generous acts you've done over the years."

Could that be true? She wanted it to be. "What do I do now?"

"What a hero would do?" her father said.

"Face everyone. Say you're sorry. Live your life."

"It can't be that easy."

"It won't be," her father said, hugging her close. "But you can do it."

She met her mother's gaze. Spoke her deepest fear out loud. "What about Ty?"

Her mom's eyes went misty. "Explain the truth. He cares about you, Juliette. He'll understand."

She wanted him to, oh, how she wanted him to. He'd faced his own past and made positive changes. Would he see that she needed to be extended that same grace?

"You can bring Bruno with you when you go see Ty," Ivy piped up. "He'll make everything better."

"I appreciate it, Ivy, but I think I need to see Ty on my own."

AFTER GOING HOME to change into a more attractive sweater and fixing her hair, Juliette parked her car by the barn and walked to the wide-open door. Her heart sank as she stepped inside. There was a good crowd for the market milling around, and once she entered, all eyes turned to her, followed by a heavy silence. She cringed, but kept walking, needing to find Ty.

Gaze straight ahead, she walked to the table featuring Alveda's pies. If anyone knew where Ty was, the seniors would be able to tell her. After she righted her wrong, that is.

Odd, that the group would have guilty expressions on their faces when she'd been the one keeping secrets. Taking a breath, she stopped and lifted her chin. "I owe you all an apology."

She turned to the people mingling in the barn and raised her voice. "All of you."

"No, my dear, you do not," Mrs. M. said in a firm tone.

Juliette turned to face the woman.

"If anything, we realize that our part in perpetuating your hero status did you no favors," Mrs. M. continued. "We had no idea what keeping that secret had done to you."

"It doesn't matter. I should have been honest."

"And I should have been born taller so I can reach the upper cabinets," Alveda said. "But we don't always get what we want."

Juliette blinked. What did that have to do with anything?

"And I wanted to be an opera singer," Bunny said.

"A singer?" Wanda Sue shuddered. "I've heard you sing hymns in church."

Bunny turned to her friend. "Your point?"

"You would have had a short career."

Before the two longtime friends could start arguing, the judge jumped in. "I think what the ladies are trying to say is that things happen in life. It's how you proceed that determines the outcome."

Could it be that simple? After all this time?

Mrs. M. smiled at her. "Never forget that you've done a lot for this town. It might have been out of misguided guilt, but it's been good, just the same."

Tears burned her eyes. How could they all be so nice to her?

"Now you put one foot in front of the other," Alveda said. "Today's a new day and all that inspirational stuff."

Brando rounded the table. "If you're looking for Ty, he's in the stable."

She nodded and turned, coming face-to-face with Addie.

"Addie I—"

Her friend held up her hand. "I'm sorry I snapped at you yesterday."

"You had every reason to. I'm not the good friend you thought I was."

Addie snorted. "Please. Who else but a good friend would sit with me after Josh died? Hold my hand while you cried with me.

Or go out with me last-minute when life is too much to handle and I need a break, even when you're tired and want to stay home." Her voice softened. "We've shared a lot, Juls. Maybe not this one thing, but everything else that matters."

With a sob, Juliette threw her arms around her best friend. "Thank you," she whispered.

Addie hugged her tight, then stepped back. "We can catch up later. Right now I think there's a cowboy you need to see."

After another fast hug, Juliette turned to go find Ty when Liz stepped in her path, her long braid swinging over her shoulder.

"Not so fast."

Juliette grimaced when Colton joined his mom. Kelsey was right at his side, the teens holding hands.

"I have just one question," Liz pressed.

Juliette swallowed hard. "Which is?"

"Do you love my brother?"

With all my heart.

As emotion overwhelmed Juliette, she couldn't get the words out, but it must have shown on her face, because Liz sent her a half smile.

"Uncle Ty took Juniper out for a ride," Colton informed her, "but they should be back by now."

The Pendergrass family looked out for each other. At all costs, Juliette had learned since spending time with them. Were they giving her their blessing?

Liz planted her hands on her hips. "So, you gonna stand around all day?"

"Thanks," Juliette whispered, her heart in her throat as she lit out of the barn in the direction of the stable.

The familiar scents of hay and horse enveloped her as she entered the dim building. She heard a nicker, then a noise near the stalls. When she rushed around the corner, she found Ty tossing clean hay into a stall. She skidded to a stop, suddenly unsure of herself.

Ty heard her and looked up. Froze. Then set the rake against the door.

She hurried over, stopping a foot away from him, her heart pounding. "Please, let me say what I came here to say before I chicken out."

He crossed his arms over his chest, his expression not revealing a thing.

"I messed up, Ty. I kept a secret that I thought was so important, only to discover that I didn't have to. I should have been honest, but sometimes we look at situations a certain way and make choices that haunts us for years. That's what I did."

"You could have told me," he said in an even tone. "Of all people, I would have understood how the past can affect your decisions."

"I thought a lot about that after we meet." She longed to move forward, but kept her ground. "I wanted to tell you my decision to come clean first, Ty. I know I could have said something before the parade, that you'd have helped me sort it out, but I was afraid you'd walk away. I was terrified to take that chance, but I was going to."

His eyes grew dark. "You think I'd have walked away? After all we are together?"

"I panicked. And lashed out at you."

"By reminding me I broke the promise? About how irresponsible I'd once been?"

She felt her confidence failing, but said, "I'm more sorry than I can ever say. You are a solid guy, Ty. I should have trusted that and I blew it. I have a lot to make up for and I don't know where to begin."

He didn't move. "How about starting with the fact that you'll never be free if you don't acknowledge that no one is perfect. It was never about being a hero, Juliette. It was always about your big heart."

Her hand flew to her mouth as a sob escaped.

"It's up to you to decide where we go now."

He was giving her the freedom to make her own decision and she never loved him more.

She lowered her hand and took a tentative step toward him. "How could I not love a man who was willing to sell his most prized possession to take care of his family. I'm so glad it didn't come to that. But still, I should have trusted us, trusted that—"

He held up a hand to stop her. "Did you just say you love me?"

She faltered. "Yes."

Would he love her in return?

As she waited on pins and needles, a slow grin spread over his lips. "Took you long enough to come around."

Sweet relief swept over her when he marched her way and pulled her into his strong embrace. "I know a little something about outliving a reputation, darlin'. Seems you came to the right guy to help you figure it out."

She laughed, then looped her arms around his neck and proceeded to smother him with a long kiss.

When she pulled away, he brushed her hair from her face. "I love you too, Juliette. I think

I have ever since you conspired to steal that sign with me the first day we met."

"I wasn't conspiring—"

He placed a finger against her lips. "Let's just go with that story. Our grandkids will love it."

She grinned, her heart brimming with happiness. "As long as we're okay?"

"We're better than okay," he assured her with a heated kiss that left her gasping for air. When she broke the kiss, he rested his forehead against hers.

"You know we can face anything together," he said.

"As long as we always tell each other the truth."

He pulled back to meet her gaze. "So, no keeping things from each other."

"No secrets."

His pirate's grin made her shiver. "More adventures?"

She pointed a finger at him. "As long as we don't break the law."

"That's no fun."

"Ty…"

He chuckled. "Fine. Let's agree we're partners in…everything."

How had she been so lucky to find this man?

Not only had she found the courage to tell the truth, but with Ty by her side, they could face anything.

"It's a deal," she told him as he pulled her into his embrace.

EPILOGUE

Three months later

"This is a fine day to hold a wedding," Harry said as he squeezed Gayle Ann's hand.

"That's because it's *our* wedding," she emphasized.

"Still, the sun is shining and there's enough of a nip in the air to keep you nestled against my side."

Gayle Ann had to admit, it had been a glorious day. Now the newly married couple, and all their family and friends, were celebrating in the Crestview Farm barn, decorated to the hilt. The rows of chairs set out for the ceremony had been moved to the round tables on the perimeter of the room. A DJ fired up the music for the couple's first dance before lunch was served.

Harry had dressed in a conservative black suit with a bright red tie for the ceremony, his thick, silver hair impeccably styled, never looking more dapper. Gayle Ann had splurged on a white suit, along with her favorite pearl necklace and earrings. Her only pop of color was the rose bouquet she'd held during the ceremony.

Who would have thought love would happen twice in her lifetime?

After the DJ announced Judge and Mrs. Gayle Ann Masterson-Carmichael—with a snort from Alveda over the ridiculously long name—she took her husband's hand and they moved to the empty dance floor.

"Your bridesmaids are scoping out their dance partners," Harry said as they moved to a classic Frank Sinatra tune.

Her bridesmaids, Alveda, Bunny and Wanda Sue, all dressed in red, had insisted on standing up with her and Gayle Ann hadn't argued. Truer friends she'd never found.

"Bunny's had her eye on Buck Watkins for a while now. I think our exchanging vows has emboldened her."

Harry chuckled. "Nothing like a wedding to make folks think about love."

"Especially those who needed a little push."

Harry's mustache quivered. "Bragging, are you?"

She lifted a shoulder. "We accomplished our mission, didn't we?"

"We did indeed."

The DJ invited others to join the couple in a dance. As they swayed, Gayle Ann smiled at her grandson, Logan, as he danced by with his wife, Serena.

"News on that front," she told Harry. "Logan told me that he and Serena want to start a family."

"Seems our plan to keep the younger generation in Golden has worked."

She nodded, adjusting his tie. "And since Reid and Heidi eloped, I suppose they'll be thinking the same thoughts."

The two had flown to Las Vegas for New Years and came back married. Not that Gayle Ann was surprised. Heidi didn't like a fuss and planning a wedding definitely fell into that category. She'd settled for a party, right here in the barn, which, much to Brando's surprise, was becoming a party and wedding destination.

As the DJ switched tempo, Gayle Ann spied Brando holding his hand out to Alveda. Her best friend seemed surprised, but a smile curved her lips. He sure looked happy, especially since Scott had moved to a nearby assisted living home and was reportedly keen on it.

Wanda Sue wiggled her fingers as she danced by on Roan Donovan's arm, but Gayle

Ann noticed that she just as quickly steered her son-in-law to her daughter's side. After falling in love, Faith and Roan hadn't wasted any time in blending their two families with a happy wedding. Four children were to become five any day now. Gayle Ann's heart melted as Roan waited on his very pregnant wife. Faith's eyes twinkled as he helped her up and she moved into Roan's arms for maybe the last dance before the baby arrived.

"Feeling pretty proud of yourself?" Harry asked, his gaze following hers.

"More like the luckiest woman in the room."

He kissed her.

"Speaking of lucky women, I heard Bunny tell you that Adam bought a ring."

Gayle Ann grinned. "Carrie has no idea."

While the young professional was using her marketing skills to ramp up Golden as a desirable business location, Adam was organizing his dream of planting roots with the woman he loved.

"And, so far, Bunny hasn't spilled the news," Gayle Ann said.

"There's still time."

"Please. Let's hope Bunny and Buck work out so she keeps from meddling in her nephews' lives."

The judge, strike that, her husband, grinned her way. "Says the chief meddler."

"Someone had to step up," she sniffed.

"And I'm glad you did. I was getting tired of golf. You gave me a new hobby."

Gayle Ann shook her head. "I never intended for you to join our club."

"Funny how fate works,"

As the song ended, Harry led her back to their table. Out of the corner of her eye, Gayle Ann noticed Ty and Juliette still on the floor, dancing to music only they could hear.

The equine therapy client list was growing, as well as the plans for the farm as they worked together as a team promoting their future.

"Ty and Juliette were quite a challenge," Harry said, his lips close to Gayle Ann's ears. "Our toughest yet."

"But with a satisfying ending."

Before they sat, the matchmakers closed in on them. Gayle Ann met each gaze. "Something you want to say?"

Alveda nodded. "We were wondering what's to become of the Golden Matchmakers Club now that you're going to be busy with Harry."

"Can't we all be busy together?" Gayle Ann

teased. "Besides, we haven't matched all the singles in Golden, have we?"

Alveda's expression turned somber. "After we almost failed with Ty and Juliette, we weren't sure."

"Nonsense," Gayle Ann huffed. "It was just a blip in the radar."

Although it hadn't felt like it at the time.

"So we're going to continue?" Wanda Sue asked.

"Why not? There's still work to do."

"Good," Bunny said, "because I'm not ready to call it quits and end up sitting around playing cards all day."

"Like you have the patience for that," Wanda Sue snorted. "And for the record, you cheat."

"What part about boring did you miss?" Bunny demanded. "I need to liven things up."

"Ladies," Harry intervened.

"So," Brando asked. "What's next?"

Gayle Ann slipped her hand through Harry's arm and leaned close. "How about we decide after we come back from our honeymoon?"

Harry winked at her. "I like the sound of honeymoon."

She playfully smacked his arm.

"That'll give us time to come up with the next couple," Bunny said.

"Without being obvious," Wanda Sue added.

Alveda grinned at Gayle Ann. "I suppose Golden is always going to need us?"

"Oh, my friend, I'd say there's nothing like risking it all for love."

* * * * *

For more charming romances in Golden, Georgia, check out the rest of the miniseries available from acclaimed author Tara Randel, and Harlequin Heartwarming, available today at www.Harlequin.com!

Get 4 FREE REWARDS!

We'll send you 2 FREE Books plus 2 FREE Mystery Gifts.

FREE Value Over **$20**

Both the **Love Inspired®** and **Love Inspired® Suspense** series feature compelling novels filled with inspirational romance, faith, forgiveness and hope.

YES! Please send me 2 FREE novels from the Love Inspired or Love Inspired Suspense series and my 2 FREE gifts (gifts are worth about $10 retail). After receiving them, if I don't wish to receive any more books, I can return the shipping statement marked "cancel." If I don't cancel, I will receive 6 brand-new Love Inspired Larger-Print books or Love Inspired Suspense Larger-Print books every month and be billed just $6.49 each in the U.S. or $6.74 each in Canada. That is a savings of at least 16% off the cover price. It's quite a bargain! Shipping and handling is just 50¢ per book in the U.S. and $1.25 per book in Canada.* I understand that accepting the 2 free books and gifts places me under no obligation to buy anything. I can always return a shipment and cancel at any time by calling the number below. The free books and gifts are mine to keep no matter what I decide.

Choose one: ☐ **Love Inspired**
Larger-Print
(122/322 IDN GRHK)

☐ **Love Inspired Suspense**
Larger-Print
(107/307 IDN GRHK)

Name (please print)

Address   Apt. #

City   State/Province   Zip/Postal Code

Email: Please check this box ☐ if you would like to receive newsletters and promotional emails from Harlequin Enterprises ULC and its affiliates. You can unsubscribe anytime.

Mail to the Harlequin Reader Service:
IN U.S.A.: P.O. Box 1341, Buffalo, NY 14240 8531
IN CANADA: P.O. Box 603, Fort Erie, Ontario L2A 5X3

Want to try 2 free books from another series! Call 1-800-873-8635 or visit www.ReaderService.com.

*Terms and prices subject to change without notice. Prices do not include sales taxes, which will be charged (if applicable) based on your state or country of residence. Canadian residents will be charged applicable taxes. Offer not valid in Quebec. This offer is limited to one order per household. Books received may not be as shown. Not valid for current subscribers to the Love Inspired or Love Inspired Suspense series. All orders subject to approval. Credit or debit balances in a customer's account(s) may be offset by any other outstanding balance owed by or to the customer. Please allow 4 to 6 weeks for delivery. Offer available while quantities last.

Your Privacy—Your information is being collected by Harlequin Enterprises ULC, operating as Harlequin Reader Service. For a complete summary of the information we collect, how we use this information and to whom it is disclosed, please visit our privacy notice located at corporate.harlequin.com/privacy-notice. From time to time we may also exchange your personal information with reputable third parties. If you wish to opt out of this sharing of your personal information, please visit readerservice.com/consumerchoice or call 1-800-873-8635. **Notice to California Residents**—Under California law, you have specific rights to control and access your data. For more information on these rights and how to exercise them, visit corporate.harlequin.com/california-privacy.

LIRLIS22R3

Get 4 FREE REWARDS!

We'll send you 2 FREE Books plus <u>2 FREE Mystery Gifts</u>.

FREE Value Over **$20**

Both the **Harlequin® Special Edition** and **Harlequin® Heartwarming™** series feature compelling novels filled with stories of love and strength where the bonds of friendship, family and community unite.

YES! Please send me 2 FREE novels from the Harlequin Special Edition or Harlequin Heartwarming series and my 2 FREE gifts (gifts are worth about $10 retail). After receiving them, if I don't wish to receive any more books, I can return the shipping statement marked "cancel." If I don't cancel, I will receive 6 brand-new Harlequin Special Edition books every month and be billed just $5.49 each in the U.S. or $6.24 each in Canada, a savings of at least 12% off the cover price, or 4 brand-new Harlequin Heartwarming Larger-Print books every month and be billed just $6.24 each in the U.S. or $6.74 each in Canada, a savings of at least 19% off the cover price. It's quite a bargain! Shipping and handling is just 50¢ per book in the U.S. and $1.25 per book in Canada.* I understand that accepting the 2 free books and gifts places me under no obligation to buy anything. I can always return a shipment and cancel at any time by calling the number below. The free books and gifts are mine to keep no matter what I decide.

Choose one: ☐ **Harlequin Special Edition** ☐ **Harlequin Heartwarming**
(235/335 HDN GRJV)   **Larger-Print**
                                             (161/361 HDN GRJV)

Name (please print)

Address   Apt. #

City   State/Province   Zip/Postal Code

Email: Please check this box ☐ if you would like to receive newsletters and promotional emails from Harlequin Enterprises ULC and its affiliates. You can unsubscribe anytime.

Mail to the Harlequin Reader Service:
IN U.S.A.: P.O. Box 1341, Buffalo, NY 14240-8531
IN CANADA: P.O. Box 603, Fort Erie, Ontario L2A 5X3

Want to try 2 free books from another series? Call 1-800-873-8635 or visit www.ReaderService.com.

*Terms and prices subject to change without notice. Prices do not include sales taxes, which will be charged (if applicable) based on your state or country of residence. Canadian residents will be charged applicable taxes. Offer not valid in Quebec. This offer is limited to one order per household. Books received may not be as shown. Not valid for current subscribers to the Harlequin Special Edition or Harlequin Heartwarming series. All orders subject to approval. Credit or debit balances in a customer's account(s) may be offset by any other outstanding balance owed by or to the customer. Please allow 4 to 6 weeks for delivery. Offer available while quantities last.

Your Privacy—Your information is being collected by Harlequin Enterprises ULC, operating as Harlequin Reader Service. For a complete summary of the information we collect, how we use this information and to whom it is disclosed, please visit our privacy notice located at corporate.harlequin.com/privacy-notice. From time to time we may also exchange your personal information with reputable third parties. If you wish to opt out of this sharing of your personal information, please visit readerservice.com/consumerchoice or call 1-800-873-8635. **Notice to California Residents**—Under California law, you have specific rights to control and access your data. For more information on these rights and how to exercise them, visit corporate.harlequin.com/california-privacy.

HSEHW22R3

THE NORA ROBERTS COLLECTION

40% OFF!

Get to the heart of happily-ever-after in these Nora Roberts classics! Immerse yourself in the beauty of love by picking up this incredible collection written by, legendary author, Nora Roberts!

YES! Please send me the **Nora Roberts Collection**. Each book in this collection is 40% off the retail price! There are a total of 4 shipments in this collection. The shipments are yours for the low, members-only discount price of $23.96 U.S./$31.16 CDN. each, plus $1.99 U.S./$4.99 CDN. for shipping and handling. If I do not cancel, I will continue to receive four books a month for three more months. I'll pay just $23.96 U.S./$31.16 CDN., plus $1.99 U.S./$4.99 CDN. for shipping and handling per shipment.* I can always return a shipment and cancel at any time.

☐ 274 2595   ☐ 474 2595

Name (please print)

Address   Apt. #

City   State/Province   Zip/Postal Code

Mail to the Harlequin Reader Service:
IN U.S.A.: P.O. Box 1341, Buffalo, NY 14240-8531
IN CANADA: P.O. Box 603, Fort Erie, Ontario L2A 5X3

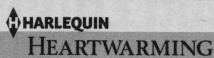
#463 HER AMISH COUNTRY VALENTINE
The Butternut Amish B&B • by Patricia Johns
Advertising exec Jill Wickey knows all about appearance versus reality. So why does she keep wishing that spending time with carpenter Thom Miller—her fake date for a wedding in Amish country—could be the start of something real?

#464 A COWBOY WORTH WAITING FOR
The Cowboy Academy • by Melinda Curtis
Ronnie Pickett is creating a matchmaking service for rodeo folks—but to be successful, she needs a high-profile competitor as a client. Former champ Wade Keller is perfect...but could he be perfect for her?

#465 A COUNTRY PROPOSAL
Cupid's Crossing • by Kim Findlay
Jordan's farm is the only security he's ever had. So when big-city chef—and first love—Delaney returns home with suggestions for revamping it, Jordan isn't happy. But Delaney has a few good ideas...about the two of them!

#466 A BABY ON HIS DOORSTEP
Kansas Cowboys • by Leigh Riker
Veterinarian Max Crane didn't expect to find a baby on his porch—or for former librarian Rachel Whittaker to accept the job caring for his daughter. Now, most unexpectedly of all, they are starting to feel like a family...

HARLEQUIN
PLUS

Try the best multimedia subscription service for romance readers like you!

Read, Watch and Play.

Experience the easiest way to get the romance content you crave.

Start your **FREE TRIAL** at
<u>www.harlequinplus.com/freetrial</u>.